JOURNEY TO THE HEARTLAND

MICHELLE WALSH JACKSON

The
Novel
Press

Published 2021 by The Novel Press Ltd,
Dublin, Ireland
www.thenovelpress.com
©Michelle Walsh Jackson 2021

Copyright for typesetting, layout, design
©The Novel Press
The moral rights of the author have been asserted.
A catalogue record for this book is available from the British Library.

ISBN 978-1-838370909

Typeset by Colin Murphy in Adobe Garamond Pro
Printed and bound by CPI Group (UK) Ltd
www.thenovelpress.com

ABOUT THE AUTHOR

Writer, novelist and broadcaster, Michelle Walsh Jackson, is a native of Howth, County Dublin, and has lived there all her life. Her seven novels include titles *One Kiss in Havana, Two Days in Biarritz, 5 Peppermint Grove* and *Six Postcards Home*. She was co-author of the bestselling popular non-fiction book *What Women Know* in 2010, published by Hachette Ireland. Her books have been internationally translated into German, Dutch, Portuguese, Romanian, Bulgarian and Norwegian under the name Michelle Jackson.

Michelle writes travel and business articles for national newspapers the *Irish Times*, the *Irish Independent*, the *Sunday Times*, the *Sunday Business Post*, the *Irish Mail*, and several periodicals including *National Geographic Traveller*.

Her website thenoveltraveller.com is one of Ireland's go-to travel websites and has been internationally awarded. She has presented a bi-weekly Travel Slot on *The Elaine Show* on Virgin Media TV for the last eight years and is Travel Pundit on Newstalk FM's drivetime show for the last three years. She has contributed on many broadcasting channels including RTÉ. For more information see

www.michellejackson.ie

or

www.thenoveltraveller.com

~

ACKNOWLEDGMENTS

This book would not have been possible had it not been for the support and encouragement of so many people, and especially my journey into travel-writing and the incredible people I have met on the way. I'd like to especially thank Matt Bates and everyone at Oklahoma CVB who welcomed me so warmly in my quest to learn about their state. Thank you, Surinder Manku, for encouraging me to delve into the world of travel journalism, and for opening my eyes to a great way of seeing the world. To all the journalists, travel trade, tour operators, travel professionals and media people who have inspired me on my travels for the last eight years in between novels, thank you and I look forward to the rebirth of travel soon.

I'd like to thank my father Jim Walsh for his love and support and for being the only family member to read all of my books. He inspired me to visit the lesser explored states of America. I grew up in a home with country music in the background and Western movies on the TV, much to the chagrin of my dearly beloved mother Pauline who passed away in 2020. It has been a wonderful journey through life with my father and my mother. I'd also like to thank Philip MacDermott who helped me to find my voice and gave me great insight into how the visually impaired cope with day-to-day tasks. I'd like to thank my friend David Tyndall whom I always said I would put into a book someday – in an entirely fictitious manner as his true story could not fit in a novel this size. Happy belated Birthday, pal!

Thank you, Clodagh Hoey, for reading every one of my books and always being my novel rock. Elaine Crowley who helped me to grow as a travel writer and broadcasting contributor, your faith and confidence in me when I was at my lowest ebb means so much. My writer pals Maria Duffy and Niamh Greene who have always just been there and are fabulous travelling companions. Thank you to fellow authors and creatives Donal O'Dea and Colin C. Murphy for helping me with the design, cover and layout of this book and for being really cool friends.

Thank you to my friends who have been such incredible supporters of my books over the years and especially those who helped me during the difficult year and loss of my mother – you know who you are.

Thanks to my darling children, Mark and Nicole, whom I have dragged to the four corners of the world and have always been the best companions, thank you for being you. My family has expanded with the wonderful love of my other half, Terry, who is my constant support.

Finally, I'd like to thank my magical editor, FG Dotier, who is quite simply a genius.

For Terry

Thank you for taking me on the
Journey to the real Heartland.

PROLOGUE

Oxford, England

I opened the front door to find a tiny bluebird dead on my doorstep and it sent a chill up my spine. It was probably a gift from our neighbour's cat, but I knew what my father would have said – he'd have called it a sign. He loved nature and was in tune with the movements of the seasons and the cycle of life and death. Living in a different country to him, with the Irish Sea between us, meant that I lived with a deep-seated fear of "the call" and knew that it would come one day – that call from a neighbour or maybe a policeman to say that he was dead.

I suppose you would call my father "a character". Proud is another word that comes to mind when describing him. Even though he'd lost ninety per cent of his vision, I've never known greater foresight in any man.

Patrick Dónal Cullen was born on 8th August 1942, in the parish of Inniskeen, a small town in County Monaghan. Being the youngest of eight children meant his mother was worn out by the time he came along. His father died a few years after he was born, leaving a gap in the family that couldn't be filled. Patrick knew what it meant to do his share and never expected much from his young life.

While his older brothers kept the farm going, he helped his mother and sisters in the house. As he grew older, his brothers made it clear that there was no room for him on the land and he would have to find another way to provide for his future.

So he made sure that he was well read and later instilled a love of prose in me that I'd never have found with normal tuition. *How Green Was My Valley, Sons and Lovers* – these were titles that none of my school friends had read but I bathed in his favourite literature.

His great love was cowboys, Indians and anything to do with the Wild West. Ironically, most people said that he looked like Clint Eastwood. He adored watching the Western movies that showed repeatedly on our black-and-white TV. It was a common passion for men of his time, especially those with a rural upbringing.

I wondered how much more he had to give to the world. A world that had left men like him behind and a world that needed men like him more than ever.

Every morning I remembered my father because it was he who always saw me to school when I was a child – not my mother.

I tried to shake the morbid image of the tiny bird from my mind as I shut the front door and got into my car. But it just wouldn't go. I sat in the rush-hour traffic, my head was filled with memories of my father. His profile chiselled, yet softened, by time. In my mind's eye he would always be tall as a tree with broad shoulders and with arms that could protect me from harm. He'd shrunk since his heyday and the gradual change was more apparent each time I returned to Dublin.

The addition of a white stick would have thwarted and stifled many men, but not my father – he used it as a contraption to start chat with a stranger and make jokes with the ladies. He lived alone, in a little fishing village by the sea. I liked to visit Dublin but hadn't stayed for long periods since my daughter turned into a teenager. Her life was in Oxford with me and I understood why she didn't want to visit the sleepy town where her mother grew up.

However, it troubled me that my father was alone – especially since he lost his sight. He always put on a brave face to me and saw his condition as a challenge to be overcome. A change most people of his age would shirk from – but not Patrick Cullen. Keeping up to date with new technology was the best way to help him to live independently.

He was concerned about me since the break-up of my marriage. I'd been forced to change with the process and was starting to come around to the new me. My confidence was shaken and old hurts and wounds around my family had been dragged up in the transition. Even though my father wanted to help, I'd pushed him away because I was ashamed. I was ashamed at the failure of my relationship, and of the uncertainty and poverty that followed my divorce from Keith.

Thinking about my father made me smile and I'd forgotten about the dead bird by the time I arrived at work.

I was sitting at my desk for only a few minutes when Gerry, the supplement editor, called me into his office. I wiped my palms on my jeans and ventured across the row of desks to his office.

"Can you ride a horse, Roz?" he asked.

I laughed and said, "Sure!" I was ten years old the last time I'd sat on one, but I was still telling the truth.

"Are you available to go on a press trip in three weeks' time? It will be for no more than eight days. It includes a stay on a ranch in Oklahoma."

I'd been working at the *Oxford Times* for almost ten years and mostly wrote features and entertainment. I did a little travel writing from time to time which allowed me to visit the odd stately home and Christmas Market, but staying on a ranch was something that intrigued me. Besides, travelling abroad when I was married to Keith Waters was more than difficult. I was now free of my shackles in one way, but a sense of adventure was something that eluded me still.

"And there's a festival too – Native American – you can pull it together with a Cowboys versus Indians feature," Gerry said in a matter-of-fact tone. "You'd like that, wouldn't you, Roz?"

Suddenly my mind was filled with thoughts of my father again. He had such a passion for the Wild West – maybe this would be an opportunity to travel with him? When I asked if I could take him with me, I was careful not to tell my editor that he was blind.

"As long as I get photos with Stetsons and Indian headgear I don't care," Gerry said."Here are the details."

He handed over a contact number and my mind clicked into overdrive, instantly thinking of barriers and difficulties that would prevent me from going. Although I was divorced from Keith, he had a hold on me that made me query every-thing I did. Whatever I wanted to do, it would be wrong or selfish or bad. I hoped that he wouldn't make it awkward for me to go. Our daughter, Thalia, was sixteen and well able to look after herself but she couldn't stay home alone. She'd have to stay with her father.

Being married to Keith had prevented me from doing so many things in my life. He hated when I tried something new or introduced new friends into our circle. By the time our relationship was over he'd fallen out with one half of every couple we'd become friends with during our seventeen years together. I'd always made excuses for him and carefully avoided the inevitable criticism and conflict that followed, but eventually people became tired of his drama and he succeeded in isolating me from friends. Our separation was dramatic and involved another woman but, even though it shook my confidence for sometime, I'd learned how to protect myself, and I did it by avoiding any new relationship with men.

But now I'd been handed a golden opportunity to spend time with the man who had given me life. If I was still with Keith there would be no way that I'd be going on this adventure or taking my father.

Once I'd put all the details in place, I called my father and waited anxiously for his reaction to my plan. And it was spectacular.

"Rosaleen, oh Rosaleen, is this a joke? If you told me I'd won the lottery I couldn't be happier!"

I knew it was the right thing to do. The joy in his voice was music to my ears and I was filled with appreciation for all that he had given me.

Even though Keith tried to make me feel guilty for leaving Thalia, as I'd expected he would, I didn't let it deter me. I was hoping for a renaissance of sorts and I was ready.

Chapter 1

County Dublin, Ireland

Time swept by and suddenly I was in Skerries, the little town in Ireland where I grew up. The taxi passed the pillar in the centre of the main street and the small stores with brightly painted frontages that lined the road. I felt my heart pump faster as the fishing boats and sailboats appeared in my line of vision, bobbing up and down in the harbour with welcoming nods.

My father was standing at the front door of his little house as my taxi pulled up. With his shoulders back, he looked staunch and proud. He must have been waiting there for a while.

It was a small house that he lived in now, compared to the one where I grew up. It was sad that he had to move after my mother died but he couldn't afford the upkeep of the house and his new home served his needs. At least he lived close to the village, making it possible to shop with ease and go for a walk safely. The move turned out to be a good thing after he was diagnosed with retinitis pigmentosa. The condition took away 90% of his eyesight, leaving him with acute blurred vision affected by bright light and also severely poor night vision. He was told that he would be able to see images on a computer screen more easily than real-life objects which meant that he could decipher photos and words if they were large and clear enough. He took this news to heart and immediately did a course in IT. He was one of the first people I knew to log on to Skype. I suppose with both of his children living abroad, it was the only thing to do. I thought I was technologically savvy but my father continued to astound me.

He watched, or rather listened to the TV with Mary-next-door from time to time, and he enjoyed a chat with Katy in the village shop – but they were no substitute for a partner. He always got on better with women than men and lately only ever spoke of one male friend, Leo in Manchester, whom he Skyped and emailed frequently.

"Come in, come in!" he said and ushered me through the door quickly. "Put your bags in that room."

I knew my father well. He liked everything put in its correct place – exactly where he knew it would be easy to find – and that wasn't just a habit that developed following his blindness.

Then it was time for a hug and, when he squeezed me, he did it so tightly I had to hold my breath. I wondered when was the last time he'd enjoyed a hug like that? Apart from Thalia's occasional embrace it had been a long time since I'd been held so tightly. Keith's hugs were only ever a prelude to sex. I wished that I could hug Dad more often. It was one of the prices of emigration.

"I'm so happy to see you, Rosaleen."

He had always insisted on calling me by my full name. He was the only person who did. Since I'd moved to London in my twenties I made sure that everybody knew me as Roz. Back then I wanted to change myself, and my name was the easiest place to start. Some of my school friends used to call me Roz but it wasn't until I took up the job of sub-editor in a newspaper in London that I truly felt the benefits of my new identity.

"Now let's eat," said my father. "I thought a salad would be nice and I got some fresh bread from the market in town." He wore a wide smile, the one that I loved.

My father often spoke about the Farmers' Market in the city centre. I'd never been there with him, but I knew it was a pilgrimage that he enjoyed after early Mass on Sunday mornings.

"Thanks, Dad, you shouldn't have gone to so much trouble."

I genuinely hadn't wanted him to go out of his way or to buy fresh food. I knew that he'd want to leave the fridge thawing while we were away, and he'd be in a panic in the morning about what to do with its contents.

"Mary-next-door is going to take the bread that we don't eat," he said as he led me into the kitchen. "I have cheese and eggs and a few other bits and pieces to give to her as well. You know how I hate waste. Now sit down while I make the tea."

I smiled to myself. He'd read my mind. It was something he did easily. He said once that we all have the power to read each other's minds – that's what the third eye was used for. He was convinced that illusionists on the TV used the power of intuition to pull off psychic tricks. I listened to his notions with pleasure.

The table was set, the crusty bread already sliced on the breadboard. A full salad bowl sat waiting on the counter.

He put on the kettle and took out the milk from the fridge. Then he lifted a china teapot down from the dresser, put in tea bags and added boiling water. When he had finished, he held the teapot upon the air proudly, like a prize.

"Isn't it gorgeous!" he exclaimed in delight. "You'll never guess where I picked it up."

I had no clue. "Tell me," I said.

He gently put the pot of tea down and started into a yarn about finding a car boot sale in the village and how he needed a new teapot. The china was called Olde English Roses and he had once had a set like it in his office. It meant that he could easily visualise its details from his memory. It never ceased to amaze me – how small things like this kept him joyous in life. I seldom drank tea from a china pot. In our house in Oxford, when we wanted a cup of tea we grabbed a mug, shoved a teabag into it then poured in some boiling water. How did he keep such interest in simple things at seventy-five? If he'd shown me the same thing twenty years before, I'd have run from the house screaming – but he wouldn't have been interested in the teapot in those days. More than likely, it would have been some tropical fruit that was newly imported into the country or some piece of technology.

"Is there anything I can help you with?" I asked.

"Not a thing. I have my own way of doing things and I like having visitors – you know that."

And he did. He insisted that I told people to visit him when they were staying in Dublin. He was a generous host, but I didn't want others taking advantage of him.

He fussed around me and I watched accordingly.

As he put the finishing touches to our small meal and laid it on the table, he brought up the subject of my brother.

"I had a call from Evan, and he wished us all the best on our trip."

"That was good of him," I replied, careful not to say any more.

My brother, Evan, was a wiz in school and went on to study medicine. He became a successful doctor and settled in Sydney, Australia. I had called to tell him that I was taking Dad away before I left Oxford and he thought it was a good idea. He never had much in common with our father – they always sparked off each other. My father thought Evan lost the run of himself after he went to study medicine in Trinity College. The wedge between them set firmly around that time.

Evan said that he could never do right by Dad and I was our father's pet – his little girl. I think because I was the first born he adored me. Evan was a threat to Dad and had reached a level of achievement in his career that my father secretly had aspired to but failed to reach. That was my understanding of it anyway.

"Evan went on to talk about his new promotion."My father sighed as he joined me at the table. "How high can you go as a surgeon?"

"I don't really know." I was keen to change the subject. "So, are you all ready and packed for the morning?"

We would be taking the early-morning flight to Chicago, followed by a two-hour transfer before landing in Oklahoma. I hoped the journey wouldn't prove too much for him.

"I've been packed for the last week. I found a new suitcase on the internet of all places. You'd think I could find one in a shop in Dublin – but it isn't easy. I'll tell you what I did."

This was a story and it was my duty to listen – I wanted to

listen. I'd been starved of his stories of how he survived the struggles with his condition and made it into a kind of game. I'd been kept away from my old life by a husband who'd isolated me any way that he could. I listened.

"I rang Clerys and they left me hanging for hours before telling me that they didn't sell Antler luggage. Then I got the bright idea to try the Great Outdoors. So I got talking to a lovely girl called Anna and she was meant to order it in, but I rang before getting the bus into town and it's just as well because the bloody thing didn't come in with the shipment when it was meant to. Then I got Mary-next-door to buy it from the shop online. It wasn't easy, I tell you, because she doesn't know one end of a computer from the other and I had some craic trying to show her how to enter the credit-card details in." He stopped to giggle. "And me not able to see the numbers on the card. I swear it was like something out of a Monty Python sketch."

I tried to imagine the nervous Mary-from-next-door taking orders and stifled a chuckle.

"If I could bloody-well see I could do all of this easy," he huffed. "Anyway, all's well that ends well – the postman delivered my lovely bag to me last Thursday and, as the Yanks say, I'm all set!"

I was all set too. Set for what I wasn't sure, but I knew that this was a journey that had to be taken.

Chapter 2

O'Hare International Airport, Chicago

The aircraft bumped through the clouds as we started our descent but only a smile rose on my father's face. We arrived on time at Chicago O'Hare International Airport. The terminal was set out like rays of light shining from stars and gates stretching like an octopus's tendrils. The flags from different countries of the world hung from the ceiling and lined the walk to our boarding gate. Daddy expected me to describe every detail to him as we took each step closer to our connecting gate.

"Are you hungry, Rosaleen?"

I wasn't. "Do you want me to get you something?" I asked. "It looks like our connecting flight is delayed."

"No, I'm not hungry to be honest."

"We've plenty of time. Do you want to go to the bar? There's one just there."

My father shook his head. "What's the delay?"

"They haven't given us a departure time yet – it just says 'check board'. Come on, let's go to the lounge and take a rest."

The Admiral's Lounge was full of passengers. They were mostly businessmen and women who spent hours alone, connected to their offices via their laptops and phones. I found a nice couch in the corner for Daddy to sit-down while I went to get a cup of tea from the food bar. I gathered some snacks and apples too and brought them over to him.

"Thank you," he said. "Can you see a screen that will give us the flight times?"

"There's one over there – don't worry, we won't miss our flight," I assured him. "Give me your iPad and I'll put the WiFi on it."

The iPad had been a lifesaver for him – it connected him to the world and especially to me, being in another country.

"That would be great, thanks."

We were settled into our new base when a tall man with a friendly face and salt-and-pepper hair walked over towards us. A jacket hung from the crook of his arm and he carried a glass of beer in his hand.

"Is there anyone sitting there?" he asked, pointing at the couch beside my father.

"Well, that's a Dublin accent for sure," my father replied.

"It is," the man said. "And if I'm not mistaken you are from the northern counties?"

"Sit you down," my father said. "I'm Patrick and this is my daughter Rosaleen."

I extended my hand. There was something familiar about this man – it was as if we'd met before, but I couldn't figure out where.

"Roz," I said. "Pleased to meet you."

"I'm Michael," he said with a smile.

"Sorry, was that Mike?" my father asked.

"No – Michael, Michael Williams – but a lot of people call me Mike. Where are you off to?"

I was convinced that I recognised him from somewhere.

"Oklahoma," my father and I said together.

"Me too. Looks like we have a two-hour delay but at least it'll still be light when we arrive."

"That's good news, Michael," my father said, though in fact it was difficult for him to see day or night. "Where are you living?"

"I'm based in Rathmines."

"What's taking you to Oklahoma?" my father probed.

I was embarrassed by his questioning but Michael didn't seem to mind.

"I'm visiting my sister – she lives south of Oklahoma City."

I looked down at the wedding ring that he sported on his left hand and was surprised by my curiosity.

"What line are you in?" my father asked.

"Dad, I'm sure Michael doesn't want to have so many questions fired at him," I said.

Michael smiled a warm relaxed smile. His grey-blue eyes twinkled as he looked in my direction. "It's okay. I came over for a chat. I had a feeling that you two were Irish when I came in. You can always spot the Irish people in these lounges. I'm in the army."

I was surprised. With a casual check shirt and denim jeans, he certainly didn't look like a soldier. Then I spotted a tattoo creeping out from under the sleeve of his left arm which made me reconsider. The way he rested in the armchair with an air of presence made me suspect that he was an officer.

"What's your rank?" my father asked.

A little too abruptly for my liking.

"I'm a colonel."

Michael wore a cheeky grin on his face that my father didn't see, but they had a definite connection with each other.

"You'll have to forgive me, Michael, if I'm not looking at you. It's difficult for me to make you out in this place – you see, I'm visually impaired."

Michael looked over at me and nodded. "I admit that I spotted the stick, Patrick."

"That's his prop for chatting up women," I said.

We all laughed. I was glad Michael had joined us and in a strange familiar vein it felt like our meeting was pre-arranged.

"Hey, we lads have to use our circumstances to our advantage. Don't we, Patrick? It's called being resourceful. Reminds me of a story I heard once."

I watched. My father had met a kindred spirit, a story-teller, and perhaps this delay wouldn't be such a bad thing.

"There was a man who had a donkey, and the animal fell into an abandoned well. He wasn't able to get the animal out, and as it was old and no longer much use to him, he decided to fill up the well with earth to prevent any other creatures falling in. He asked his neighbours to help and shovel the clay in on top of the donkey."

My father was engrossed in the tale and so was I.

"The poor animal was sobbing when he realised that he was being buried alive but after a short while the sobs stopped. The man looked over the edge of the well and was surprised by what he saw. As each shovel of soil had landed on the donkey, he'd shaken it off and taken a step up to the next level of ground. The donkey continued to step up as the farmer and his friends filled the well, until eventually he was able to hop out to safety."

Michael looked over at me mischievously – he wasn't finished.

"That's incredible. So what's the moral?" my father asked.

"Well, the donkey was pretty peeved off at what his owner had tried to do to him, so he dug his teeth into the man's buttocks and sent him running. I suppose you could say the moral is – when life throws shit on you, shake yourself off and take a step up, but if you throw shit on others prepare to be bitten in the ass!"

We laughed. Michael was someone who brought warmth into a room. But I could sense that he wasn't telling his full story. There was something strange about his openness that didn't sit with the English manners I'd become accustomed to in the people that I usually met. It was one of the reasons why I loved being with my father who embraced his Irishness so naturally.

"Is there any change in the time for our flight?" my father asked.

I checked the monitor. "It looks like we'll be taking off at 4 o'clock, so there's only an hour and a half delay."

"It gives us a chance to get to know each other – will you have a drink?" Michael asked. "I'm getting another beer."

"I think I had too much on the flight from Dublin," my father said.

"I'd better not," I said. "I'll be driving when we get to Oklahoma."

"Sparkling water then?" he suggested.

When Michael was out of earshot my father leaned over and whispered to me. "He's a lovely fella – how old is he, do you think?"

"I'm not sure . . . he looks like he's in his forties – fifty at a push."

"He's quite a character."

I knew exactly what my father was up to. Matchmaking in an airport lounge was just his style.

"He reminds me a bit of you," I said with a grin.

My father always liked a compliment even if it was backhanded.

Michael returned with his hands full and a bottle of beer in his pocket. "I got you a refill, Patrick," he said, putting a cup of tea on the table.

He handed a large glass of sparkling water to me and smiled. It wasn't a flirtatious smile exactly but it was directed at me. Michael was the first person to pay me attention in a long time and it was a very nice feeling.

"Have you any more stories, Michael?" my father asked.

"I bet you have a fair few, Patrick, huh?"

My father enjoyed centre stage but seemed perfectly happy to let Michael take it for the moment. "You must have good stories about the army? You know my daughter had a plan to get rid of all the soldiers when she was a little girl – she figured out that it was a way of ending wars."

Michael raised his brows and looked over at me with a smile. "I think she had a point. It would put a lot of my colleagues out of a job – but you know much of the work we do is peacekeeping. I've done tours of Bosnia and Lebanon and made some great friends with local people. Not all armies are like our Irish one but there is a place for protecting communities. In an ideal world we wouldn't need armies, but this is where we are at the moment and we have to do the best we can."

"You don't strike me as a soldier," I said. His body-language didn't fit in with what he was telling us about himself.

"Well, I've done other things on my way to the forces but I can honestly say I've never been happier. It's not all about guns and battles – when you go into a territory and see the devastation left by brutal regimes, you know that you've a job to do that nobody else can. It's the rebuilding and rescuing that motivates me."

"And where are you going to next? Or can you not say?" my father asked.

"Officially, no."

"Go on, you can tell us," my father pressed him.

"I'm going to Thailand, actually."

"On a tour of duty?" my father asked, surprised.

"Nah, just on holiday," Michael replied. He raised his eyebrows towards me with a cheeky grin.

It sounded less likely that he had a wife. He could be a widower – if he was divorced, he wouldn't still be wearing a ring. It wasn't an appropriate question to ask a stranger even though I was riddled with curiosity. I didn't look at men as potential boyfriends – Keith had taken away more than my confidence. But Michael was oozing testosterone and I was feeling teenage flutters in my stomach every time my eyes connected with his.

Even though we weren't flying, time certainly was. I glanced over at the departure board and the flashing light beside our destination.

"Oh, it looks like we're boarding earlier than expected," I said.

"Isn't that grand now, and the time has flown with Michael to entertain us," my father said.

We gathered our hand luggage and walked together out to the thoroughfare. My father held on to my arm and Michael stayed close by.

"What number are our seats?" my father asked.

"3a and b."

"That's funny – I'm 3c," Michael said.

"So we would have met anyway," I said.

"Well, I always say there's no such thing as a coincidence, don't I, Rosaleen?" my father prompted.

He did and he firmly believed it. I used to think like that before I left Ireland and carved a life for myself in England, but those natural feelings of intuition and gut instinct left me with the same shocking alacrity as my husband.

The crowds pushed past us, but we quickly arrived at our gate and sat on three chairs close to the steward's desk.

"I don't even find it odd anymore," Michael said. "The amount of coincidences I've come across over the years is unbelievable."

"I think it is amazing that coincidences happen," I said. "It's especially strange that they happen more to people who believe in coincidences."

"It's like finding the free parking space just where you need it to be," Michael said.

"I'm surprised to hear you talk like this," I said. "Makes you sound like a bit of a hippy, Michael."

Michael nodded. "I've been called worse. The army has certainly opened my eyes and given me a different perspective on life. I just believe there's another force on hand that we can call on when we need it."

I could feel myself getting on my high horse. I couldn't see any good in army life.

"What about all the corruption associated with the armed forces?"

"You'll find that in all institutions of power really." Michael shrugged.

"Wherever you find two men together you'll see a power struggle," my father interrupted.

Michael grinned. "I know what you mean, Patrick. But I've seen some amazing things over the years. There is always hope and resilience in the human spirit. There have been wonderful men and women inspiring and helping us to find the beauty in life through the hard times."

When we got the call for boarding, we lined up as a united group.

~

Just before takeoff I looked over at my father. His face glowed, with clear skin showing barely a line. He certainly did not look his years. I hoped that I would radiate his healthy glow if I ever reached his age. I then turned to my other side and Michael was messing with the controls on his personal-entertainment system.

"It's great," he said, without realising how loudly he was speaking over the din from his earphones. "I've found Mott the Hoople on here – they're my favourite band!"

I smiled at the excitement in his voice. He reminded me of my father in so many ways – his enthusiasm and love of life were characteristics that my ex hadn't shared.

The two hours went by too quickly. Michael and I were children of the eighties and nineties and, although we hadn't known each other then, it seemed we had both been busy doing the same things such as going to the same concerts, frequenting the same bars in Dublin city and even attending the same sports events.

"I used to go to all the rugby matches in Lansdown Road in the nineties too," I said. Evan used to get tickets and I'd go along with the girls and we would party in the city afterwards.

"Strange that I never ran into you!"Michael paused for a moment. "I was refereeing in those days."

"At rugby matches?"

He seemed to become a little uncomfortable. "Eh, yeah, I used to do some B-team matches and the odd A-team."

Michael certainly was a man of many talents. As we made our descent through the clouds, I wanted to know more about him. This was the first man that I'd met since my marriage ended that I felt a real connection with, and he made me feel better about myself.

I wished we had a longer time to spend with Michael Williams.

We said goodbye at Will Rogers Airport and I was aching for him to ask for my number.

He shook my father's hand. "Have a wonderful trip, Patrick."

Then he turned to me and I held out my hand. He took it and put his other arm around my shoulder in a half-hug. "It's been really lovely meeting you, Roz. I hope we meet again."

I was about to ask him for his number, but something stopped me. Besides, I figured social media had made it possible to find almost anybody. How many colonels could there be in the Irish army?

Chapter 3

Oklahoma

"Tell me what you see now?" my father asked. He insisted that I left a gap in the car window so that the balmy breeze crept in to cool us –he hated the harshness of air-con.

"Some cows," I replied.

"What cows?" he asked, his voice a mixture of impatience and excitement. "Are they black, longhorned, what?"

I couldn't understand why he wasn't exhausted – it was one o'clock in the morning by my biological clock.

"No, they don't have long horns – they're all black though." I kept one eye on the Sat Nav and another on the road ahead. "Would you like to hear some music?"

He shook his head. "Maybe tomorrow. Right now I don't want to miss a thing."

My eyelids were heavy and I had to concentrate hard on the road ahead.

We came to the Cimarron River. Over small bridges we

criss-crossed the rambling, snakelike, winding water. These bridges resembled the ones in Iowa and Ohio and others scattered across the middle of America, in towns forgotten by the big cities that lined the east coast.

"There's one of those windmills like you see in Westerns." I pulled over slowly so that he could open the window wider and try to see.

"That's a water pump," he said. "The windmill works the pump to draw the water up. I want to take a photograph of one of those on my iPad before we go home."

I smiled – my dad the techie.

We continued on our journey.

"What's that red flashing by – on the ground?" he asked.

"That's the earth – it's a deep pinky red."

"Ah yes, I remember the description of the red earth in Steinbeck's *Grapes of Wrath*. I downloaded the audio book onto my iPod before we came away. I hadn't read it in years, and it was even better the second time. The young girl sharing her breast milk with the starving man had me in tears."

I felt a bit uncomfortable when he described the scene. I wasn't at such ease with myself so instead continued with my descriptions of the topography.

"The earth is deep red, and the fields are scattered with large bales of hay."

"Can you see any tractors?" he asked.

"I've seen some massive, big yellow ones that look like combine harvesters."

"It's early to be bringing in the hay. They must be having a dry spell," he said with a knowing smile.

I almost missed the sign for our accommodation. It was chiselled into a piece of log and the skull of a Longhorn hung on the side of the post holding it up.

"'*Long Island Guest Ranch*' – it looks like we're here at last, Dad."

"That didn't take long at all!"

I chuckled quietly.

We drove down a track covered with stone chips and it became windier and rougher the farther we travelled. After about two miles I began to wonder if we were in the right place – but then I saw an oil drill and storage unit.

My itinerary read that the daughter of the Black family, Casey, would be there to greet us. I'd texted her on our departure from Oklahoma City Airport so she had a good idea of our arrival time. Finally, we came to a wall that marked a dwelling and two large farm gates.

Then the gates swung open and a woman was there.

Her eyes were like pools of brown ink, large and bright with traces of Native American ancestry.

"Hi, how y'all doing after your long trip? I'm Casey." Her skin too was tanned by her genes. "It's so great to see y'all. I was thinkin' you couldn' find us."

We got out of the car and were met with a hug from our hostess. I was too used to English ways and found her warmth a bit strange, but my father was overjoyed with Casey's welcome.

He pointed his nose up to the sky, in the same way a Labrador would, and sniffed the air.

Casey took him by the arm. I'd told her before our arrival that he had only limited vision and she seemed to know exactly how to make him feel relaxed and comfortable.

The guest lodge was surrounded by pine trees and small flowerbeds. Outside on the porch, three people sat on rocking chairs, awaiting our arrival.

"This is my paw, Joel," Casey said proudly, pointing to an

old cowboy dressed in denim and a straw hat. "And my brother Rick. This 'ere's Amy and she helps us with the horses."

Rick wore boots with spurs and Amy's straw-likehair was piled on top of her head in a pony-tail. Her dungarees were two sizes too big but didn't take away from her beauty.

We shook hands and I sensed we were with kindred spirits.

Then I was reminded of the feeling that I used to have whenever we arrived at my grandmother's house after the long journey to Inniskeen.

Casey led us to the dining table in the old guest lodge. Pinned to the walls were deer and buffalo heads. In between the animals, beautiful paintings hung – one of a Native American woman and another of a cattle drive. The smell of beans and brisket came wafting from the top table. Fresh salad and dumplings filled large ceramic bowls to the side.

"Will y'all have some lemonade?" Casey wiped her palms on her dungarees and lifted a jug.

"How lovely – and that food smells delicious, Casey," my father said. His sense of smell had become more acute since he lost his sight.

Casey pulled back one of the dark-pine chairs. "Why don't you sit here, Patrick," she said, "while I get you some supper."

"Not at all – I will serve myself like everyone else," he insisted.

It was dark in the lodge and I knew this would cause him difficulty, but I didn't want to put a dint in his pride. I stood beside him while he asked for a description of the food laid out on each platter.

"Can you smell that wood?" he whispered into my ear.

I hadn't until he'd asked me. The logs that made the lodge had their own unique aroma and although we were indoors it felt like we were outside in nature.

"This is flipping brilliant!" he said. Then he carefully lifted his plate with its cowboy food and took it over to the red-check-covered table where we all settled down to eat.

"What are all those things on the walls?" my father asked Casey and the others.

Rick started to explain how some of the animals had been hunted, and when and where they came from.

I let them talk on and ate hungrily. I was exhausted. It was not the journey but more the responsibility of getting there in one piece that had drained me. Perhaps I'd bitten off more than I could chew by bringing my father. I was aching for a shower. The humidity of Oklahoma was a world away from Oxford and even further from the fresh coastal breeze I'd enjoyed in Dublin the night before.

"Do you think we should go to our chalet, Dad?" I asked when we had finished eating.

But my father was having none of it. He was in his element, chatting to Joel about his own childhood in rural Ireland.

"Roz, why don't I help carry your luggage to your chalet?" Casey suggested. "Then I can bring your paw over when he's finished."

I appreciated her help, so that was what we did.

Our room was similar to my grandmother's house in Inniskeen. The sheets had a type of floral print that she used to have. A fan overhead brought relief from the dense thick air that wafted in through the doorway.

Twelve hours on airplanes and in airports had taken their toll and I needed to feel water on my skin. I turned the dial on the shower and the tepid water dribbled out. It did just fine. I closed my eyes as it ran down my body and thought of my daughter and hoped she was alright.

"I'm coming in – are you decent?" my father called through the door. "Not that I can see much anyway!"

"I'm taking a shower!" I shouted, but I needn't have – there was nothing wrong with his hearing. He had told me some time before that he could hear better now than when he was a child. He could hear sounds that he hadn't before his sight left him and he could tell so much from a breath or a sigh that he often didn't need to understand the words to know what someone was saying.

"I'll only be a minute."

"Take your time," he replied. "It'll take me a few minutes to figure out how to unpack."

There was a time when I would have done it for him, but now he berated me for treating him like an invalid. I knew to help when he asked for it and not before. His pride had never left him.

I dried myself and slipped into my cotton pyjamas. I would be warm but decent.

"I can't manage to open this drawer," he said.

His lack of sight and strange surroundings didn't stop him from throwing himself into his task, but his frustration reminded me of Thalia when she was small.

I went over to help him, pulled hard on the drawer and it opened.

"Are you sure you want to unpack everything?" I asked.

"I like to get my things out of the case. You know I do."

He wasn't to be swayed, so I let him put his carefully pressed shirts into the drawer, on top of each other. There wasn't a crease to be seen and I wondered how long it had taken him to press them like that.

I checked my watch, and it was now the equivalent of 4am in Ireland.

"Are you tired yet?" I asked.

"Rosaleen, I've never felt more awake in my life. There's something about the sounds out there. That grand girl, Casey, led me to the step of our chalet and as we were walking I listened out for every sound, but there were so many I couldn't quite catch them all. I did hear the whip-poor-will though and I checked with Casey and she said that there are coyotes around too."

"Do you want to go out onto the porch and hear some more?"

He nodded and we slowly stepped out into the night. The sounds of wildlife filled the air. .

"I wonder how Michael is getting on. We never got his number and it's such a pity." Dad sighed.

I'd been thinking about him too but would never mention that to my father.

"I'm sure he's easy to look up – there can't be many colonels in the Irish army?"I said.

"That's true," he said, nodding. "I always hoped that you would meet a man like that. Such a fine lad."

"Well, he was wearing a wedding ring on his finger!" I said and my mind wandered until my dad brought me back to the moment.

"Oh! I suppose that's that then … but he didn't strike me as married. I thought he was interested in you."

"Don't be silly, Dad."

"Alright but I know these things. So tell me then, what are the stars like?"

I looked up to be overwhelmed. Earlier I hadn't stopped to look up, and what a sight I'd missed.

"Oh my, I don't think I've ever seen so many!" I craned my neck to find Cassiopeia, my favourite constellation, but I couldn't. There were so many stars piled on top of each other I could barely make out the Plough. The night was deep velvet blue – pure – not contaminated by city light.

A shooting star shot by and then another.

"Tell me, is it beautiful?" he asked.

"Yes, it is."

"When I was a lad in Inniskeen you could see every star in the universe. There wouldn't be a light on the street for miles and I would sit out on a summer evening and look up until I was dizzy with the beauty of it all."

In that moment I got it – it was a sight that could only be described as magical.

"That's what we are all made from, you know," he said.

"What is?"

"Stars. Every substance out there is down on this planet and forms every part of us. We are stardust!"

I giggled. "It's typical of you to come out with something like that, Dad."

"I remember when I was about eight years of age and hiding out under the stars by myself. We didn't have electricity until I was older, and you went to bed with the stump of a candle and by God you made it last as long as you could. There was no light for reading, or books to read anyway unless you were in school. This particular night I was out lying on a pile of wood that I'd gathered for my brothers that day. It was a spectacular night – kind of like this one in many ways. And the shooting stars were bouncing around the Galaxy like ping-pong balls. I used to call these nights 'magic nights' and I'd make all kinds of wishes. I was in the middle of dreaming up all sorts when my mother came out and caught me lying there. I thought she'd be mad."

"And was she?"

"You know what she did? She climbed up on the pile of wood and lay down beside me. She said she often came out to look up at the stars when she wanted to talk to my father. Now, I knew my father was dead and I knew what dead meant. But my mother said that he'd dissolved into one of the stars above our head and some day we would be stars too because we'd all come from the stars and would go back there."

I couldn't imagine my granny speaking that way – it was almost a new-age thing to say. She was a strict Catholic woman who kept a picture of the Pope and the Sacred Heart above the mantelpiece in her parlour.

"Did you not think it a bit strange when she said that?" I asked.

"No, it made perfect sense. I was confused before she told me that and then I understood. It used to drive me mad in the head trying to figure out what was in the universe before there was the universe. When my mother explained that it has no beginning and no end and we are all part of it, it helped. Have you never thought about what you are made from?"

"I did honours biology and chemistry, Dad – I know exactly what I'm made from."

My father tutted. "You don't need science to know what or who you are."

"I know that I'm energy and everything in the world is energy."

He winked at me. "Then you know that energy has to go somewhere – it can't just disappear, can it?"

Since when had he become a scientist? He was giving new meaning to Einstein's theories and philosophy, and he wasn't finished there.

"Remember always that you are energy – like those stars up there – and we can talk about this again."

And with that cryptic message he beckoned that it was time to go back into our chalet and sleep.

I didn't realise it on that first night, but it was the start of my lessons.

Chapter 4

Newcastle, Oklahoma

Michael often found new people to put into his prayers at night. His evening office was a requirement of his occupation, but he saw it more as a meditation at the end of the day. When he'd met Roz and her father at the airport, he knew that he had new candidates for his prayers. Sometimes there was a reason for meeting new souls and then at other times the people who touched him were never seen again.

He threw himself onto the bed. His brother-in-law, Ben, had opened a couple of beers on his arrival and his sister had ordered a takeout Chinese meal. He was made feel welcome by his sister but realised that he was on borrowed time. He liked to check in on Claudia every couple of years because she seldom made it back to Dublin. Although she was cheery and upbeat there were times when he felt she was hiding something from him. Michael didn't like Ben but would never use his personal feelings to judge someone and Ben was part of his family. Michael figured the best thing to do was to pray for those that he didn't like.

He would say his office on his back as he had done on so many occasions. The life of a priest was taxing in the twenty-first century with so many different parts to play. Michael often considered how lucky he was to have joined at a time when he could be truly himself and not hide under a guise of fear and servitude. The hugely controlling Archbishop McQuaid had long gone from the Irish bishopric before Michael took Holy Orders and the Catholic Church was an institution in demise before the scandals of the last century had hit. There were times when he felt lonely and at low ebb, but he considered that to be part of the human condition.

Only when he came across people like Roz and her father did he question his station in life. There was something about Roz that made him feel real inside – like he had done in the past. There were people he'd loved and had to leave because of who he was and how he chose to live. He could have chosen a different faith and allowed himself the freedom to commit to another but deep down he knew that was not his destiny. It didn't make it easier when he came across people like Roz who aroused his emotions and feelings of intimacy. It made life more interesting but also more testing.

Roz was lucky to have her father in her life. Michael guessed that she was in her early to mid-forties and she looked well with the years. Her father was a character and the sort of man that he would enjoy getting to know better. They were in his soul group. It's not something he'd say to them or to anyone, but he knew what it meant to share soul connections with people and he was spiritually connected to Roz and Patrick. Sometimes he felt he could travel back in time and imagine when people had crossed his path before. On first impression he would put Roz and Patrick back in the nine-teenth century and the height of the Great Famine. When he first saw them he felt as if he were thrown back to the stone walls of Connaught and roars of the bailiffs. He could see in his mind's eye Roz carrying her family's pain. But, then again, sometimes he reckoned that he just had an overactive imagination, and his historical metaphors were ways that he picked up on people's personal issues.

Claudia called out *"Michael, come for a nightcap?"*

Michael lifted himself off the bed and walked out to the hall where Ben brushed by him with a frown.

"Good night, Ben."

"Yeah, y'all sleep well, Michael."

Ben was gruff and short usually and Michael wondered if he was hiding something.

When he went into the kitchen Claudia was sitting at the table drinking a large glass of white wine. Her auburn hair was lighter than the last time he had visited and her skin not so sun-kissed. She looked as though streaks of tears had dried into her cheeks a few minutes before.

"Is everything alright?" he asked.

Claudia sighed. "Sure, it's been a tough year on the farm. Ben's afraid we're going to lose it. There's a big drive by the banks to get people off their ranches. They want to industrialise the land."

"But what about you, Claudia? How are you doing?"

Claudia was a teacher and it was getting harder to keep positive in a system that wasn't feeding and nurturing the minds of the young people that she dealt with everyday. There was always the threat of trouble in the public school where she worked, and it was becoming more common for kids to come to school with weapons in their bags. She shook her head.

"Everything just feels so pointless, Michael."

This was what he had been afraid of. He was worried for his sister's mental health. She had been so lethargic about everything the last few times they had spoken that it had spurred him on to make time to visit. He knew that he had to be in Oklahoma and hoped that the week would be enough for Claudia to open up completely to him about what was really wrong with her world.

"Well, I'm here if you want to talk about it," he said.

"Not tonight – it's good to just see you. It's been a long time. How are Mam and Dad?"

"They'd love to see you all. They haven't seen the kids in a long time."

"We can't afford to fly over – not all four of us. We barely have enough to get by at the moment."

"I can give you the money for the fare. I don't have anyone else to spend my money on."

With that Claudia stood up. "Ben would never agree to that. I'd best get to bed. The kids have summer camp tomorrow, and we are up early. Goodnight."

Michael watched her walk out the door and he realised he would have to be more assertive next time they spoke – because he wasn't going home without some answers.

Chapter 5

Long Island Guest Ranch, Oklahoma

I woke shortly before six and the birds trilled with song. The whip-poor-will was at the forefront and the sound of horses' hooves shuffled in a paddock nearby. My first thought was of Michael and I wondered what he was doing now.

My father lay stretched out on the bed with his eyes closed but I could tell he wasn't asleep.

He spoke first.

"Did you sleep all right?"

"Yes, thanks. I'm glad we slept until this time. I usually wake at four when I'm this side of the Atlantic. How about you – did you sleep?"

"Yes, I slept but I was enjoying the sounds from outside. I'd swear a coyote came up to our door."

I lifted my iPhone and checked for messages. I saw none and was relieved that all must be okay at home.

"I'm going to pop outside and call Thalia," I said.

"Say hello to my lovely granddaughter."

"I will."

"And if that blackguard answers the phone, tell him I'll kill him someday."

My father never referred to my ex-husband by his name. Maybe it was the fact that he blamed Keith for settling me across the Irish Sea. In the end he was right. Thalia was the bond between us and my father said that Keith used it to get at me still.

My wedding day was a sad occasion – largely because of my father's speech. He spoke that day about marriage taking me away from my home and my family – like so many emigrants, never to return. He implied that Keith had stolen me from him forever and how much he would miss me. It set me off on a tearfest for the rest of the evening and even my girlfriends who'd come from Dublin to share the day with me were howling.

Keith's solitary disposition irked Dad. It troubled him that he never knew what Keith was thinking and he said to me once, 'That's a bad thing in a man!". Maybe because he found it so easy to read other people's thoughts, the fact that he couldn't read Keith's frustrated him. Or maybe he *could* read Keith's thoughts and that was why he was frustrated with me.

By the time our marriage ended I realised that I should have listened to him.

Keith treated my father with a certain amount of respect from the beginning. However, he hated my father's Irishness.

Keith was always controlling me, and I spent most of my time trying to cope with his moods. But my daughter had the measure of him now and had developed a strong character that reminded me of my father.

Truthfully, my dad and I had been under strain since I married Keith.

"He has no backbone," were the exact words he had used when I told him that we were getting married. "And why hasn't he asked me for my permission?"

"That's very old-fashioned," I'd said at the time – but secretly I'd wondered the same.

"That's good manners," my father had retorted.

Then immediately he'd wrapped his arms around me and hid his head in my shoulder. He did the same thing when I had to tell him ten years later that my marriage was over.

It was a difficult time for him during the summer that I got married. My mother had started having lung problems and her body became weaker. We weren't sure if she would make it through to my wedding. But she went on to survive the birth of Thalia and my brother's wedding five years later.

"Your mother's not going anywhere," Keith had said a few days after we got married.

He'd been right and it meant that my father was left to pick up the pieces alone. I still felt terrible guilt for leaving him to bear the burden of caring for my mother for all those years. I cried a lot at that time, but my father never gave a hint of any of his hardship. Instead, when I visited – usually just Thalia and me – he would show us a fantastic time, touring places like Glendalough and Newgrange. He wanted Thalia to be knowledgeable about her Irish identity and when she was little it was an important part of her development.

But the teenage years were proving difficult, not just for Thalia but for me surprisingly. Keith's relationship with her was fraught with tension; he was paranoid that his daughter was turning wild and it meant that he interfered in our lives too much. Thalia went to a good school and was doing well with her studies. She was just about to begin her summer exams. I was proud of my daughter and didn't feel the same need to restrain her that her father did.

Thalia was hyped up before I left about a party in Woodstock. I knew that Keith wouldn't allow her to go so I'd organised for her to stay with her friend instead.

I dialled the number for Keith's apartment and was overcome with mother-love when Thalia answered.

"Hello?"

"Tally, darling, it's me."

"Hi, Mum!"

"How are you getting on?"

"Dad has just left and I'm going to Emma's after school – her mum said she'd pick us up."

I'd told Emma's mother, Paula, about my trip and she'd assured me that she would look after Thalia as if she were her own while I was away. I trusted her good sense to keep Thalia safe, but it would be a balancing act to keep Keith feeling he had control over our daughter and not push him out of the equation.

"Is everything okay?" I asked.

Thalia hesitated and I was immediately worried.

"How did you get on with your father?" I asked.

"I can't stand him, Mum. You know how he creeps around the house and then locks himself in his room."

I did know exactly what she meant, and it was foolish of me to think that it was normal in the past – I didn't miss his idiosyncrasies. It was another reason why I'd organised for Thalia to spend time in her friend's house.

"Don't worry. I'm going out now so ring me in Emma's if you want to later."

I reluctantly said goodbye.

I'd learned to get on with my life because there was a time when I'd let Keith's moods affect me – especially when Tally was younger. I was proud of myself for taking my father away like this and had faith and trust that my daughter would be okay.

I hesitated outside the door of the chalet. The air was heavy and humid, but I felt life all around me from the bees buzzing in the hedge and the redwings flitting from branch to branch. The calm and serenity about the ranch imbued me with a new sense of peace.

I opened the door to see my dad standing at the sink with his electric razor in hand.

"Can you show me where the plug socket is, please, Rosaleen?"

I took the razor from him and surveyed the plug.

"You'll need an adaptor," I said and went to search in my bag.

"It's been so long since I've been to America that I forgot the plugs are different."

His frown said a lot. When he got frustrated like this, I realised how much I took my sight for granted.

"What do they look like?" he asked.

"The pins are thin and flat, and slanted."

"Oh yes, I remember now. Let me attach it."

I handed him the adaptor and he attached the razor.

"I'll need you to show me how to turn on the shower."

The roles were now reversed. He was the one who used to show me how to do everything.

On holidays to France when I was a child, he would explain the cultural differences to my brother and me. Those holidays were fraught between moments of bliss and others of terror – especially when my mother had one of her turns. I know now what those turns were but then it was all unclear. Daddy always tried to cover up – to make things better for us kids. He did his best and I was determined to make this trip exceptional for him.

We made our way to the lodge where a hearty breakfast awaited, prepared by Casey and Joel. Thick pancakes rested on plates with the sweetest maple syrup dripping all over them. The bacon was cut in chunks and the eggs were a bright yellow the colour of sunshine. We relished every bite.

Afterwards, Rick and Amy led the way to the paddock, followed by me and my father in a state of high excitement.

"Are you sure Rick won't mind taking me out? I haven't been on a horse in fifty years," he whispered.

"It's part of the experience, Dad – he knows you can't see."

"I don't want to mess things up for you – you have to write your article."

But when Rick directed my father over to a brown mare called Cowgirl, it was as if he had introduced two old friends.

Cowgirl nuzzled into my father's shoulder and he took a deep breath.

"Good girl," he said, rubbing the mare's nose.

My father had a way with animals. I'll never forget how he built a hutch for the guinea pigs that I brought home from school when I was eight years old. There were two of them because I'd promised a girl that I'd take two so they wouldn't be lonely. My father told me afterwards that the girl's mother was so keen to get rid of all the guinea pigs that had mated in her shed, she had to give them away in pairs. I was lucky that I was given two females so there wouldn't be more guinea pigs, but my father looked after them long after I lost interest in them. He used to feed the creatures cornflakes and hot milk on cold winter's mornings. He connected easily with animals and made time for them despite his own busy schedule.

Cowgirl took off around the paddock with my father on her back. I hadn't the same connection with four-legged creatures.

Rick looked me up and down in a genial manner but suggested he might have difficulty finding a suitable animal for me to ride. It would have to be a mild-tempered horse. I handed over my sanity as I put my foot in the stirrup and Rick lifted me up onto a mare called Pongo. She leered at me with suspicion.

We were led on a trail through the pine groves and I began to loosen up as I watched my father sit upright and straight. How was he able to ride his horse so well when he couldn't see where he was going? He was certainly at ease.

Perhaps it had something to do with the instinct he'd gained since losing his sight.

Rick gave a running commentary along the way and this pleased my father, who didn't ask one question – he just patted his horse on the mane every now and then. The balmy breeze blew over us and I started to enjoy the experience.

"That's the Yellow Rose of Texas right there," Rick said, stretching out his heel at a cactus.

I listened as he talked about the plants and cursed the cypress trees that sprouted up all over the landscape.

"And that there's a hangin' tree – was a time when these prairies was filled with outlaws hiding out from bounty hunters and the like. My gran'paw told us stories he got from his pappy who came here for the Land Run."

My father's ears pricked up and he started a buoyant conversation discussing the Irish who had come to escape the harsh times in Ireland during the 1800s.

"Yeah, *we's* all got Irish in us *and* Injun. *We's* in the heartland – that's Oklahoma."

I watched the expression on my father's face and it was angelic – calm and relaxed in a way that I hadn't seen since I was a child.

Each step our horses took brought us further along the trail and out into the open prairie. We stopped at a waterhole and a strange-looking tree with branches hanging forward as if it were bowing.

"That there's another hangin' tree," Rick said. "Folks say plenty of fugitives met their end at this tree. In the ol' days they'd hide out in the Gloss Mountains and boun'yhunters'd came seek 'm out."

A wild turkey flew up from a ditch and startled my horse, and my father instinctively leaned forward and touched my shoulder.

"Are you all right?" he checked.

I was surprised by his touch. How did he know how to find my shoulder so precisely?

"I'm fine, thanks." I was a little girl again and my father was so sure and strong in his stride. The warm breeze enveloped me with emotion.

He had always made me feel safe like this in the past and I tried not to remember when it had changed.

Riding on this land reminded me once more of Inniskeen. My father loved to spend his time helping his brothers on the land and taking care of the Friesians. I remembered the first time he showed me how to milk a cow. We sat on small milking stools in my grandmother's cowshed and he gently put the teat into my palm.

"Now squeeze hard and pull down," he ordered.

My little hand made no impression at first but, after he showed me a second time, I managed to squeeze a few drops of milk from the cow.

A great sense of accomplishment always followed after he showed me how to do things. Like the first time I rode a bicycle. He would take me to the local demesne where the trails wove through scores of sycamore trees and hold on to the back of my saddle. We did this every Sunday for about a month and then I finally got the sense of balance needed to propel myself forward. My brother never came with us – in hindsight my mother liked to hang on to her little boy and was happy to leave me be with my father. That disconnection between us as a family unit was not natural but it was what I was used to. It didn't concern me then as I knew no better but, after the failure of my own marriage, I did wonder if I knew how to be in a family. When I had my daddy to myself I was happy and those were the years that formed me as a person.

It was like that now even though Rick and Amy were riding beside us.

We rode into the paddock just as Casey rang on the old tin bell. It hung in the porch and was our call to lunch.

"We done good," Rick said and smiled at me.

I felt huge relief as my feet touched solid ground. My legs were left bow-shaped and yet lightened from the experience.

"I've had spa treatments that didn't make me feel this good when they finished," I said.

"Ah, you were squeezing on to your horse too tightly – let your legs hang straight next time," my father said.

"You done real good, Patrick," Rick said as he helped my father down.

He reached for my father's stick which had been resting against a fence which had the skulls of three Longhorns tacked to it.

"I never thought I'd be up on a horse again," my father sighed.

I wasn't sure but I thought I saw a tear in his eye.

"Come now or Casey'll be mad at us," Amy said.

She was confident but quiet in a mild-mannered way that put those around her at ease.

The smell of cowboy stew filled the air as we entered the lodge.

"I've worked up some hunger," my father said.

We sat at the table and dug into the mix of meats and beans held together with a warm broth. Fresh white crusty bread was dipped into our stew and we ate without saying much until it was finished.

"What's that black shape up there?" My father pointed to the head of a buffalo looming over the door to the kitchen.

"Why, that's a buffalo Paw shot and that buckskin beside it was my first kill," Rick said proudly.

Coming from my sanitised world, I'd have normally found this type of conversation difficult to stomach but I was beginning to understand that this land was not like mine – although it was just as real. These people hunted and killed as part of their way of life – the same way as the Native Americans had before their arrival.

I listened as Casey talked about her mother. It was the first time her mother had been mentioned and we were taken into the Black family confidences as the story was told.

"Momma was half Cherokee and so, so, beautiful," Casey said. "Her name was Elizabeth. People use' to stop and talk to her wherever she went."

I observed Joel's expression as his daughter spoke about his wife, his eyes half closed as if he was seeing her in his mind's eye.

"Casey's righ'," he said. "She loved having people here – would stay up all night talkin' about differen' countries and stuff. She'd tell ye what the weather was gonna be and if there'd be trouble comin'."

"In Ireland we'd say she had the gift," my father prompted.

"Oh, she had that awrigh' – she even knew the day she was gonna die," Casey said softly.

Her mother was a missing piece in this little family unit, and I could tell that since her passing the dynamic had changed dramatically. Casey fussed over her father like a spouse. I wondered if this was an attempt to make things better for her or for her father. They were settled in their body language and I'd seen this type of relationship before.

One of my oldest friends had nurtured and minded her father for all of her adult life – to such an extent that she hadn't married. She walked the path of his widow on the day of his funeral while his other children skulked in the shadows. That wasn't a right way to live either but, since I'd been divorced, I realised that there was no right or wrong way to live – only life.

I watched the banter between Casey and Joel as they described Elizabeth some more.

"She was the warmest, most welcoming woman," Casey continued.

"She sure was," Amy said, making one of her infrequent contributions.

"Deirdre was the same," my father piped up. "She loved to have visitors and was always ready to throw a good party."

I almost choked at my father's words. My mother certainly loved a good party, but I would never have described her as hospitable. Could time have faded his memory so much? Still, this was his chance to speak and I would never contradict him in company. I did feel hollow inside and wished I could paint up the past in pretty rose-tinted frames the way he obviously had.

I excused myself and went out to the pool where the bees buzzed busily and the butterflies danced in synchronicity over the pond. The past needed to be laid to rest but I wasn't ready to do it yet.

Chapter 6

I was stretched across a deckchair when my slumber was broken by Casey.

"Hey, Rosaleen, do you want to join us on a trip to Enid? I was telling your paw 'bout Simpson's Cowboy Museum and he said he'd love to visit."

I was surprised that she'd called me Rosaleen. My name was Roz and it was printed clearly on all the literature that I'd sent her.

"You okay?" she said.

"Yes, fine thanks, Casey," I said with a laugh. "I'm just not used to anyone apart from my father calling me Rosaleen."

"Oh, it's such a purty name, but Roz is too – I jus' kinda think you're a Rosaleen."

Maybe I was Rosaleen while I was with my father. I did feel different being on my own with him like this. It reminded me of those days spent in the park on my bike and fishing down at the harbour.

"I really don't mind what you call me," I said. It wasn't Casey's fault that I'd tried to change myself. She knew nothing of my inadequacies. "Yes, let's go to the museum – is it far from here?"

She shook her head. "Heck no – only abou' thirty mile."

I laughed to myself – thirty miles was quite a trip in Oxfordshire. But I guessed if my driveway was three miles long like Casey's I would have a different perspective on distance too.

"Where's my dad now?"

"He's gone to freshen up – he's such a great guy – you wouldn' guess he was blind only for 'is white stick."

"He's very independent."

"I worry about my paw – he's been poorly since Momma died. Taking lots of tablets now and not able to ride the way he did."

Her expression told a multitude. Living in this isolated way on a ranch, eight miles from the nearest town? I understood exactly what she meant. The Blacks were a solid family who lived and worked and moved together in much the same unity as the bees that buzzed in the bush nearby. That sense of oneness was something missing in my family. We were never one strong unit and I envied Casey that. But something in the closeness of Casey and Joel reminded me of the relationship that my father and I had shared before I married Keith… and already we were becoming closer again.

We drove in an old jalopy as Joel wouldn't hear of us taking our rental car. The wheels bumped up and down and spat stones up into the air as we came to the main road. My dad and Joel sat in the front while Casey and I took the back seats and bounced in harmony with the lumps on the road. We looked like two little girls who'd been taken out for an ice cream. I tried not to think of my aching muscles after the horse-ride.

"The Gloss Mountains out that way are real purty – we can swing by on the way back," Joel said.

"We won't have time to do both, Paw. Rick's girlfriend's comin' for supper and Amy asked her friend too."

Joel grunted. "I'd forgo'en that."

Again they showed the habits of an old married couple. I hadn't asked Casey if she had a boyfriend. It wasn't my place. I figured that the Blacks would tell us more about their lives at their own pace. So far we'd told very little of ours.

"The roads are just great," my father piped up once we left the track to the house. "So long and straight. I notice the bends and bumps more than most as I can't see the way the road turns."

"I'd never've known you couldn't see – wasn' I jus' sayin' that, Rosaleen?" Casey said.

"Yes – Dad is very independent – he lives alone."

"Oh! I figured you guys lived beside each other – or together."

Casey seemed startled and I felt guilt creep over me.

"Dad lives in Ireland and I live in the UK. Maybe you've heard of Oxford."

"Oxford!" Joel exclaimed. "We've been to Oxford, haven't we, Casey?"

"We sure have – Momma was with us and we went to see Winston Churchill's grave – what was the name of that palace where he was born, Paw?"

Joel looked thoughtful.

"Blenheim Palace," I prompted.

"That's the name of it," Joel said, thumping the dashboard.

"I live very close by, in Bladon."

It was a remarkable coincidence but maybe, as Michael had said to us at the airport, there's no such thing as a coincidence. I hoped that meant the universe would provide the opportunity to bump into him again.

The old truck hit a pothole in the road and I hoped it wouldn't fall apart – another couple of smacks and it easily could.

"Well, I never," my father said, as he ran his palm along the bars of the makeshift jail.

"Come over here, Patrick." Casey took my father's elbow gently as she guided him over to the sheriff's desk.

"Isn't this flippin' great?" he chuckled as Casey pinned a sheriff's badge to his shirt.

"Did anyone ever say y'all looked like Clint Eastwood?" Joel said.

That made my father's day.

"My wife Deirdre used to say she fell in love with me after watching *The Good, the Bad and the Ugly* – I can't see the resemblance myself."

He made me laugh. Over the years dressing as Clint Eastwood was his party trick. He took out a well-worn poncho and cowboy hat every Halloween since I could remember. When I was a child he always dressed in his cowboy gear at the end of my birthday parties when handing out the goody bags.

"I see the resemblance awrigh'," Joel said.

"Well, on the other hand," said my father, "maybe I do

resemble him a bit. He's a Monaghan man like myself after all."

"What do you mean?" asked Joel, frowning in puzzlement.

"Yep. At least according to the *Irish Sun* back in the nineties. Apparently he was over in Ireland, touring and golfing, and he told them his mother's family had roots in County Monaghan – where I come from. 'The best part of me is the Irish part,' he said. So, you see, I could be related to him."

The Blacks were suitably astonished.

The museum was an old mercantile store, now converted to hold lines of LP records and movies in video and DVD cases. It doubled as a film set and meandered around corners displaying salon bars, boudoirs, a stable and a church.

"The owners make movies here too," Casey explained. "Heck, maybe you'll get a part in the next one, Patrick."

Everyone laughed and my father looked chuffed.

I watched the wonder on his face as he ran his palm over the surface of all he surveyed. He held his iPad in his other hand and took photographs liberally. His plan was to decipher them on his return to Ireland.

He was childlike in his excitement and I was reminded of his demeanour many years ago. It was Christmas Eve and I was ten years of age. Mother always loved Christmas time because it gave her free reign to indulge in the thing she loved the most – alcohol. Christmas Eve was the day that the relatives came to our house. My father had finished putting the lights around the front of the house – he'd got them from a man he knew and we were the first house on our road to have fairy lights outside. Even though it hadn't snowed, our porch sparkled and a plastic Santa Claus that said "*Hohoho!*" greeted people when they rang on the doorbell. Technology like that was rare and Daddy loved to bring home a new gimmick or something the neighbours wouldn't have. Our tree was always the biggest too – stretching up through the middle of our hallway.

Granny had come from Inniskeen to spend Christmas with us and I was waiting for Santa Claus to arrive.

But before the last of our relatives left the house Mammy had one of her turns. She had a tendency to sing and dance after a certain amount of vodka and on this occasion got very giddy, slipped and lost her balance. My father had to spend the evening in Jervis Street hospital while my brother and I stayed at home with Granny. It was a disaster and after my mother came home in the small hours with her arm in a sling and a broken shoulder, we had a very sombre Christmas Day.

I hoped that this euphoria my father was feeling would last until the end of the holiday. Mammy wasn't around anymore, and he was free.

We sat on the porch as the sun slid down the sky in front of us. Casey came out with glasses and a large jug of iced lemonade.

"I thought y'all would be tursty."

She was right. We'd had an exhilarating day and the contentment on my father's face, as he rocked to and fro beside Joel, was priceless. This day was a gift from my editor, Gerry – I would remember him gratefully for giving us this time.

We dined on BBQ ribs and crusty chunks of bread before Casey produced some cinnamon cake made from a traditional cowboy recipe, topped with a big blob of vanilla ice cream.

My father ate his with relish and swore it was the best dessert he'd ever tasted.

"Deirdre was a terrific cook – she used to make the best apple crumble, but I think that cake tops it," he said.

I nearly choked. My mother was never a great cook. She would be in the kitchen every evening when he came home from work, that was true, but she was usually cremating a chicken or some lamb chops. She never made cakes or pastries – everything was shop-bought. I wondered when she had made him apple crumble – probably on one occasion and she got credit for it for the rest of her life. Funny how the mind remembers only what it wants to recall and how my memories remained so morbid about my mother.

The heat of the day was withdrawing as the red ball of sun disappeared from the sky. Only the stars were left to start their show overhead. We sat and watched them turn on one by one, like sparklers on Bonfire Night.

The old men continued their chat about the cattle and the museum. They were both *au fait* with every cowboy actor that ever starred on the silver screen. They reminisced about their favourites and agreed that Jane Russell was the most beautiful and John Wayne the best. Like two peas in a pod, they rocked merrily while I sipped on a glass of lemonade and the cries of the coyotes grew louder.

I had forgotten about my real life. This slow easy living was all that mattered, and the stress of running around from work to home and caring for my daughter dissipated, until all I knew was the peace and ease of this place entangled in nature.

Chapter 7

Next morning my father was itching to go riding again and I was more confident about his abilities. He was dressed and showered before me and eager to taste Casey's pancakes.

I knew he was keen to ask me something by the way he fussed about as he dressed. He stalled at the door of the chalet and asked, "Will we be able to get to Mass on Sunday?"

I had been waiting for the question. He knew how I felt about Catholicism and the fact that I'd married a fervent atheist hadn't helped. The way divorced women were still viewed in the Church didn't sit easily with me either. Secretly I had hoped that he would miss it just this once.

It made me uneasy going to church in Ireland – still more so in the Bible Belt of America's heartland.

I pushed myself up on my elbows in the bed and said gently, "I'll have to see where we will be on Sunday."

"Maybe Joel will know a good church in Oklahoma – he told me that he's a Catholic."

The idea of worshiping a God who allowed the world to turn in such a state of chaos and imbalance had jarred with me since I was a teenager. I'd attended the local Catholic girls' school and, although it was not an institution known for academic excellence, I'd scraped together enough grades to study English in UCD. This was the start of my career in journalism and my father was always supportive of my education. He had said then that he prayed for me to do well and he had been doing it throughout my entire life. Sometimes I found it a burden to carry on my shoulders. Life was complicated enough without having an omnipotent Master looking over my shoulder and judging everything that I did. I reached my own understanding and logic about creation and how the world was made in my own simplistic scientific way. I didn't need fairy stories and myths to guide me on what was the right way to behave in my life. The idea of saying a few 'Hail Marys' to bring forgiveness to a soul was ludicrous but I couldn't say that to my father.

It was too early in our adventure to have a row, so I decided it was best to say nothing. And for the moment my father was prepared to do the same.

"We'll ask on Saturday – I promise I'll try," I said.

It was the best I could offer, and it seemed to satisfy him as he nodded on his way out to the lodge.

I threw myself back down on the bed and closed my eyes. When had I become so disconnected from my father and our religion? Was it when I went to college? Or was it when I married Keith? Maybe it was when I ran away from home and the reason for doing it – my mother. I would have to figure it out. I thought that I was going away to leave my issues behind but instead of sweeping them under the carpet they were sweeping down the Oklahoma plains and coming at me like a freight train.

My father went with Rick and Amy to bring the Clydesdale mares down to the paddock and I offered to help Casey tidy up the breakfast dishes. I was in journalist mode and wanted to find out more about life on the Cimarron River from a woman's perspective.

Every task Casey started she seemed to do with such joy and relish. I envied the satisfaction she derived from the simplest chore.

"How can I help, Casey?"

"Oh, Rosaleen, jus' keep me company if you wan' – I like dryin' the pots and pans."

And I could tell that she meant it.

"Tell me 'bout your work, Rosaleen," she said. "It must be wonderful to be a journalist."

It was something that I'd aspired to as a child. I took my position for granted now and only wrote trivia and about holidays.

"I always wanted to write – my father taught me more about books and authors than I learned in college."

"He's one clever ol' dude, Rosaleen. You mus' be so proud of him."

I was proud of him. He could turn his hand to anything.

"What was his work?"

"He had a market garden in the city centre. Shops and people from all over the country would buy produce from him and some imports too."

"That's good work – feeding people. Proud work."

I'd never thought about it that way before. There was a time when he employed ten men in vans who delivered around the country. Certain vegetables and fruits could only be bought from my father as he had the vision to bring exotic fruits into Ireland before anyone else.

"I am proud of him – he was an advocate of organic produce before anyone knew what *organic* meant. He was suspicious of science and technology getting involved in what he calls God's work."

"It's hard to get organic produce even now," Casey sighed. "Everythin's gotten so closed. The government tells us what we can grow, how much we can grow – what we gotta put on the crops, an' the antibiotics we mus' inject in the cattle."

"It's like that all over Europe too," I agreed. "Makes you wonder sometimes where it's all going."

Casey threw the dishcloth on the counter and wiped her palms along her pants.

"Amen. The good Lord made this world and he made all of nature. I have faith in the Lord and hope things will change for better – how I'm not sure but I'm praying hard."

I agreed with the nature part of our conversation. We were a world apart, Casey and me, but we both knew what was right and wrong.

"What's your man workin' at?" she asked.

"Oh, I'm divorced."

"I'm sorry – I didn't mean to pry – jus' your pappy was talking 'bout your daughter. . ."

"Keith is still in our lives though – my daughter stays with him every second weekend." I felt awkward and then answered her question. "He's a fund manager."

"Wha's that?"

"He invests money for companies and helps them gain the most profit possible with their portfolios." I hated what I'd just said. Keith's job description sounded ruthless. Standing in the heartland of this wild and rural world, it felt like such a waste of time and energy to play around with numbers and money in bank accounts to make more for those who were already wealthy. Casey had awakened my consciousness and I wondered when I had decided to use my voice as a journalist to write about things that didn't really matter, instead of changing the world the way I'd set out to do when I left university.

"Well, he's gotta lot of responsibility with a big job like that," Casey said.

She was right, he did have a lot of responsibility and he used it to protect those that *had* so that they could have more. It didn't sit comfortably with my father and he'd chastised me about it when Keith took the position.

Keith was a stockbroker when I met him and it was a fun and crazy time to be in London. He drove a fast car and brought me to the best restaurants – Quaglino's for dinner on Friday evenings followed by cocktails in some trendy Mayfair bar. He had an apartment at Canary Wharf near the City and he made me feel like I was on top of the world. The truth was it was a shallow existence and he reluctantly agreed to move out to the country when Thalia was born. It worked out well and he didn't seem to mind the commute to work. He used the time to do work on his laptop and make calls on his cellphone.

In return we could afford a comfortable home in Bladon, not far from Oxford City, and assurance of good schools for Thalia for her future. Was it then my life became so compartmentalised? All I know is that Keith fell out of love with me when he got the big job and we bought the big house. He had to have the mistress to complete the package and I wasn't really surprised when I found out. He still hadn't married her, which made it easier for Thalia to be in his life, but it was uncomfortable for me whenever I called around.

I was half a person in Oxford and I realised this looking out on Casey's big back yard. I was thriving in the ruggedness of this vast and wild land and questioning my very existence. Who was I anymore? I wasn't sure – but I could see that Casey knew exactly who she was.

I decided to relax by the pool with my book for the rest of the morning, but my head was full of thoughts that wouldn't go away so I decided to call my daughter as she would be settled in her friend's house by now.

"Thalia, it's Mum."

"Hi, Mum, are you having a good time?"

Her sweet voice brought an instant smile to my lips.

"I'm grand, love. What about you – are you still at Emma's?"

"Yes, tonight's the party – did you say anything to Dad about it?"

The excitement in her voice resonated with me more than the words that she used. I hoped that I'd done the right thing by letting her go without her father knowing.

"I haven't spoken to him – he won't know about the party. I'll ring him later, but I wanted to talk to you first."

"We're going to La Galleria with Emma's parents and then Alan and his friend are collecting us and driving to the party."

La Galleria was a great Italian restaurant in Woodstock, so at least Emma's parents were close to where the party was going to be held. I hoped this Alan chap was reliable and trustworthy and that Emma's parents would check him out before letting our daughters into his car.

"How will you get back?"

"Alan is going to drive."

"Emma – I hope Alan isn't going to drink – and that there will be no alcohol at this party?"

"I promised you, Mum – Emma and I don't drink. Alan doesn't either and he's borrowing his mum's car."

"So does Emma's mother know him, then?"

"Yes, she does – and she knows his parents well."

A well-off family then, if they were acquaintances of Paula's.

I felt torn – the way a mother feels when separated from her child. I was especially scared that something would happen, and Keith would never let me forget it. But, if she lived by her father's rules, she would never have any fun in her life, and I remembered how important my friends were to me when I was sixteen.

"Have a great time, love," I said, "and call me tomorrow at about lunchtime."

"I will, Mum. How's Granddad holding up?"

"He's on horseback as we speak – he's having the time of his life."

"I'm pleased. You deserve this time together. Enjoy it."

She sounded so grown up and I realised that my little girl wasn't a little girl anymore – Sweet Sixteen and almost a woman.

"Be safe and have a good time, love."

"Bye, Mum."

When she hung up, I missed her. It was time to call Keith.

His mobile phone went straight to voicemail, so I left a

message and took my book out to take my mind off the thoughts that I was having.

My father slurped on his broth. "That's absolutely gorgeous, Casey," he said, complimenting another fine cowboy recipe, and everyone agreed.

"Eat up, y'all – we's goin' on a long trolley ride after supper," Rick said.

My father's redundant eyes danced in his head in anticipation of the jaunt.

"They are fine horses – beautiful horses," he said.

"Like the ones in the Budweiser advert," Casey said.

"I've never seen that advert," my father said. "I find it difficult to make out the TV – it's good for sport and the news but movies are difficult to follow unless I'm in the cinema."

"My father loves going to the movies … don't you, Dad?" I prompted.

"Indeed – I get the over-55s rate in the film centre in Dublin. I go in at least one morning every week with my friend Rita. They had a special showing of *High Noon* last week."

Casey looked at me with raised eyebrows and I had to laugh. My dad loved dropping hints that he was a bit of a ladies' man.

"Let's get going while we have sunlight," Rick said as he stood up. "We'll keep that apple pie 'til we get back, Casey."

"Awrigh'," she said and started to gather the dishes into a clumsy pile on top of one another.

The night was creeping in, but the air was still balmy outside. I looked at my watch on the way out. It was almost midnight in the UK. I thought of Thalia and hoped that she was all right. Something caught my breath as we got up on the trolley and I couldn't understand why I felt so anxious. Thalia kept coming into my head and I couldn't shake the feelings in my gut.

I looked across at my father who beamed widely as Rick shook the slinky bridles on the two big mares. With a clatter and clang the wheels of the big old wooden trolley started to move slowly over the rough terrain. We were all on board – even the old sheepdog who skulked by the doorway of the lodge from dawn to dusk.

"This is just great," my father said, loudly enough for everyone to hear over the clamour of the horses' hooves.

"I'm gonna feed the cattle some pellets, Rick!" Casey called.

As we drove onto the open prairie the Longhorn cattle appeared in shades of tan, black and white. Some had calves by their side and others seemed to be hiding theirs behind the tufts of cypress trees.

It was natural to try and protect the young in this way. I wondered about the instinct and nature of motherhood. It was something that couldn't be taught, and all of the animals knew exactly how to care for their young. My father knew how to care for me – he'd been my father *and* mother for much of my young life. I closed my eyes and bemoaned the loss of my mother and the sadness that I felt whenever I thought of her. Why was she such a narcissist and why couldn't she just have been a normal mother like my friends' mothers were? I hoped that I was a good mother to Thalia. I tried my best to get the balance just right – to be there for her in the ways my mother wasn't for me. To create a careful balance of allowing her to do the things she wanted but with the guidance and rules in place to show her that I cared. Being a single mother wasn't what I'd wanted for my daughter. But Thalia seemed to be maturing well without the baggage of dodging two parents at each other's throats all of the time.

We stopped at the edge of the herd while Casey cut open a bag of pellets.

"Don't get too close to them – they're protectin' their youn'," Rick warned.

I watched the beasts, with the long sharp horns, eye me suspiciously and had no intention of getting any closer. With my camera in hand, I zoomed in on the herd and photographed the cattle feeding. This taste of rural life would appeal to the readers of my article and, as I breathed in the moment, I felt completely at one with the herd, my father and our new "Okie" friends.

I climbed down from the trolley as we came to a halt at the lodge house. I couldn't understand why I felt so tired. Perhaps part of it was letting go of the tension that I lived with in my day-to-day routines. I hadn't realised how much I rushed as I travelled into the office on High Street and back to collect Thalia from her school and bring her to the places she needed to go. I took the role of being a single parent for granted without regarding the toll it was taking on me. The things that I did on a daily basis seemed to fade into oblivion and I wished for a moment that I was back in Inniskeen with my granny, so that I could rearrange the past.

But the past was, and had been, and the present was all I was sure of. The lovely family connection that the Blacks held was missing from my life and I wanted to experience it. Why was my family scattered around the world and my poor father on his own in the dark?

I took his arm gently as we walked up the steps to the lodge – he was still reeling from the ride.

"Thank you," he said. He wasn't thanking me for helping him up the steps – he was thanking me because he was happy to be there and to feel the connection with the land.

The apple pie was even more delicious than it had looked when Casey had taken it out of the oven earlier. We ate it on the porch as the crickets played a cacophony of choruses and the coyotes howled and moaned in the distance.

"I don't want to leave this place," my father said as he drained the last sup from his cup of coffee.

I didn't either, but in the morning we had to leave and travel to another part of the state that was printed in clear black ink on my itinerary.

"We don't want y'all to go," Casey said. "Y'all are more like friends than strangers. Promise to come back."

I agreed and said we would – but we all knew that we wouldn't.

Chapter 8

Newcastle, Oklahoma

Michael woke up in the middle of another restless night's sleep. It was deathly quiet in the house except for the odd snore coming from the lounge where Ben had fallen asleep. It was 3am.

He thought over the struggles Claudia had shared with him as he'd helped her dry the pots after dinner.

"It's so difficult to survive on what we get from the farm," she'd said. "Every year my wages are used to cover our ever-increasing taxes and it's getting worse."

Michael knew the answer to the question before he asked it, but he had to see where his sister was in her head.

"What are you going to do, Claudia? Would you all not move to Ireland?"

Claudia paused. "Not a chance Ben will move from Oklahoma. Besides, you know things aren't good between us. That's why you're here, isn't it?"

He put his dishcloth and pot down and turned to his sister.

She instantly did the same and allowed her brother to wrap his arms around her in a warm and loving hug.

"I've been worried about you for some time. Would you not just take the kids back to Ireland on your own?"

"American law states I can't take them out of the country without his permission," she sighed. "The Land of the Free and the Home of the Brave is right! We have more laws and regulations than anywhere in Europe. We are weighed down with debt over here that you can't imagine, and there's no getting out of all the taxes unless you're super-wealthy."

"It's getting like that in Ireland too, from what people are telling me. You can't stay with him, Claudia. I know I'm a priest and to the Church the family is sacred but the way you live isn't good for you or the kids."

Claudia lifted her dishcloth and returned to her chore.

"I have no way out. The kids are being affected, it's true, but there is nothing I can do."

"There's always something you can do. Will you let me talk to Ben?"

Claudia looked at Michael fearfully. "No way. He can't know that we talked like this. He'd be really mad."

"I know you won't want to answer this, but I need to know. Is he ever physically abusive?"

Claudia didn't answer. Then she looked her brother straight in the eyes. "Why is it always about physical abuse with you men? There are other types of abuse much worse than a thump or a black eye. What about words? If you tell someone that they are shit, eventually they start to believe it. If you're told you can't do anything right, eventually you lose confidence in everything that you do." She threw down her dishcloth again. "I've got to go to bed, Michael, I'm tired. I'm just really really tired."

Michael let his sister walk away, feeling inadequate and as if he had let her down in some way. It wasn't his place to interfere between a woman and her husband, but he had to do something. He had no experience of living with a woman or maintaining a relationship. He wondered if he'd ever be capable of such a thing. He'd set himself up for a life where that wasn't an option anyway and a small part of him wondered if he liked the fact. Then he remembered Roz and wondered how meeting someone for such a short time could etch such an impression on his mind. He wondered if she was happily married or if she was another in a line of unhappy relationships that he witnessed all around. Either way nobody else had ever lingered in his mind after only a fleeting acquaintance.

Chapter 9

My father felt for any socks or other articles of clothing that might have got stuck at the back of the drawer. I checked under the bed and every inch of the bathroom and soon we were packed.

I hated taking him away from this place. The ease he'd felt with these people meant that we'd had space to be ourselves.

"Have you phoned home yet?"

I hadn't – I wanted to be sure that my father had packed everything.

"I'll ring her now," I said and slipped outside.

It was lunchtime and Thalia would probably still be in Emma's house.

Her phone rang out but there was no reply. I heard her sweet voice on the message mail and told her that I would call later.

Then I rang Keith.

"Hello," he answered gruffly, as if I'd disturbed him from a meeting.

"Hi, how are you?"

"I'm on lunch – with a client. What's wrong?"

"Nothing's wrong – I called to see how things are."

"Busy," he answered abruptly. "Have you spoken to Tally today?"

"No – she's still in Emma's."

"I hope she didn't go to that party."

My heart leapt, like a child being reprimanded by a parent.

"That party wasn't on last night – she was just staying with her friend," I lied.

The way he clicked the roof of his mouth with his tongue, I could tell that he didn't believe me.

"She'll be going to stay with you tomorrow."

"I have to meet a client tomorrow night."

"Okay then, but will you be back early or should I ask Mrs Higgins to check up on Tally?"

"I'll tell her myself. I'm in the middle of a huge portfolio break-up – you couldn't have picked a worse time to go away."

I sighed. No time would have suited Keith for me to travel.

"Well, if you're sure."

"I have to go, Roz. I'll talk to you later in the week."

And then he was gone. I was uneasy about Thalia and tried to call her again but she didn't answer.

My father came out to the porch and asked if everything was all right.

"Sort of – Thalia's not answering her phone, so I'm worried."

"Why don't you ring the people she is staying with?"

I wished I'd thought of that first and acted on his suggestion.

There was no response from Emma's house so I called her

mother's number but still no reply. All I could do was leave a message.

I led my father out to the paddock where he sadly said goodbye to Cowgirl, his horse.

"I think she understood ya, Patrick," Rick said.

"She's a lovely horse. I hope you got a good photograph of me riding on her, Rosaleen."

"Of course I did, Dad."

The bees circled the bush beside our car before we got to it.

"Oh, they're moving," Casey said with satisfaction in her voice. "I was hopin' they'd be gone before the weekend."

Then an entire hive moved as one entity, flying in formation like the Red Arrows from one tree to the next before darting up into the air and off to another part of the ranch.

"Did you hear the noises they made? Aren't they just fabulous?" my father said. "I could feel them swoosh by me."

We hugged our goodbyes to Joel, Rick, Amy and Casey and waved our arms out of the car window until they and the lodge were out of sight.

"Don't you think it significant that the bees came out as we were leaving?" my father said with a beaming smile.

"They were just moving to a new hive – that's what bees do."

"But of all the times the bees had to move they chose the very moment that we were leaving. Can't you see the connection?"

"I really don't know what you mean."

My father took a deep breath and began to explain as the car bumped and chugged over the rough track.

"The bees work in a collective – each has their role and knows the effect that their being has on the entire colony. That's what's wrong with the world now – everyone is so concerned with the 'I' they have forgotten that we are all part of the 'We'. When a community stops living as 'We', it means hardship for everybody. We can learn a lot from the bees and good folks like the Blacks. I was chatting to Joel last night about the hardships the farmers are facing – it's the same old story that happened during the Great Depression. The men in suits decide the prices of the produce and don't think about the people who are growing it or how they will be affected. Then big department stores sell it at prices that are too cheap and the farmers can't make a decent living."

I understood what he was saying even though it didn't affect me in the same way. "But it's difficult for people at the moment – everyone is trying to survive."

"And why are they trying to survive, Rosaleen? Because the stock markets and the bond holders want to make more money than they need and those at the bottom of the rung are paying the price – it's all about crowd control. Separate the man from his responsibility to his fellow man and then it's easy to send fear and loathing into the masses. What's going on now in the economies of the US and Europe is exactly the same as what happened to the crop farmers in Oklahoma during the Dust Bowl years and the Great Depression."

"Aren't you being a bit dramatic?"

"More like realistic – it's the nature of greed in man and it's been the same since history was recorded. The only thing we seem to learn from history is that we don't learn from it at all."

That was my father's favourite quote from the German philosopher, Hegel, and although it didn't sit comfortably with me, I knew that he was right.

He continued. "I remember when I was a lad there was this man who had a store. He employed some local lads and paid them a fair wage to sell the farmers' produce and the few bits of luxuries that he would get up in Dublin – like hats and confectionary. He was kind to the poor women who didn't have much and God knows there were many of them. They fed their families from hand to mouth and were constantly on tick, owing from week to week for their groceries." He paused for breath. "Anyway, this other fella came down to Inniskeen with the idea of putting a store in a petrol station and all the farmers were delighted that they had another point of sale for their produce. It was a small community and we all relied on each other. After a while the farmers got greedy as the petrol station was paying more for their goods and soon only the poor creatures who could afford to buy on credit were going to the local man. He couldn't afford to pay his workers and kept the shop himself but couldn't go to Dublin anymore to buy luxuries. His little shop was run down to the ground and the boys who worked for him went to work in the petrol-station store. Then he closed down his shop and the women with no money couldn't afford to shop in the petrol-station store. When the man who owned the petrol store realised that he had a monopoly, he cut the wages of the lads that worked for him and gave the farmers less than the other store owner for their produce."

"That was just awful – what happened to the poor families?"

"Well, the farmers' wives felt sorry for them and they used

to let the women buy directly from them. But the fella with the petrol station went on to open stations all along the roadways and caused terrible upset in the villages and towns around my way."

"But we live in a capitalist society and that's the way of industry and business." Maybe I'd listened to Keith too much in the past.

"What do you think is going on now in India and China and countries where children are sent to work in sweat shops day after day for a few pence? There's no clothing industry in Ireland now or most of Europe because everyone wants stuff made cheaper and cheaper. It can only end badly – there's a price to be paid for your cheap swimsuit or the pair of shoes that you throw away at the end of summer." He paused and drew a deep breath. "During the Great Depression in this country, the labourers who worked on the peach farms in California for 2 cents a box cost their brothers their earnings because they had been paid 5 cents before. You only have to look at the harrowed faces of the poor creatures in those depression photographs to see the real cost of cheap labour. I guarantee you could take the very same photograph in Asia or Africa right now. And what everyone forgets is that by protecting themselves they will eventually get it thrown back – call it karma or whatever you want with your newfangled new-age talk but it all amounts to the same thing."

He dropped his shoulders like a deflated balloon and I realised that he had expended every bit of energy to make that speech.

"Always remember that you are part of the great big 'We', Rosaleen. Only selfish people see the world as 'I'. You are young and in a position to do something about it – as a journalist, as a mother. People like Keith can help people rebuild their companies instead of ripping them apart."

His little personal story and global viewpoint resonated with me. I was beginning to see that there was another purpose for our trip.

This was my second lesson.

Chapter 10

Ponca City, Oklahoma

Ponca City beckoned and I slipped a Neil Young CD into the player on the dashboard. He sang about his search for a 'Heart of Gold' and it made me think. My father didn't speak as the entire album played in the background – the perfect antidote to my lesson as we set off on our new quest. We arrived at the city limits by Route 77 and I could tell my father was mourning the loss of his friends back at the ranch.

"What's this place we are going to now?" he asked.

"It's Ponca City. We are meeting a lady at a monument and then going to see the 'Palace on the Prairie.'"

"And what is that?"

I hadn't a clue yet but I was sure there was a story to be told. We pulled up to meet our guide at the Pioneer Woman statue and she stepped out of her car wearing a bright-yellow sundress.

"Hi, I'm Caitlin," she said, holding out her hand.

I shook it. "Lovely to meet you. I'm Rosaleen."

"And I'm Patrick – come closer so I can see you – I've only got ten percent vision and it's such a pity I can't see your pretty face."

Caitlin blushed. She was pretty. But my father used to say that as you got older every woman got prettier. She came closer and shook his hand.

"The monument is beautiful," I said. "And who exactly was the pioneer woman?"

"The Pioneer Woman represents all the women who came out to the west. See how she is walking in a south-west direction as most settlers came from the north-east. She stands forty feet tall and is made of solid bronze. EW Marland commissioned Bryant Baker to make the sculpture for a sum of $100,000 in 1930."

"That was a lot of money then – still is today," my father said.

"Yes, sir," Caitlin agreed. "But EW Marland was one of the wealthiest men in the country at that time. He lost his first million at the turn of the century but made another million when he struck oil in Oklahoma City a few years later. He wanted to make this statement about all the mothers and women who had formed the West and never got a mention like their men folk did – it was the men who wrote the history books, I guess."

"That's very admirable," my father said. "Good man himself!"

"Come on, let's get a photo on your iPad so you can see it better when we get home," I said.

After, we got into Caitlin's car to drive to the Marland Mansion.

I was concerned that tiredness might have set in for my father, but he seemed bright, and we hadn't far to drive.

The mansion wasn't exactly huge. It was Italianate in style and architecture. Our guide spoke as if EW was in the building and whispered at times about his marriage to his wife Virginia.

"EW and his wife didn't have children," she said as she led us through the large double doors of the porch, "so every summer they took her niece and nephew, Lydie and George Roberts, on holidays to Europe and all the other wonderful places that they visited. The children loved to travel with their aunt and uncle so when George was nineteen and Lydie was sixteen EW adopted them and formally educated them."

As we walked through the house from the breakfast room to the kitchen, Caitlin described the fine life the family had and for a moment I switched off as I took photographs of the architecture and wondered how best I could make this story interesting.

"Then in 1926 Virginia died and EW took Lydie back to Pennsylvania where she came from, to annul the adoption," Caitlin continued.

That caught my attention. "Gosh, that was a bit harsh, wasn't it?" I said. I felt for the poor girl, being taken from rags to riches and then being thrown back to her original family again by her uncle.

"Well, not exactly," Caitlin said. "You see, the reason he wanted to annul the adoption was because he wanted to –"

"Marry her?" my father butted in.

"Exactly!" Caitlin beamed at my father's astute guess. "He married Lydie in 1928."

I was gobsmacked. Not just at what EW had done but the fact my father had instinctively known such a bizarre scenario.

Caitlin continued. "She was twenty-eight and he was fifty-four. He built this mansion for her. But they didn't get to enjoy the fruits of his success as shortly after this he lost his second fortune. He tried to stop the monopoly Rockefeller had with his pipeline pumping oil to the west coast and wanted to create a new, more competitive pipeline, but the banks foreclosed on him, the way they do today. He had to sell the mansion to a religious order at a great loss – a fraction of what it had cost to build it. So he lost everything expect a cottage on this estate. And that was where they lived after they were married."

"So what did they do then?" I asked, as I scribbled notes on this man who had suddenly become fascinating.

"Well, he decided that the way the banks worked was dirty and unfair, so he went into politics to try and change the legislation and take the power away from the banks. He became the tenth governor of Oklahoma and Lydie was the First Lady."

"Well, clearly he didn't succeed in changing the banks as all those crashes and depressions followed – a terrible bloody shame," my dad said. "Remember what we were talking about in the car, Rosaleen?"

I agreed – it was the same story repeating itself and my father's words were sinking in. But he expected too much of me. There was little I could do about it.

The tour continued and the story unravelled as Caitlin told us of Lydie's disappearance for twenty-two years after EW's death. She roamed the States working as a waitress and doing bit jobs to get by until she returned to persuade Ponca City to purchase the mansion and preserve it as a historic property. She personally oversaw the restoration of the mansion before her own death."

"That's quite a story – do you mind if I run around and take a few more pictures?"

She told me to go ahead so I left my father in her company.

It took a good deal of digestion to comprehend the strange incestuous relationship of the father with his adopted daughter. There was no doubt that Lydie adored EW until the day that she died. Her whole life was absorbed by him and in photographs they made a lovely couple, and of course there was no blood relationship between them. Still, it sat uncomfortably with me. The attraction of a father to his daughter, adopted or not, was ugly and wrong and evil and everything bad.

I went to the hall where a marble statue of Lydie stood in prominent position. One of the tour guides came over and asked if I'd like my photograph taken with the statue.

"It's okay, thanks," I told her. "I'm a journalist and taking these for the paper I work for."

"You know, Lydie stood over the destruction of her statue after EW died. It had been removed from the mansion after the sale to the religious order and stored at the cottage. But Lydie was heartbroken and didn't want an effigy of herself anywhere in sight. So she got one of the workmen to bury it."

"She was beautiful, wasn't she?" I said.

"She was very beautiful, but she hated herself after his death. But the workman couldn't stand to see her statue lost to the world forever so he placed the pieces very carefully in a plot that could be easily found again, and she was reinstated in her rightful place after her death. Can you see the crack along the skull – that's exactly where she hit it."

"Did she hate herself for loving the man who was her father?" I wondered.

"I think she hated God for taking him and not her. They made no apologies for their love. When he came home from a trip, she'd be running down to the station all alone to meet him – this was afore they were ever married. It was true love all right."

I returned to where Caitlin was showing my father all the delicate details in the furniture and helping him to run his hand along the carefully painted decor and stucco work.

"Fine place this – what do you think, Rosaleen?" my father asked.

I nodded. "Yes, indeed, it's an incredible story." I turned to Caitlin and thanked her. "We have to move along now and see Standing Bear Park before we return to Oklahoma City."

"Oh, that won't take you long," she said. "Go back straight down 77 and take a right on to 60 – that'll get y'all there."

When we got back into the car I sensed my father's unease.

"Did you take plenty of photographs?" he asked. "I'd love to see what that place was like on my computer when I get home."

"I did," I replied. "What did you make of Marland?"

"It was some story all right," he sighed.

"Wasn't it creepy?"

"I suppose they weren't related by blood. But, you know, Rosaleen, you always were and will always be the prettiest girl that ever walked this earth in my eyes – well, in my mind now. Because I can still remember how you looked as a little girl with your hair in pigtails and your frilly dresses. When you became a teenager and dressed in all that crazy stuff ... I can't remember what you called it now ..."

"Grunge?" I prompted.

"That and the rest – when you had your lips black and your beautiful eyes covered in all that muck you were still the most beautiful girl and you still are. I don't think many men admit how much they admire and love their daughters. And you are the picture of your mother."

I was like her. I sometimes felt a jolt when I looked at myself in the mirror since I'd reached middle age. The woman staring back at me had my mother's face and sometimes I felt like an imposter to myself.

"It's true that little girls adore their daddies. I read somewhere recently that your father is your first love," I admitted. "A girl's thoughts when picking a man depends much on her relationship with her father."

"It's the way to love someone in safety. Unfortunately, not all little girls are lucky enough to feel safe with their daddies and there is nothing worse a man can do to his daughter than break that trust."

It was strange having this conversation with my own father, but we were both adults now. I'd known a friend thwarted and tortured her whole life because of an incestuous relationship with her father. Did these men realise the damage they were doing or did they not care? It was a sick and sorry side of human nature that made me feel ill to the core.

As we drove along the road my mind meandered. I had modelled my first boyfriend on my father. He was so like him in looks and stature. He even had my father's sense of humour and fun. He was perfect in every way. My father thought he was good enough for me – just about, and my mother used to flirt with him. But as time passed I couldn't stay with this boy who was a replica of my father. I needed to meet others who might be better for me. I finished our relationship at the tender age of eighteen and set about dating other boys –

several other boys, until I found that I was searching for someone identical to my own first love. I never found him again, or anyone who was similar to him. When I was dazzled by Keith in my mid-twenties I had given up on ever meeting such a man again and that was that.

Then my mind drifted to our stop in Chicago and the lovely Michael. He was worthy of comparison with my father. He was a strong good man. It was stupid to be thinking of someone whom I had only briefly met and would probably never see again but something inside me stirred and in my gut I believed that our paths would cross again. I don't know how I knew but I just did.

Chapter 11

Standing Bear Native American Foundation was set at the side of the road – the complete opposite in stature and lavishness to the Marland Mansion from where we had come. Surrounded by lush parkland, the minimalist round building was marked by a small bronze statue of a Native American in front.

"Do you want to ring Thalia before we go in here?" my father asked.

"Oh, good idea. It's hot, isn't it – will you stay in the car and have some water while I call?"

"Yes, whatever suits."

I took some water out of the boot and passed it through the passenger window to him while Thalia's phone rang.

"Hello, Mum, is that you?"

"Tally, it is – why didn't you answer your phone earlier?"

"Oh, I was in Oxford with Emma's parents. They said I can stay here until you come back – is that okay?"

I didn't like the tone of my daughter's voice. She sounded distressed.

"That's a big burden and responsibility for Emma's parents – have you spoken to Keith?"

"No, I've decided I'm staying here – you can tell him."

"Why are you staying?" I was suddenly suspicious.

"I just am – I'm better here. Please, Mum, trust me."

There was anxiety in her voice but I wasn't in a position thousands of miles away to push the issue.

"How was the party?"

"Oh, it was all right. I won't be going out with that crowd again though."

"Why not – what happened?" I was suddenly very nervous.

"Nothing much – look, I'm just going to stay at Emma's – tell Dad, okay? I've got to go for my dinner."

I felt a pain as she hung up, a discomfort that I hadn't felt since leaving her.

I opened the car door for my father and helped him out.

"How is my granddaughter?"

"Very strange and she won't stay with her father."

"I don't blame her for that!" my father quipped.

I wasn't concerned about that. But I was concerned about my daughter. There was little I could do about it. It was getting late and we still had a ninety-minute drive to Oklahoma City after we finished here.

As I led my father over to the bronze statue, a woman emerged from the building. She was draped in a maxi dress with feathers hanging from her ears and her long black hair beaded in braids. There was no mistaking her native pedigree.

She welcomed us warmly to her place of work and said her name was Nancy and she was Osage Indian.

My father was examining the statue, feeling his way around the drum that the figure was holding.

"That feels like a bodhrán – does it look like a bodhrán, Rosaleen?"

I explained to our guide that a bodhrán was a type of drum used in traditional Irish music – animal skin wrapped in the same way as in the statue and easy to hold on the lap or under the arm.

"The drum represents the sound of the earth's heart beating for my people - six tribes are represented here - Osage, Pawnee, Otoe-Missouria Kaw, Tonkawa and Ponca. The beat of the drum is thought to bring the world back into balance."

"Well, the world could certainly do with a good bit of drumming at the moment," my father said with a chuckle.

We walked in through the entrance of the centre with installations on all sides.

"Yes, my people and those of the tribes you see here have been treated badly by the government. We were promised an Indian state in Oklahoma which was to be called Sequoia, in the 1800's." Nancy pointed to a map. "It never came to pass but we keep our culture and traditions sacred."

"Who was Standing Bear?" I asked.

"Chief Standing Bear did much for the rights of all tribes. He was the first Native American to look for protection under the 14th Amendment for his people after they were unjustly moved in 1878. He and the other Ponca chiefs were promised that if they moved from their farmland in Northern Nebraska that they would be well catered for here in Ponca. But after an arduous trek over 500 miles, where his young daughter Prairie Flower lost her life along the way, he quickly realised that they were fooled – there were no farm implements or provisions for the coming winter when they arrived."

"That's despicable," my father huffed.

Nancy continued. "His people starved and the tribe was

reduced by two-thirds of its size from smallpox and starvation. Then more tragedy followed for the Chief when his twelve-year-old son died and he asked in his last breath to be buried in the land of his fathers in Nebraska. Standing Bear and some more chiefs became fugitives and walked the long trail back with his body to Nebraska where they were arrested."

We walked through rooms of images and maps describing the trials and tribulations of the Poncas and our guide stopped at a photograph of Standing Bear in a court of law.

"What's going on here?" I asked. Then I explained to my father what we were looking at – a photograph of the Chief in court.

"This is the trial when Standing Bear argued for protection of his people. He had to first prove that he was a man the same as any white man. This he did in court, as he stood and held out his right hand. He explained that the colour of his skin was different to the judge's but if he cut it his blood would run red the same as the blood of the judge and everyone else in the room. He was created by the same God as was every person in the courtroom and America. When the judge heard this, he immediately awarded Standing Bear the right to be protected by the court of law and allowed him to return to his homelands in Nebraska."

"Ah, the poor divil – imagine having to prove you were a human being," my father said and he wiped a tear from his eye.

"Indeed, sir. There are still Native Americans seeking that respect today."

"Sure there are poor divils all over the world looking for that," my father said with a shake of his head.

When we left Nancy, my father was quiet. She'd urged us

to walk around the park and observe the sculptures and points of rest along the trail to where the Standing Bear statue stood.

We walked the park shoulder to shoulder, and I thought I saw another tear in my father's eye.

"It's such a sad story, isn't it?" I said.

"Jesus, those poor people, and the thought of his daughter dying on the road as they were driven from their homes like that is just awful. What was her name again?"

"Prairie Flower, I think."

"What a beautiful name! Dear God, why does mankind do this to one another? And you can see it again all over the world – in the middle of Africa and the Middle East while the rest of the world just looks on."

I could feel that pain in my stomach again. A kind of guilt for letting the world be the way that it is. As a journalist I had a responsibility to do something about it – to educate others at least.

"Do you think most people believe that now?" my father asked.

"Believe that Native Americans are human?"

"That every person no matter what their colour is human! I wonder if we've evolved at all as a species."

"Standing Bear really put it up to them. He clinched it when he said they all shared the same god. Do you believe that, Dad?"

"Of course I do. There's only one God."

"So the Muslims and the Hindus and the Jews all worship the same God as you?"

"Absolutely," he said with a firm nod.

"So, then, it doesn't matter what religion you follow as they are all doing the same thing? Following the one God but controlled by men who run big institutions to control the population?"

I felt that I'd made my point and won the argument.

My father stopped on the path and stood squarely in front of me.

"Look, I'm not going to argue with you over this again, Rosaleen. I'm sure of my God and my faith and when my time comes to meet my Maker I want him to know that I've done my best to honour him through my religion."

I'd lived with an atheist too long. My life was clean-cut and orderly, and I hadn't acknowledged my spiritual self since I was a teenager. I used to say my novenas to St Francis to help me through my exams or to grant me a kiss with the boy that I fancied down the road but that was all superstition as far as I was now concerned.

He shook his head. "Where did I go wrong? I tried to do my best, to instil a respect for God in you."

"Where was God when Mammy got cancer?"

My father looked shocked.

I huffed. "Where was God when all those poor divils you were talking about earlier were driven from their land? Where is God when bad things happen to good people?"

"That is why we have faith."

"Oh yeah – everything happens for a reason? Well, that's not an answer. Why is it that most of the wars that are waged are caused by rival religions? The Crusades, Gaza, even bloody Northern Ireland and both parties were so-called Christians. I just think the world would be better off without religion."

My father relaxed and swallowed hard. "Rosaleen, I'm going to tell you about an audio book I've read on my iPad that might startle you. It's called *Anatomy of the Spirit* by some American woman."

I had no choice but to hear him out. My father sometimes had a jewel of literature to share but he wouldn't be convincing me of anything else.

"It's very clever and says that all religions are based on the same principles. The Kabbalah's Tree of Life and Christianity's Seven Sacraments are all one and the same as the seven Hindu chakras. You see, we are all following the same rites of passage as we journey through our lives. Even Shakespeare wrote about the seven stages of man – and why did he do that?"

I was silenced.

"This life we are given is a blessing. We have a duty to respect it and do our best with it. If we didn't have the structures of religion, there are some that wouldn't know how to behave. Do you remember an old friend of mine called Richard? He was Jewish and worked as a craftsman in the buildings beside the market in town?"

"Kind of – there were lots of friends in those days – too many to remember."

"Well, Richard had a son and when he turned thirteen he had his Bar Mitzvah and Richard asked me and your mother along. You and Evan were invited but you had things to do with your pals as you were getting a bit older. Have you ever been to a Bar Mitzvah?"

I just shook my head.

"It's the same as a Confirmation. The young lad is brought into the community as an adult and sure the timing is perfect as he is about to become a young man and his body is changing and he is getting a new perspective on the world. In my day, when you reached that age you had to get out and find a job after you made your Confirmation – unless you were extremely fortunate and could afford to stay on in school."

"I understand what you mean but can't a young person have these rites of passages without religion?"

My father shook his head. "Sure they can, but would they?"

I shrugged. Thalia's thirteenth birthday had come and gone without any ceremony other than the usual trip to the cinema followed by dinner with her pals. In fact, she had a sleepover and the girls watched a movie.

"The difference with religion is that it gets a community to celebrate their rites of passage in the presence of God. And that's what you have your Confirmations and Bar Mitzvahs and weddings for."

He seemed exhausted from the story and the little speech.

I wasn't finished though as I didn't completely agree with him.

"Ceremonies are all very well but what about the rules and regulations of these man-made churches? What about the repression of women exercised by them? What about the women being forced to suffer female genital mutilation or to wear burkas – their feeling of inadequacy amplified as they hide behind a veil? What kind of 'rites of passage' are those?"

He was quick to retort. "And the girls who wear miniskirts and drink in bars in Spain doing all sorts with boys they don't know?"

"At least they are free!"

"But we should use that freedom wisely and respect our bodies and souls. Look, I agree with you on the terrible FGM. I can't understand male circumcision either to be honest. But Muslims are at the same stage that Christians were one hundred years ago. Don't forget Christianity had five hundred years on them before Muhammad came along, and we are only getting our act together now. But it's not the communion of people that is wrong. People need to feel connected to their god and it is important to share and experience these rites of life and passage together. Religion is the vehicle we use to do this."

"What do you think about the Native Americans then? They have their rituals and practices."

My father nodded. "And they are just as relevant as all other religions, but I'll just say this and let it be the end of this conversation – it's important to believe in something, Rosaleen. I know that you lived with Keith for too long, someone who doesn't believe in anything except the colour of money and I'm not bothered about him – but what do you and my granddaughter believe in?"

We'd walked to the end of the path and finally reached the tall imposing bronze figure of Standing Bear. He held out his right palm in a gesture of peace and acceptance. The eternal flame burned in a circular stone furnace below his feet.

I had just been given my third lesson even if I didn't necessarily feel any wiser from the debate.

Chapter 12

Oklahoma City

Michael liked Peter's company. They'd been through a lot in the old days, when they were in the seminary together. They'd led very different but equally interesting careers. It was a strange coincidence that Peter should end up living in the same city as Claudia. Michael's life was a merging of strange coincidences that weren't really coincidences at all. He truly believed that we are all part of God's plan and every soul had a part to play in others' lives – no matter how small. Sometimes he wished that the connectedness he experienced in the past was a part of who he was today. Too many people in the western world didn't have room for God and too many others chose to be selective about the right God.

As far as he was concerned there was only one God and he wished that everyone else could see that. He would probably go to the grave without managing to help all the people that he met along the way, but he would do his best to spread the only true word – Love. His planned trip to Thailand was about finding solace in eastern philosophy, the same as it now appeared Christ may have done, going to live in the Far East to learn about yoga and transcendental meditation before returning to perform his first miracle at the wedding at Cana. His eyes had been opened widely since joining the army, exposing him to more pain and joy and humanity than any of his previous occupations.

It was a world away from the pilgrimages he used to take during his days as a rugby referee. He had enjoyed a spectacular time in places like Biarritz and Cardiff with international squads. But then, again, the camaraderie he enjoyed during that time was another way of experiencing the essence of being at one with the world. His rise to the top of that profession was merely more confirmation that an action accompanied by love brought joy and success. All he wished was that everyone around him could see the world in the same way but that was not a possibility. He also realised that he had the ability to embrace any new task without the responsibility of a wife or children. Michael's contract was between himself and God. He'd sacrificed those things and in turn was able to throw himself completely into every new challenge and task.

In ways his life had been a sort of kaleidoscope of human experience and emotion through education, sport and community and he'd been a part of the pain and joy of those who he came in contact with. If he could write it all down it would take several years and he would surely forget some of the precious moments of joining people in marriage, bringing babies into the community and helping friends and family say goodbye to their loved ones forever.

The sacrifice was simple. He was now alone. While he was

such a big part of everybody else's lives at those special times, he would always be alone in the end.

This seldom troubled him except on the rare occasion when he felt a deep attraction to someone. He couldn't explain why he was so fascinated by the woman he'd met at the airport. Roz Waters was an attractive woman but he had met more than his fair share of beauties, especially during his college and rugby days. But there was something sad about Roz that he felt he could heal. He sometimes felt this way about a parishioner but hadn't for a long time. She was the sort of woman that he could have a holistic relationship with. Or maybe it was just lust. He wasn't sure – which made him question how he really felt about her.

He knew that he didn't like being alone in this dull magnolia-coloured house. He resented the time that he was missing with his friend. It was just a shame that one of Peter's brethren had taken ill and needed Last Rights the very evening that Michael had chosen to stay with him. He'd to give Ben and Claudia space because she had promised to speak with Ben while Michael was staying with Peter. Michael hoped that she would have the nerve to carry it through because he couldn't go home and face his parents and lie by saying that she was okay.

Michael's parents had shared fifty happy years together and spent only a handful of nights apart. They were an exceptional example of how matrimony is at its very best and he knew how lucky he was to have that secure family experience that was being experienced by less and less people these days. He'd asked his father once what the secret of his happy marriage was and he had said it was simple. *"Every morning when I wake up I do everything possible to make your mother as happy as she can be and everyday when she wakes up she does the same for me."*

The secret of a happy marriage was one of selflessness and always putting your partner first. It was a simple rule of wisdom that he had shared with many young couples in their preparation for marriage, but he wondered how few actually had taken on his advice or could even think this way. As he'd counselled couples over the years he realised that very few put their partner first and that was why there was an ever-increasing divorce rate in Ireland. It was only for a short while that he had served in a parish but it was enough time to make him feel far from an expert in the area of family and relation-ships and filled with admiration for those that did take their vows to love another for the rest of their lives.

He was feeling restless and decided to go for a walk. Peter's house was only four blocks away from an Irish bar and Michael thought he'd kill a couple of hours while he waited for him to return.

Chapter 13

The sun dipped behind the Devon Tower as we drove into mid-town Oklahoma City. According to my itinerary it was the tallest tower west of the Mississippi River, but not as tall as some in LA or Seattle. My list was getting shorter but there were still five more pages of content to visit and explore.

We pulled up to the Ambassador Hotel – a world away from the simple chalet we'd shared in Northern Oklahoma and I knew already my father would rather be back on the ranch. But we had come to experience all that Oklahoma had to offer and as we entered the foyer our bags were taken by porters with wide smiles and warm welcomes.

We were appointed a room each to enjoy some space and get a good night's sleep. The clouds were gathering overhead and the wind whistled through the plantation shutters in our rooms. A darkness that carried tons of water overhead warned that we were in for a deluge.

After I had unpacked our luggage I knocked on my father's door, in the room next to mine, to see how he was getting on.

The TV was blaring and he had worked out how to fill the bath. He was wearing a fluffy white robe and had poured himself a whiskey from the mini-bar.

"Isn't this just gorgeous?" he said with a wide beaming smile. "And did you smell the bath salts? And the shampoo?"

It made me happy to see his delight in little things.

He held out a bottle of mouthwash to me.

"I've been trying to figure out what this is," he said. "It's so small and the top is difficult to get off."

I pressed down on the lid and turned the cap, then held it up to his nose.

"Oh, it's mouthwash! Isn't that very clever – I've never known a hotel to give that away."

He chuckled as he put the lid back on.

"When would you like to eat dinner?" I asked. "Would seven-thirty be okay?"

"I'll be finished by then – where are we going?"

"I thought you might like to try the Irish bar, McNellie's? It's just across the road."

"I wouldn't say no to a pint of Guinness. Mind you, I didn't miss a drink at all while we were on the ranch. It was the best couple of days I've had in a very long time."

I was happy that our mood had lifted since leaving the park in Ponca. It was good that we were able to have a debate without arguing over our differences. We'd always been able to do that. I could look forward to a couple of drinks and a nice meal with him later.

The Irish bar wasn't very Irish – it had a Scottish, Welsh and English flag flying from the rafters.

"At least the Guinness is good," my father said, licking the white frothy moustache from his top lip.

I sipped on my Californian Cabernet and let him chat about Standing Bear. The story had left an impression on him and I wondered how many similar stories could be told by tribes all over America.

"It's sad that he lost his son too, but I couldn't figure out how a twelve-year-old would ask to be buried with his ancestors," I commented. "He must have been very mature."

"They are a proud and noble people, Rosaleen," my father said. "With a strong belief in the spirit world."

My brother didn't often come to mind but now, thinking of Standing Bear and his son, I thought of Evan and his relationship to my father.

"I think a man and his son have a different sort of bond and relationship to fathers and their daughters. There's always an element of competition between fathers and their sons."

My father had read my mind once again.

"Why don't you visit Evan sometime?" I said.

"Ah, Rosaleen, it's too far away. He did ask me when he heard that I was coming away with you."

I wondered if it was sibling rivalry that had prompted him to invite our father.

"And will you go? You're doing great with all of the travel here, aren't you?"

My father shook his head. "It's just too far. I don't want to go to Australia – there's something hedonistic about that place. I think the English and Irish and all those who colonized it ripped the heart and soul out of the country. What they did to the Native Americans over here was terrible but the way the Aborigines were treated was even worse. I'd miss old things – everything is too new in Australia. I went there once with your mother and that was enough for me."

It was a miracle that my mother had made the journey to see her son before she passed away and it had meant the world to Evan.

"He's happy enough in Sydney," I said.

"I regret the relationship I have with him – I think I was too hard on the lad," my father said as he lifted the glass of black liquid up to his lips.

I agreed. Daddy was always stricter and firmer with Evan than with me but there was resentment between them that I never understood. Daddy wished he was the main man in my mother's world but the bottle of vodka was my mother's true love. As Evan and my father vied for her attention neither had a chance. I seemed to be the only one who realised this.

"Why do you think he became a doctor?" I said.

"Because he wanted to fix your mother, I suppose. He adored her, probably more than even I did."

How lucky my mother was and how little she appreciated the love of those around her! I gave up on ever reaching her and guarded myself by channelling my love to my father and later to Keith. I hardened myself against my mother from a very young age but still the men in her life were powerless to her charms. The dynamics of family were responsible for the way we all lived and for who we each became.

I sometimes think my father lost his sight after my mother died because he couldn't bear to live in a world where he couldn't see her in it. It was just a hunch that I had.

"Are you finished? We have a busy day tomorrow," I said.

He nodded and I went to the restrooms. When I returned he had company.

A man with salt-and-pepper hair sat with his back to me,

wearing a cream polo shirt over a pair of denim jeans. I recognised his friend instantly. He'd been in my thoughts several times since we met but it couldn't believe this could be just a coincidence. I felt my heart flutter and a wide smile sneaked across my face.

"What a coincidence to see you again! Are you on your own?" I asked.

Michael jumped up and gave me a warm hug. He oozed charm and kindness and was happier to see me than Keith had ever been when we were together – I realised that I'd have to stop comparing him to my ex-husband.

Michael's hand rested on my arm and his smile was as wide as mine. He had tanned nicely and was looking great.

We sat down.

"Yep, I nipped out to get a pint – and am very glad that I did now. I'm staying with a friend tonight in the city and I'm going back to my sister's tomorrow. I can only take her husband in small doses."

I found it difficult to believe that anybody would have a problem with Michael's company.

"Is your friend not with you?" I asked.

"He doesn't drink – besides, he has to work – but I knew there would be someone to talk to in an Irish pub!"

"Did he not get the night off when he knew that you were coming?"

"I'm afraid he's on call most of the time."

I presumed he must be a doctor and didn't pry any further.

"Well, it's good luck for us, isn't it, Rosaleen?" my father said.

I hoped that I wasn't blushing.

"Dad's been dying to talk to someone other than me about our stay on the ranch, haven't you, Dad?"

"Oh my, we've had the best time! I'd no idea that Oklahoma would remind me so much of home and, as for the stars, well, I could picture them perfectly. Rosaleen took a photo of them on my iPad. I got up on a horse too. It was my first time in fifty years and it felt like I'd been on it the other day."

Michael grinned. "I'm sure that you looked the spit of old Clint on the back of that mare, Patrick!"

He knew exactly what to say to please my father.

"You know, Michael, I bet you could say Mass!" I said, surprising myself by resurrecting an old saying to compliment his charm and eloquence.

"I have been known to. "Michael held his tongue firmly in cheek.

"That's it – I knew it!" my father exclaimed. "You're a padre!"

I looked at Michael for his reaction to my father's joke. He looked blankly at me and then the penny dropped. He wasn't messing. How did my father know that?

"You're a priest!" I said in disbelief, trying to hide my dismay.

He nodded apologetically. "People are inclined to jump to conclusions about me if I tell them that I'm a priest when I meet them. I seldom have to wear a collar, being an army chaplain. I've been a chaplain in schools in the past and didn't wear one there either. When I was based in a parish I used to wear one the odd time. I don't like labelling myself or putting labels on what I do because at the end of the day my job is to be there for others."

I didn't know what to say. This was just my luck. The first man that I actually found myself attracted to for more than a decade turns out to be a Roman Catholic priest. Then I remembered where I'd seen him before. He'd officiated at the wedding of a college friend of mine about ten years ago. I could see him wearing his white ceremonial robes and remembered being very much attracted to his warm smile and bright eyes.

"We were talking about religion earlier, weren't we, Rosaleen?" my father said.

But I still couldn't hide my emotions or focus on the conversation. Being a priest meant I disagreed with his beliefs in so many ways, because the Catholic Church stood for things that I hated. But in a strange way the fact he was unobtainable made him more desirable in my mind.

I had to get back to the conversation because my silence was deafening.

"We were having a religious debate alright," I said. "Sorry, I'm just surprised because you don't act or look like a priest."

"I'm a soldier too. But I know what you mean. I wouldn't be like a lot of the priests you've met."

"The Church has taken quite a hammering in recent years," my father said.

"And rightly so," Michael agreed. "It needed a shake-up."

"I just figured you were married when I saw your ring," I said, immediately regretting giving so much away.

He shrugged it off. "I'm married to everyone. I'm here to serve people —some might say it's easier to do this job than to commit to one person."

I'd never heard anything like it.

"I wish I hadn't told you now," Michael said, seeing my expression. "Don't let your opinion change, I'm still me."

I blushed again. My opinion hadn't changed and I still felt awkward.

"Don't mind her," my father said. "She's had it in for the Church since her marriage broke up –actually since she met that idiot ex-husband of hers. Maybe you can talk some sense into her, Michael."

I didn't know where to look and didn't want my father to suspect my feelings for Michael either.

"Roz's opinion is as right as anyone else's," Michael said and gave me a smile.

"My daughter has some strange ideas on life which she might tell you about," Dad said with a shake of his head. "But she's had me traipsing all over Ponca City today, Michael, and I'm exhausted – do you mind if I hit the sack? It's just across the road. I can make my way up to bed if you just help me cross the road."

Michael drained the last drop from his pint of Guinness. "I'll walk you back to your room," he said.

I stood up. "I'm finished too and, if you like, Michael there's a rooftop bar in the Ambassador Hotel which I was told is nice – we could have a nightcap."

I surprised myself with my forwardness, but the words flew out of my mouth before I could stop them.

"Great idea," my father piped up.

We walked together over the road and up the steps to our hotel.

The lift stopped on the second floor and Michael held the door open while I took my father to his room. When I stepped back into the lift, the air was tinged with the excitement of a date night.

Michael leaned against the wall, hugging his elbows in a confident manner, and I desired him. Like Casey on the farm, he was comfortable in his own skin. And I wondered what it took to reach that stage in life – to be happy being you?

"Hey, this is swanky," he said as we stepped out of the lift and into the bar. The wall-to-wall glass windows gave a spectacular vista of the city skyline all the way down to the Devon Tower in the distance.

We chose a little table in the corner of the lounge. I sat on a sofa and Michael took the armchair beside it.

"What would you like to drink?" he asked.

"I don't mind. I think something exotic?"

"I bet this place specialises in cocktails."

A waiter came over and beamed his shiny white teeth as he handed us a drinks menu. There were cocktails. Instantly Michael ordered a Mojito without looking at the menu.

"I'll have one of those too," I said.

The lights were low and the city sparkled outside like rows of gems on a jeweller's tray. Inside was plush and warm with small groups of beautiful young Oklahomans watching each other to see who was the most desirable.

"It was a surprise to bump into you again," I said.

"Just a little coincidence… but is that just another word for fate, do you think?"

"I'm not so sure I believe that there's any big significance to this coincidence. I mean, where else in Oklahoma would you get a decent pint of Guinness other than an Irish bar?" For a moment the pragmatic Englishness in my tone jarred on my ears. "You and I probably thought the same so as Irish people we increased our chances of meeting each other."

"I thought you'd say something like that, but what would your dad say?"

"He believes in the power of coincidences or God's doing or something crazy and spiritual."

Michael shrugged. "And what do you say about God?"

"I'm not sure really. I can't say how I feel about God or spirit. I think we are all just blood and bones and when we die it's lights out and goodnight."

"Maybe it is," he said.

I was surprised he didn't try to debate my opinion. I'd been questioning what I believed for some time and being with my father meant that I had to think about it some more. But surely it was Michael's duty to convert me.

"I thought you'd say something else."

Michael slapped his hand across his thigh and shook his head indignantly. "It's my night off, I'm on holiday and I'm sitting next to a beautiful woman. That's all I know at the moment."

With that the waiter came over with two glasses glistening in the light on a shiny silver tray.

He leaned forward and placed a glass in front of each of us.

"Thank you," Michael said, and put a fifty-dollar bill inside the wallet that rested on the tray.

The waiter disappeared and I hoped my blushes weren't visible in the darkness.

Then he held up his glass and clinked it off mine. As our glasses touched, he looked straight into my eyes and I saw the grey-blue colour clearly despite the darkness. He was kind. It was something that one of my teacher's had told us in school during our talk about relationships. "Find a man who is kind." But I'd married a man who was cold and had lived with that chill for years and I no longer knew what kindness felt like.

Michael was kind, he was confident and his light dazzled me. When I was in his company I felt better about myself.

"I think I might have seen you before at a wedding – did

you marry my friend Louise Moran? It would have been in Wicklow, about ten years ago?"

Michael tilted his head, trying to remember. "I've married so many people it's difficult to remember them all. Did she marry a rugby guy, Tony?"

I nodded. "Yes, that was his name. I can't remember his surname."

"Tony Doyle, good lad. Ref'd with me in rugby. I don't think I stayed around for that reception – sometimes I'm double-booked."

I could see why people wanted Michael to perform their wedding ceremonies and suddenly I realised the importance of a religious ceremony for them. Then I remembered my own miserable marriage in a civil ceremony. We hadn't even done it in a castle or somewhere romantic or special.

"Do you still hear from your friend?" he asked.

I shook my head.

"I seem to have lost touch with all of my Irish friends. Keith didn't like them and he wouldn't allow them to visit."

Michael's eyebrows rose.

"Is Keith the ex-husband your father mentioned earlier?"

"Yes. Louise was one of the last from my college days that I was still friendly with. I can't seem to juggle like I used to. I like to be organised but keeping up friendships is beyond me."

"Organised is good! So what are your plans for the rest of the trip?"

"We're going to the Red Earth festival tomorrow and then the Paseo district tomorrow night."

"You'll like that. What then?"

"We're driving through Chickasaw country and visiting a cultural centre."

"The Chickasaws have the right idea with the way they live their lives. You're going to love it down there."

"What flight are you taking back to Dublin?" I asked.

"I go home Saturday."

"So do we – maybe we'll be on the same flight."

"If you're going via Chicago we most certainly will be. I've a tour of duty coming up in Syria and I'm not looking forward to it."

"You must have seen some strange and difficult things as a chaplain."

Michael nodded. "Probably the strangest of all is the sad rate of suicide in Ireland. You expect to see the horror when you go to Bosnia and Beirut but sometimes it's harder to take on your own doorstep. Life is hard for so many people, Roz."

Suddenly his phone rang and he answered it.

"Peter. . .I am. I met the Irish folks I told you about on the flight and I'm in the hotel across from the Irish Bar."

"The Ambassador," I prompted.

"The Ambassador, Peter," Michael said into his phone and then listened. "Alright, I'll be back in a few minutes – glad that went well."

He turned off his cellphone. "That was my friend – he's a padre too – we were in Maynooth together. He was called out to give the Last Rites tonight."

"I presumed your friend was a doctor or something like that. I'd never have imagined that you were a priest."

Instantly I knew that I was treading on thin ice. A blind man could see that I was attracted to Michael and he was such a good judge of people he knew that I liked him. I hoped so much that he felt the same way.

"How long were you married?"

"For twelve years."

"And did you not have to give up a lot to be in that relationship?"

I had given up a huge amount – I'd given up my soul. I nodded.

"And now you see another way of living and how is that?"

"I hated it at first. My husband met someone else quickly after – in hindsight he probably had her before we split up, and it was very difficult. Thalia, our daughter, was only twelve at the time. When my marriage failed I felt like a complete failure too."

Michael put his hand on my thigh and although it was a friendly gesture I felt a thrill.

"Don't ever say that anything you try or put work into is a failure. It was a marriage that had an expiry date, that's all. Not everything in this life is meant to last forever – very little is actually. What matters is that you love when you can and you don't do anyone harm. To stay with your husband is wrong if you don't love each other, especially for your daughter."

"But doesn't the Catholic Church say that you must marry for life?" I was beginning to wonder about Michael. What he'd said went against one of the main doctrines of the Church.

He leaned forward, still with his hand on my thigh and I wanted it to stay there.

"The Catholic Church doesn't have all the answers. We are in new times and things need to change. I didn't give up anything and neither did you. We all have the power to love and be loved by everyone that we meet in the course of every day."

Our eyes fused and I felt as if he could see right through me. The silence wasn't awkward or strange. It was perfect. I wanted him to stay so badly and to continue our conversation.

There was so much I wanted to know about this man and so much I wanted to say to him. I was swaddled in a pink aura of joy in his company.

"Do you have to go?" I asked.

He nodded. "I have to meet Peter – he's had a long evening. Maybe we can link up on Facebook?"

I nodded. "I'll see you on the Dublin flight for sure on Saturday."

He stood up and my eyes scanned his torso. I hadn't felt this way since I was a teen.

I watched as he walked away. I couldn't take my eyes off him – then he turned around and smiled, leaving me feeling like a lump of blancmange on a plate.

Chapter 14

I sat on the bed in my room in the Ambassador Hotel. It had been a long time since I had felt that sheer electro-magnetism between me and another person. A part of me wondered if the attraction was heightened by the fact that he was a priest and any sexual relationship forbidden, or if it had just been so long since I'd actually felt anything for another soul. The life I led was filled with should-dos and I seldom related emotionally to anyone apart from Tally.

I glanced down at my thigh where Michael's hand had been and tried to recreate his touch.

It was late but a bath would help me to relax and take my mind off this elusive character, who might as well have stripped me bare and touched me in all of the places that I yearned to be touched. He had touched me somewhere that I hadn't even touched myself ... my soul.

I watched the bubbles form in the bathwater and ran my hand over them to test the temperature. As I undressed, I watched myself in the mirror. My body was like a Picasso portrait from his rose period. I lacked the curves of most women my age. My breasts were still unusually high, and I didn't have a midlife gut just yet so there was something to be grateful for. But I didn't feel vivacious and I certainly didn't feel beautiful. Keith used to call me skinny but I wasn't that anymore. The lines on my face were faint and covered a multitude of anxieties and were mostly hidden under my dark fringe. I wanted to know what Michael thought when he looked at me. Could he see my flaws the same as I did?

Michael had to remove himself from that situation. He knew he was being cool and distant with Roz, but it was more for his own reasons that he had to leave. Peter had called at the right time. If he had stayed he was in danger of doing something that he would regret. The lethal cocktail of alcohol and distance from his usual life had presented itself to him on several occasions but this was a particularly difficult challenge. He looked down at his phone and went onto Facebook. On his third attempt he found Roz and he floundered over the friend request. There were still a few days before he would see her at the airport. If he arranged to meet her again, he knew that something could happen. But it was inevitable that he had to see her again. He thought of the line of her thigh and where he had rested his hand. It had been a long time since he'd been intimate with a woman. He sometimes felt guilty for remembering the time that he had slept with the PE teacher at the school where he was chaplain or the woman who kept the parish accounts a few years later. Those dalliances had been infrequent but enough to remind him of what he had given up and how much he needed intimacy like everyone else. Celibacy suited some of his colleagues who were hiding from their homosexual feelings or others who were asexual and didn't seem to have a sex drive at all. But if he were true to himself, he needed to be touched – and that yearning to be intimate and close to another soul was the ultimate experience of love.

He jumped up and went into the bathroom and ran the shower. It was warm and balmy in Oklahoma City but his head and loins were hotter. As the jet of water ran down his face and over the hairs on his chest he thought of Roz again and wondered and wished that she could be there with him right now.

I slipped into the warm water and sank under the bubbles. I closed my eyes and imagined that I wasn't alone in the bath. I sensed his muscular body in the water next to mine and imagined my foot running along his thigh. The bath was big enough for two. It was such a waste spending my time in this beautiful haven alone. There was so much to be relished that was good in life and instead of devouring and savouring delicious experiences I was just surviving. I wasn't really living.

I made up my mind to change when I returned to Oxford. I needed to connect and enjoy my life. I needed to let go of any fear I had to connect with a man because all men weren't like Keith. I had known that in the past but somehow I'd forgotten over time and although I wasn't open to love again I knew that there was the possibility that some day I would be.

Chapter 15

Next morning I couldn't wait to hear my daughter's voice. I was giddy and invigorated after meeting Michael and needed to ground my thoughts. So I lifted the phone and waited.

But Thalia was distant when we spoke. She didn't want to discuss what she was doing and said that she was studying hard for her exams. I had an uneasy feeling about the tone of her voice and the way she was speaking.

I put down the phone and lay back in the bed, thinking. I was trying to figure out ways to be the best that I could, and my father was challenging me to question who I'd become. Meeting Michael made me question what I wanted in my life. I was set in my opinions before coming to Oklahoma but this heartland of America had a strange way of unravelling emotions and feelings I had no control over.

I got up and was dressing when the phone rang beside my bed.

"Are you up, Roz? Are we going for breakfast?"

"Yes, Dad," I said. "I'll be in to get you in a few minutes.

My father sat squarely in the car as we drove to the Red Earth Festival. It was held at a race-park on the outskirts of Oklahoma City and he expected a running commentary of all that we passed on the way.

"How did you get on with Michael last night?" he asked.

"We only had one drink and then he went to meet his friend Peter who's also a priest."

"Did you get his number – I meant to ask you to keep in touch with him."

"He's on the same flight home as we are so we'll see him again."

"Perfect. It never ceases to amaze me the way people come into our lives for a reason."

I didn't answer because I didn't know the reason and I didn't want to indulge my father who might lose the run of himself. But he did have a point and Michael perhaps was here to help me wake up and realise that I could be attracted to the opposite sex and ponder the possibilities of falling in love again or at least explore them a little.

In the distance I saw feathers and flamboyance. Tribes assembled from every corner of the country for what was to be one of the biggest annual powwows in America. I had my camera ready to capture the colourful costumes and head-dresses of the performers.

I parked the car up in a regular parking spot – my father hated to use a handicapped space. "They should be left free for the poor divils that really need them," he always said stoically.

He could walk and move freely and had use of his limbs. He never saw his blindness as an affliction – more of an inconvenience.

I could still remember how he explained the way that he felt after his vision got so bad that he was diagnosed as blind.

"I can picture the sky above my head and the sea lapping against the shore. I know what a forest looks like and a flowerbed. I just use my other senses now to conjure up the images and it's even better."

I used to think that he was being brave but there had come a contentment and acceptance with his hardship and I think he saw it as a bonus.

"It's great to be able to hear sounds so clearly and to smell aromas that I couldn't before," he'd say.

I wondered if it was his cup-half-full attitude that had helped him through his life – the way he'd thrived in adversity where others would have perished.

"Oh, do you hear those drums?" he said as we stepped out of the car. "They're having a right old shindig."

Crowds swarmed around the entrance to the park where the festival was in full flow. I held tightly to the crook of my father's arm and directed him. It reminded me of times in the past when he'd brought me to town as a child. He always held me tightly in case I would get detached and panic, but I sensed the nervousness of his step and was reminded that the roles were now reversed. I was the parent and he the child and, although he was excited and happy to be here, he was unsure of his step.

I grabbed my press pack from reception and gently led my father towards the performing arena, ensuring constant contact between us at all times.

The cacophony of voices and sounds was frightening and I sensed his relief as the path brought us out into the sunshine

"There's an art exhibition on in the main building so I can

leave you here in the sunshine if you like while I buzz around it?"

"No – I want to see the art! I'll be able to make out some of the colours and touch the sculptures."

I led him along the stalls as we surveyed beaded jewellery and handcrafted musical instruments. My father took photos on his iPad of the larger, most colourful pieces of art to inspect when he returned home.

"Miss Comanche Princess 2014 has just passed by," I whispered in his ear.

"Oh, is she pretty?"

"Very."

"Ask her if I can have my photo taken with her – I'll wave the white stick so she'll have pity on me!"

I laughed and followed the princess. She beamed widely at our request and put her arm around my father's waist – to his delight. I took the picture and thanked her and then we followed the crowd out to watch the Men's Fancy Dance Competition.

As we found a seat the rhythm from the drums pulsated through the arena with thunderous beats and the accompanying crying and wailing reminded me of sean-nós singers I'd heard when I was a teenager in the Irish Gealtacht. The loud crying sounded sad to the spirit, while the men on stage moved flamboyantly around the arena, springing like gazelles and bounding like deer on their hind legs. Their costumes were all shades of fluorescent and primary colours mixed in a myriad of repeated patterns that must have taken hundreds of hours to make. The heat didn't deter the men's energetic exertion and they gave every ounce of themselves for the pride of their tribe. And, even though the off-stage performers were sending texts on their cell-phones and eating hotdogs, this tribal tradition was sacred and part of the indigenous America that would live on after the hotdogs and cell-phones.

"I really would love to see them," my father said, his eyes closed as he breathed in the sound of the music.

It was the first time I'd heard him say that and I sensed his frustration. He had bravely weaved his way through the stalls but there was so much going on it was terrible that he couldn't see.

Just as I was wondering if we'd done enough for one day, I felt a tap on my shoulder and turned to see a woman with a young man in a wheelchair by her side.

"Excuse me, could you tell me where I can get one of those catalogues?" she asked, pointing at the guide in my hand.

I could tell she was European by her accent.

"I was given this as part of a press pack but I'm sure if you go to the information stand you can get one." I was curious to know where she was from. "Are you German?"

"Yes, I'm from Cologne."

"We are Irish. My name is Roz and this is my father Patrick."

The woman was tall and athletic and definitely ten years older than she had looked at first glance. The young man by her side appeared to be in his late twenties.

"This is my son Norman and I am Martina," she said.

There was a free seat beside me and I asked her if she'd like to join us. Her son wheeled up to the end of the line of seats, came around and shook our hands.

We made a space for the wheelchair.

Patrick was curious about our new friends and sat upright like a turkey in a pen about to be inspected.

"Is this your first time to Oklahoma, Martina?" he asked.

I could tell by her body language that she had no idea my father was visually impaired and it was good to leave it like that. He knew which way to move his head by the sound of her voice.

"Yes," she replied. "We are travelling on Route 66 and this is our second week. Where have you been?"

My father relished the opportunity to tell about his time on the ranch. "Mind you, this was a real working ranch with genuine Longhorn cattle. We went out for a ride on a trolley cart and that was the best bit of the trip. Well, that and the riding."

"Can you give me details of the ranch because we would like to stay on a working ranch – do you know if they can cater for people with disability?" Martina asked.

"There's nothing wrong with my arms, Mother – I can hold myself straight," Norman piped up.

"You sound like a grand strong fella," my father started. "Sure what would you need –"

Martina seemed confused until I interrupted.

"Martina, my dad can't see the wheelchair," I explained.

"What? What wheelchair?" my father said, shaking his head.

"Can you not see my wheelchair?" Norman said and laughed out loud. "Are you blind?"

"Well, yes, I am actually!" my father said.

We dissolved into hysterical laughter.

"What a motley crew we are!" I said.

"I was in a motorbike accident two years ago," Norman said. "I can stand but I cannot move my muscles yet."

"The doctors said that he would never walk again but he has got so much stronger they are not so sure anymore," Martina said.

"I mountain-climb and am stronger now in my shoulders."

"He's made great progress," said Martina.

"I'm driving now," he added.

"Yes, but he won't park in the special parking areas!"

I laughed out loud. "My father won't let us use those either!"

I'd known we'd found kindred spirits the moment Martina had approached me. There was a glint in her eyes that in a strange way made me feel as though we'd met before, which was unlikely of course as I'd never been to Germany. It was the same familiarity I'd felt when we met Michael for the first time.

We watched the Boy's Fancy Dance and the Women's Shawl Dance. Norman described the details as they unfolded before our eyes to my father, while Martina and I shared stories of our life. She was an artist and travelled to find inspiration for her work. I should have known by her appearance that she was an artist, as she dressed much more youthfully than her years and she wore her dyed-black hair so well.

"Would you like to meet up later?" Martina asked. "We are staying one more night in the city before we have to find a ranch. We must keep to schedule as we have to fly back from LA in two weeks."

"I'd love that, wouldn't you, Rosaleen?" my father said excitedly.

"Where are you staying?" I asked.

"The Ambassador Hotel," Martina said. "And you?"

"The same place," I answered.

"There you go then – we would probably have met up anyway," my father said. "Some things are meant to be."

We went together back to our cars which happened to be separated in the parking lot by only one car.

As my father and I drove back to the hotel I laughed and shook my head. "What a remarkable coincidence that they should be parked beside us. There were thousands of people at that festival but she came up to us."

"As I keep telling you, Roz, when you get to my age you realise that there's no such thing as a coincidence."

I felt a lecture coming on. The day was balmy with thunder in the air and I wasn't ready for another one. But that didn't matter because when my father had something to say then he said it.

"Martina and Norman are good people. They are part of our DNA group and it is no coincidence that our two families found each other. My friend Leo in Manchester told me a funny thing a while ago. He said Yale University can prove we are attracted to people with similar DNA to us. Look, have you never been somewhere and found people that were like you or, as in this case, they found you? It's the same as when we met Michael and then bumped into him again. Not just coincidence but destiny. It was so much easier when I had my sight. I miss that connection with strangers when I walk along the road and somebody nods hello – it's like a sign that we're meant to meet. Sometimes you would never speak to that person but other times you'd start up a conversation and it leads to passing on information that helps both of you."

"Well, it certainly seems to happen a lot in Oklahoma."

"It's been happening to you your entire life whether you've noticed it or not. A nod or a wink and there's the connection. I can usually sense it in other ways now by the tone of a person's voice or the emotion in their language – when one sense leaves, the others compensate."

"Have you always been aware of this power of coincidences, Dad?"

"I've had signs my whole life . . ."

And then my memory was jolted back to the dead bird at our doorstep in Oxford and I realised how his philosophy had rubbed off on me. I said nothing and let him continue.

"You know, the way I met your mother was a coincidence."

He had told me before of course when I was young, but I let him reminisce.

"I had met a girl at a dance in the IRN ballroom and she was from Roscommon and she had a great smile. I arranged to meet her at Clery's clock a week later at seven o'clock and we were going for an ice cream in the Forte's Café."

"You lived on the edge, Dad!" I chuckled.

"Well, anyway, I turned up to meet her – but she was a nurse and there was a terrible accident in D'Olier Street that night and she couldn't get off duty to come and meet me. So I stood and waited for over an hour under the clock and while I was there a pretty girl with long brown hair and wearing a blue coat was standing there as well. We looked over at each other now and then. We both knew that we'd been stood up. As it turned out she was seeing a policeman who was also involved in the same accident. We didn't have mobile phones in those days and, if you had to stay on in work for some reason, you couldn't tell people that you were delayed. Anyway, I got chatting to the girl and she was meant to be going to the Forte's Café too with her policeman. We decided to go, just the two of us, and that was my first date with your mother."

Something struck me. "So how did you know the other two were involved in the same accident?"

"The next time that I went to the IRN didn't my nurse and your mother's policeman come into the dance together!"

"Really?" I didn't remember this part of the story.

"And, would you believe, we bumped into them in Jameson's jewellers two years later when we were all going in to buy engagement rings and they had the very same day planned for their wedding as we had. Now what do you call that?"

It was an incredible story. "It was a remarkable series of coincidences but you would probably have met Mammy anyway as you all went to the same dances in those days."

"But we all married the people we were meant to."

"You might have had an easier life if you'd married the nurse?"

My father tilted his head and raised his eyebrows. I hoped he wasn't going to snap at me for mentioning the unmentionable.

"Maybe," he said with a shrug, "but I wouldn't have had you."

I felt myself well up, so I swallowed hard and continued the conversation.

"How can you tell that Martina and Norman were meant to meet us?"

"They wanted to find a real ranch to stay at . . ."

"And lots of people come to Oklahoma looking for ranches!"

". . . and the fact that we've just come from one that will be perfect for them is more than a coincidence."

If my father wanted to believe this there was no point in arguing with him and, after meeting Michael, I was more open to the idea that he could be right. He'd been inclined to crazy notions his whole life and these notions were part of the idiosyncrasies that made him charming.

"What are we here for in this life, Roz?"

This was too big and crazy a question and I was too tired for the debate. Wisely, I gave him the opportunity to prolong the lecture. "What, Daddy?"

"We are here to help each other and share our life experiences with each other. Do you remember when you saw those stars on the ranch and how infinite and beautiful they were?"

How could I forget?

"We come down to this earth to experience life together and if we can help each other along the way then our life has had purpose. Every sign that there is a coincidence is a message that you are on the correct path. Meeting people like Martina and Norman confirm this belief I've had my entire life."

He spoke with sincere conviction and, as I recalled times that had resonated with me throughout my life, they too were cemented by coincidence. Meeting Michael again last night was most definitely a strange coincidence and a very nice one.

When we pulled up to the Ambassador Hotel the porter pounced on our car so that he could park it for us. I was beginning to relish these words of wisdom that my father seemed compelled to give. I was beginning to understand my fourth lesson.

Chapter 16

As arranged, Martina and Norman were waiting to meet us at seven-thirty in the foyer of our hotel. I didn't see Norman as an invalid because he didn't see himself as one. He insisted on taking himself without help to the hotel transport and then we were on our way to the Paseo District.

Dusty, our driver, was a local kid who chatted incessantly from the moment we sat into his jeep. It took some of the tension out of the situation as a certain anxiety had crept into my stomach about dining with complete strangers like this. On the other hand my father was hyped up like a schoolboy about to go on an excursion.

When we arrived, the Paseo Grill was buzzing with life inside and out. Our reservation had been made for two people and I wished I'd called to tell them that we were now four. They could accommodate us if we sat outside on the decking and the others agreed that they preferred to sit in the sunshine.

The streets heaved with people in search of art as every other shop was a gallery. Buskers sang in a tiny park where two roads joined, surrounded by stalls selling jewellery and souvenirs.

"This is a nice place – we would not have found it," Martina said. "Thank you for including us in your evening."

"My father says it's more than a coincidence that we met the way we did, and we must have a message for each other," I said.

My father frowned at me. "My daughter thinks I'm crazy sometimes but I'm a firm believer in fate and when you get on with people you should get to know them better as they usually have a message for you."

"My message is to stay away from motorbikes," Norman said.

The way he said it raised a laugh and put us all at ease.

The waitress put beers down on the table as we scanned the menus.

All seemed right with the world until our jovial group was interrupted by howls coming from the table next to us. A man was arguing loudly with a woman who sat stone-faced opposite him. It seemed the louder and angrier he became, the more aloof her reaction was. It was unsettling for those of us sitting nearby and, as the argument grew louder, the waitress came and apologised.

I watched as a waiter tried to calm the man down. The woman he sat with wore a perverse smirk and seemed to enjoy the man's reaction.

"I did not order that bottle of wine – it's the most expensive on the menu."

"I'm sorry, sir, but that's the bottle the lady asked me to bring," the waiter replied.

The man lifted the bottle and slammed it back down on the table hard. "She only drank some of it!"

"I'm sorry, sir, but we cannot sell the remainder now."

The man huffed and asked the waiter to put a cork in it to take home. The row was not going to be resolved easily and he realised that everyone was looking at him.

My father leaned over the table. "What's going on with that pair over there?" he asked.

"I'm not sure but it seems that couple are looking for a public argument," I replied.

Martina appeared to be enjoying the display. She shook her head and grinned. "Classic drama – he is trying to interrogate her and she's withdrawing and aloof. I would think there is a lot of fun in that house. He reminds me of my ex-husband."

"He was much worse," Norman replied, taking a sip from his bottle of beer.

"What did you call it – drama?" I was intrigued by her choice of language.

"Yes, it's a control drama. We all use them when we try to take energy from other people. It is the reason so many relationships fail. I wish I had realised this at the time when I created dramas too."

Martina spoke so articulately I wondered at her comprehension of the English language.

"Your English is really superb," I commented.

"I lived with an Englishman for many years – Norman's father was English. But he died when Norman was only six."

"That's why my English is not so perfect, I guess." Norman shrugged.

"It's better than my German," I said with a laugh.

My father had remained silent, trying to listen to the couple at the next table.

"My, my, what a terrible waste of energy all that kerfuffle was," he said with a shake of his head after they had left.

"That's what it's all about, Patrick," Martina said. "We spend our entire lives trying to take energy from people until we learn not to do it anymore and that there are more creative ways to bring energy into our lives."

"How was the woman reacting?" my father asked Martina.

"She was aloof and driving the man crazy with her silence," she sighed. "This is the way that I behaved with my ex-husband."

"And how did he die?" my father asked.

"Oh, he's not dead – he wasn't Norman's father – I married a man when Norman was eight, thinking that it would be good for him to have a father figure . . . what a mistake!"

"Matteus was, how do you say . . . a control freak?" Norman was drinking his beer at a rapid rate.

"I let myself slip into dependence with him and it was difficult to get him to leave once I understood the way he was controlling Norman and me," Martina continued.

Controlling – the word resonated with me. I'd been in a controlling relationship and used travel to run away in the past.

"Control dramas are how we get our energy from other people," she said. "I learned about this years ago when I read a book called *The Celestine Prophecy*. It made great sense to me and I am careful not to fall into this trap now. There are four types of personalities and when an argument takes place it is one of these that is used – Interrogator, Intimidator, Aloof and Poor Me. That man was trying to intimidate his wife because he couldn't get a response from her. She was being aloof which is frustrating for an Intimidator. It may have looked like the man was a bully but the woman was controlling the situation by doing nothing. They were fighting for each other's energy."

"What a waste," I said. She made sense. I could put my relationship with Keith into a similar context.

"That's a great way to put it," my father said. "And what does a Poor Me do?"

"They make the other person feel guilty and draw energy from them that way."

"That's feckin' brilliant. Every day's a schooldays – I've always said it!"He thumped the table. "I knew you'd have a gem of wisdom for us, Martina."

"My mother has the answer to everything," Norman said, with obviously genuine admiration for her.

"Not to everything," she said with a laugh. "But when I paint, lots of ideas pass through my head and I think to be creative releases a lot of the negative thoughts we have and brings about positive change."

My father was in his element and hanging on Martina's every word. Norman seemed like a young man with no hang-ups and content with life, which was miraculous considering his condition. I wondered if his mother's wisdom had helped him.

I felt a terrible urge to hear my daughter's voice and just then my phone started to ring and I asked to be excused.

I found a quiet corner of the veranda and answered.

Keith's hostile voice was at the other end of the line.

"Roz, what is this message I got from Thalia saying that she is staying longer with her friend? I don't like it – she needs to stay with me."

"I couldn't get you on the phone to explain. She is studying in her friend's house and wants to stay there."

"This is all your fault – if you weren't away like this, Thalia would have more stability in her life."

My energy built up into a small ball of light as I watched it being sucked into the phone and sent on its way to England. My heart thumped and like a lightning bolt I got it – I understood exactly what Martina had been explaining. This was our control drama and my reaction was always to remain aloof or to run away. It was why our relationship had ended so badly.

"Keith, I cannot do anything about it now – I'm four thousand miles away and my main concern is that Thalia is happy. You already explained that you had a lot of business and meetings and wouldn't be around for her. Let's discuss this when I return." I tried to be as clear as possible and not allow him to take any more of my energy. But he had been draining me for years.

"This is typical of you, Roz. You suit yourself and try to fix things up with a Band-Aid."

· I'd had enough. "I have to go now, Keith. Goodbye."

I felt a renewed strength as I turned off the phone and returned to the table. A huge plate of nachos covered in cheese and jalapeños had arrived.

The others were deep in conversation and an epiphany swept over me. My father had been right. Martina did have an important message for us and it was up to me to do whatever I needed with the information when I returned to the UK.

I lay flat on my comfortable bed in a shroud of soft white cotton with a feather-and-down duvet and pillows. I'd had my share of dramas in my life. My father had lived with the same objective and protected my brother, but more so me, from my mother's dramas over the years. I couldn't say when they started. My mother drank too much as far back as I could remember. When Daddy had to be at the market early to buy the vegetables and make sure there was plenty of stock for the shopkeepers, I would be in the house wide awake and sometimes I'd hear my mother get up and go to the bathroom. The moaning and groaning meant that she was still in a stupor and more than likely vomiting. She threw up so often it was no wonder that she maintained a skinny figure her entire life.

I envied her as my shape developed during puberty and flesh formed that I had no control over. She was svelte as always and, with a chiffon scarf hung loosely around her neck or a flowing skirt, she remained elegant and stylish.

She never worked a day after she married Dad. I wondered why she was so thwarted and needed to avoid reality through the copious bottles of vodka and wine that she consumed.

I gained a new perspective on my mother from her brother, hours after we had buried her. He told me that my mother was always troubled and there was nothing his parents could ever do to please her. Her family hailed from County Cork. Her parents were fortunate to be shop owners and well-heeled enough to send their daughter to a private school. She attended university in Cork and this was where her troubles started. She fell in love with a man from the same village as herself. He was training to be a doctor while she was doing a language degree.

When she arrived home from her studies at midterm she went to meet his parents and was squarely told that the relationship could not continue. She was angry with her lover who did not stand up for their relationship and, under pressure from his parents, he finished the affair.

There was suspicion in the small community that the couple's parents were related by blood. In those days the landed gentry owned every scrap of land in Doneraile and the locals paid rent to them in terms of service and goods. Dark secrets lurked in the history of almost every villager and, as my mother's boyfriend was a direct descendant of the gentry, the story was that his kin had at some stage impregnated my grandmother. It was never clear who was the love child and who was a child of the man of the house in this rural town of secrets, but this grey veil was enough to stop the liaison forever.

My mother never recovered from the rejection and ran off to Dublin where she took a flat with a girl from the same village. Excited with new prospects and possibilities, for a short while she worked in the bank but once she met my father she was content to let him look after her. That was what he did until the day that she died.

She controlled my father for the duration of their thirty-year marriage. I'd listened to Martina talk about control dramas over dinner and wondered how my father felt on hearing her words. But, instead of being upset, he wholeheartedly agreed with her as if he knew that was the part he had played in my mother's life.

I tossed and turned on my pillow as the thunder rolled in the distance. The air hung heavy under the brooding darkness and I wallowed in my maternal drama all alone. I found it difficult to forgive her for the way she led my father around for so many years but he seemed relatively unscathed by all that he had endured. Perhaps it was my perspective alone that was twisted and thwarted? I had run away from her my whole life and selfishly neglected the fact that by doing so I had left my father on his own to bear the burden of a woman who needed constant care and attention. I never quite believed that my uncle's story was the underlying reason for her discontent but, if it wasn't that, then I couldn't see any other.

I would never know now. But in turn I was left with unexplained emotions and bitterness that would return every time that I thought of my mother. I had to let those feelings go but didn't know how. There was no way that I could discuss them with my father as it would only upset him but, most importantly, I didn't want them to transfer onto my daughter with whom I had a fragile yet respectful relationship.

By going away to the heartland of the United States, I was delving further into my own heartland. I let the emotion pour through my eyes and run down my cheeks. I was so engulfed in my feelings of rejection that I had to do something about them. And I wondered what Michael would say to me if he was here. Every time I pictured his kind smiling face, my heart lifted. Suddenly the pain I carried around with me, the rejection from Keith and distain of my mother, seemed trivial and stupid, a bit like the control drama we had witnessed at dinner. Why was I carrying around other people's issues when they didn't serve me? I needed to clear out my head and fill it up with more thoughts of Michael and the positive loving energy that he emitted every time that I saw him. I slipped off to sleep with a renewed picture of love and how it should be in my mind's eye.

Chapter 17

Newcastle, Oklahoma

Michael drove into Claudia's driveway and parked up at the back door. His sister waved through the window and opened the door to him.

"Did you have a good time with Peter?" she asked.

"Yes, he's good, thanks. How did you get on last night?"

Michael threw his bag on the kitchen floor and went over to get a beer out of the fridge.

Claudia shrugged. "I didn't have the guts to talk to Ben. I don't think we can talk anymore. I feel like I don't know him."

"I met a woman last night that I'd met on the flight from Chicago. She reminds me a bit of you and she's been through a bad break-up. It's not your fault, you know, and it's not hers. Sometimes we go through tough times to learn life's lessons."

Claudia shook her head. "Don't go all religious on me, Michael – you know it doesn't work with me. And don't say anything to Mum and Dad – I couldn't stand their disapproval. It's easy for them."

"Do you really think it has been easy for them their whole lives?" he said.

"Yes, really easy. They've always been crazy about each other and only had eyes for each other."

"But do you not think it's their philosophy that has made their relationship work? I mean the way they do everything for each other and put each other first?"

Claudia pulled a chair back and sat down at the table beside Michael.

"Jesus, Michael, you can be so bloody annoying – you've hidden under that stupid collar since your twenties and never been in a relationship with anybody. You've never had to share yourself with another person 24/7 and you've never been rejected or had to watch your relationships disintegrate."

This wasn't like the Claudia that Michael knew and loved. This woman was feisty and bloody-minded and he felt uncomfortable because she was right – he didn't have the experience of a long monogamous relationship.

"I'm sorry. I didn't mean to upset you, Claudia, but I've plenty of experience of talking to married people who need help."

"Yes, but you're hardly qualified. It's easy to preach when you have your own life boxed away neatly. It always infuriates me the way people with one child feel they are qualified to be parenting experts – they haven't a bloody clue what it's like to deal with siblings."

Michael couldn't argue with her. She was speaking the truth. "I just want to help you, Claudia."

Claudia nodded. "Yes, I know, and I'm sorry if I hurt you but using Mam and Dad's relationship as an example of how marriage works doesn't really help. They are perfect for each other and they are probably that one couple in a thousand or several thousand that find their soulmates and spend their lives in bliss. I do believe in soulmates and finding that perfect fit but it's bloody difficult and it's miserable when you are married to someone who isn't that person."

Michael hadn't had that deep connection with the women he'd slept with, it was true. He had never experienced that complete profound joy and ecstasy of meeting his other half. He wondered if it was just something that people read in romance books or movies. As far as he was concerned love was just love and it was his choice to love everyone equally and respect them and make their lives better for meeting him. He had given up any idea that there was the possibility of a soulmate and was happy with his beliefs, but maybe he was hiding too behind his parents' marriage and the idea that he couldn't replicate it so why would he try?

Claudia stood up. "It hurts when you wake up one day and realise you're not living the life that you've dreamed for yourself. It was romantic to meet Ben, a tourist in Dublin wearing cowboy boots and a Stetson, and following him back to Oklahoma fifteen years ago but my dream hasn't worked out."

"I'm not leaving until you do something about it," Michael said.

"Of course you are, Michael. This is my mess, my life, my kids and my bloody miserable husband. You'll go back to your cosy barracks with your soldiers and hide behind the collar you've been wearing and I'll get on with my existence here… and Mam and Dad won't know a thing, okay?"

Michael felt sick in the pit of his stomach. He found it easy in his job to make people feel better, to heal them and to be the light in someone's day, and it frustrated him that he couldn't do it for his own sister.

"Take the kids away for one of the days before you go back – that would be a help," she said.

Michael nodded. "Whatever you want. I'm sorry."

Claudia smiled. "It isn't your fault. It's nobody's fault. It's just the way life is for some of us."

Chapter 18

The Chisholm Trail, Oklahoma

The next morning after breakfast it was time to set off again on our travels. Taking Route 81 we headed for Duncan. The road followed the famous Chisholm Trail and our destination was the heritage centre.

My father was silent for the first few miles of the journey but then he started the conversation that I didn't want to have.

"Did you enjoy last night?"

"I did," I replied. "Did you?"

"Yes, I wasn't sure if you were upset – you didn't give much away after your phone call."

"It was just Keith again – it's fine."

My father's deep sigh and silence meant that it wasn't fine.

"Martina made some interesting observations," I said. "She was open and honest and helped me to see things differently. Is that what you want me to say?"

"Something like that. She explained something to you that I couldn't have."

"We talk about Keith and me and our flaws but we skirt around our own family issues," I said, and regretted it instantly. "It can't have been easy for you with Mammy. I know Evan and I ran away and left you to cope with her alone and I'm sorry that we did."

"I was listening closely to Martina last night too. I know the way your mother and I lived and it wasn't perfect – no relationship is. But I can't change the past – if I understood then what I do now, believe me I would have done everything differently."

Sadness hung over his words and I wished I wasn't driving so that I could hold him.

"I've let the past rest, Dad. Whatever way you and Mammy chose to spend your lives was up to you. It can't have been easy living with someone so aloof."

"It can't have been easy for your mother living with me . . ."

I was perplexed. My father was a wonderful husband who had done everything he could for his wife. What did he mean?

"Dad, we both know that Mammy was an alcoholic. You tried to hide it and keep Evan and me away from it, but you only ever did your best."

"I wonder, if she'd travelled and done all the things that she wanted, then maybe she wouldn't have ended up in the state that she did."

"Dad, you can't blame yourself for Mammy's alcoholism – it was in her genes – you even said yourself that her father was a heavy drinker."

"Your mother had such potential in her life. She had

education – she went to a real college, which was a mighty achievement in the sixties."

"But look what she chose to do with that. She was a spoilt woman who expected you to do everything for her and for us. She was never there for Evan and me."

"She was unhappy with her lot. I wasn't much of a catch for her."

I hated the words he said. "You gave her a good life," I put my hand over and rested it on his knee, "and you were always there for me."

"If I hadn't limited her, though, she would have been happier. She wanted to travel – she spoke three languages and she only got to use a foreign one when we went on holidays to France. She was such a beauty – I couldn't believe it that she would go out with a poor lad like me."

"What do you mean 'limited her'?"

"I interrogated her into feeling disabled. An Interrogator wants people to behave a certain way. I wanted your mother to need me and as I took away her power by doing too much for her, she became dependent on me for everything. It made me feel better about myself. If she had been with someone who'd let her stretch her wings and fly, she would've been happier for it and mightn't have taken to drink."

There it was – he had said it. He'd admitted for the first time in his life that he was married to an alcoholic. Why didn't he realise that she was controlling him always with her 'aloof' attitude. I didn't tell him what I knew from my uncle and had mulled over in my head the night before. But perhaps my mother's condition was wrapped up with regret and maybe my father had smothered her with too much love.

"You did your best for her. No one could ever say otherwise."

"I know what I did and I'm not proud of how I was as a husband. We all want so much from the one that we love. That's why I feel so sad that it didn't work out for you and your husband, Rosaleen. You deserve better."

His words stung me and not in the usual way – with hurt – but with real caring.

"I'm fine – maybe I've been aloof and not realised it these last few years, but Tally and I are doing fine."

"Is 'fine' good enough?"

"Fine is what I have."

My father heaved a loud sigh that penetrated the entire car.

"It's because of Tally you need to ensure that no more control dramas are carried on in our family. I messed up. I know I did, but I always tried to protect you and Evan. I wish I had the vision then to rectify what I see so clearly now."

I had to make him feel better. "I don't know, Dad . . . if only this sort of stuff was taught in schools, it would prevent so much suffering and hardship. People draining each other of energy sounds crazy but it is a reality and something that we all do."

"I just want you to be happy," he said. "But I also want you to promise me this . . ."

"What?"

"Before you or if you do decide to have a relationship with anybody else, I want you to promise me one thing. Make sure that he is absolutely stone-crazy about you – that's more important than anything."

"I can't see that happening anytime soon, Dad – but I'll keep it in mind."

There was no answer to it. The more wisdom my father

imparted and the more I learned from those that we met along the way, the less I was sure of anything.

I almost missed the sign on the motorway, welcoming us to Duncan.

As per our itinerary, Stacey was there to greet us when we arrived at the Chisholm Trail Heritage enter. A massive bronze monument of a wagon and cowboys leading a herd of Longhorn steers along the trail made an impressive display at the entrance.

With a plump and gentle face, Stacey blinked her lavender-blue eyes and brushed away her blonde fringe. She ushered us into the foyer of the centre away from the heat of the day. Inside was a reception desk and doors leading to the various exhibits.

"I'm pleased to meet y'all," she said and shook our hands warmly. She then turned to my father. "I've heard tell you're quite an expert on the Old West."

My father rolled his shoulders back proudly and nodded. "I've followed the old stories over the years and watched a Western or two."

It was good to see him smile and back in the realm of happy thoughts and adventures. I was still reeling from our conversation but trying to focus on the job at hand. I had an article to write when I returned to Oxford – my head had been filled with so many personal reflections on this journey but I couldn't let my work ethic slip at the expense of the feature. But I did wonder if my father was right. If my mother had been exposed to a more varied life and had the opportunity to travel like I did, would she have been so dependent on alcohol?

"We enjoyed the drive here, Stacey – it's lovely countryside," I said.

"That's great – I was wonderin', as it's comin' up to lunchtime, would y'all like to have lunch at the Chisholm Trail monument over in Comanche? Then we can come back here for the full tour of the centre"

"Is it far?" I asked.

"Abou' twen'y miles."

And I realised that was a stupid question.

She packed some sandwiches, iced tea and cupcakes into a paper bag from the fridge in the souvenir shop and ushered us out to the car park again.

We sat in her SUV and the air-conditioning blasted me in the back of the car. Stacey turned on her CD player and I felt a jolt as I recognised the first song. It was Neil Young's 'Heart of Gold' and I was about to say what a coincidence that was, but my father beat me to it.

"Great song, Stacey. We have that track in our car."

"Aw, that's one of my favourites!"

Our guide drove erratically for about ten miles but made the journey feel short.

The word '**Comanche**' was printed on the town's water tower next to the image of a Native American Chief in full feathered headdress. As we'd driven through the small towns across Oklahoma, the water towers had been our signposts telling us the name of each town. I spotted a building with '**Trading Post**' printed across it and stalls with scattered knick-knacks outside. The house beside it resembled a saloon, and I thought my father might find this place interesting.

"Would you mind if we pulled over and took a look in that store?" I asked. While I'd been driving the country roads, I was constant navigator and tour guide for my father. It was nice to be a passenger for a change.

"Sure, we got plenty of time," Stacey said and swerved onto the grass verge in front of the store.

My father was confused and wanted a description of our new destination.

"It's a really old building, painted red, with 'Buzzards Nest Trading Post' written across the front. It has a porch – like something you'd see in a Western. I think we might find some nice bits and pieces inside," I said encouragingly.

My father was keen to make the most of every special moment that we shared, and I appreciated that. There were times when I suspected he hid his tiredness in case it prevented me from doing the job at hand.

We opened the door to the store, accompanied by a ringing of the tiny bell above the door.

A lady wearing a colourful printed top appeared from behind the counter and smiled welcomingly.

"Hi, I'm Stacey from the Chisholm Trail Center," said our guide, "and I'm taking these folks on a tour of the area – this lady is a journalist from England."

"Oh, from England!" The shop lady was impressed that we had come to visit her small shop.

She quickly turned to hostess mode and brought us on a tour of all the antiques and novelty items on display. I was surprised to see handmade garments and jewellery as well as chocolates and ice cream for sale.

She stopped at a stall piled high to the ceiling with elaborately decorated handbags. "And these are concealer bags," she explained, taking one down from the stand and unzipping a pocket at the side behind an embossed Christian Cross.

I wondered what the local ladies concealed in these bags – liquor? My mother came to mind and I stared vacantly at the bag.

The shop lady handed it to me and told me to look inside.

Stacey could see my confusion and explained. "This ol' pocket is where y'all keep your handgun."

I was shocked. But this was the culture of these warm and friendly country folk who thought nothing of carrying a gun around.

"Do you have a gun?" I asked Stacey.

She laughed. "Not on me now," was her answer.

But I could tell that she saw situations where she would.

I was unnerved but at the same time amused by my father's reaction – he seemed totally unfazed by the exchange.

We trod the boards until we found an old duck egg that was hand-painted and signed by the artist. The image of a butterfly on a flower in pastel shades had caught my eye. I let my father touch it and described the detailing.

"Do you like it?" he asked.

"Yes, it's really pretty."

"Then let me buy it for you. It will be something to remind you of the trip as I don't think you'll ever use one of the handbags," he said, chuckling.

I appreciated the gesture and took the paper bag from the shop lady with a thrill that sent me back to my childhood. My father would let me pop into shops on the occasions when he brought me into Dublin city and I never came home empty-handed. Whatever took my fancy that day he would buy it for me as something to remember the day we had spent together. Over the years I had thrown out most of my belongings from my childhood and now I felt a longing to see again all the little gifts that he'd bought me that made me feel like his special little girl. It wasn't a coincidence that this place had caught my eye – this was a sign to remind me of the little girl inside who was craving for the love and attention that had passed between her and my father. On the wild and lonely roads of this territory, I was beginning to find myself again.

We said goodbye to our new friend and set off on the long straight road again. But something had happened in that store that changed how I felt inside. I was open now to emotions that I had hidden as a little girl and my father and I were back on track to continue on from where we had left off when I was a child and before I'd moved to England.

Stacey drove for ten minutes then pulled off the main road, and up a dirt track that seemed to be going nowhere until we started a gradual climb.

"This here's private land but the folks are real proud a' being part of the Chisholm Trail, so they put up a big monument to mark that ol' spot."

She stopped at a fence where an obelisk monument protruded from a pinkish marble base. The words **'Chisholm Trail Lookout Point'** were chiselled on to it. This land was flat and had been for most of our road trip but this vantage point was on a hill high enough to see far away in every direction.

My father ran his palm along the base of the monument and his fingers stopped at the indentations where letters were etched.

I read out the words on the pillar: *The wagon tracks of Jesse Chisholm across Indian Territory became known as Chisholm's Trail and Texas cowmen using this route gave his name to the entire cattle trail from South Texas to Kansas. The Cherokee-Scot trader was known to Indians as an honest and trustworthy man, a reputation that served his country well in his activities as an interpreter and peace negotiator with the Indians.*

Stacey went on to explain that the trail was started shortly after the Civil War ended when millions of wild Longhorns roamed the plains of Texas with a value of $4 a head. Jesse Chisholm figured that by herding the cattle up to the railways in Kansas they could be exported to the east coast where they could command a price of $40 per head. It was dangerous work bringing thousands of wild beasts with sharp horns over rough terrain and rivers. The cowboys were given a dollar a day for their work which lasted one hundred days before they ended their journey at Abilene in Kansas. Many died along the way, drowning in the rivers, bitten by rattlesnakes or spiked by the cattle's horns.

"It's the stuff that Westerns were made from – cattle trails and wild adventures," my dad said.

The Route 81 that we had driven up and down was real cowboy territory and my father was living and breathing every word of the story that passed from Stacey's lips.

"Let's sit over there and have lunch," Stacey said.

It was difficult to navigate my father over the harsh terrain, but he found his feet as we settled on a spot.

We sat on a rock as Stacey produced our picnic and we ate in the sunshine, chatting about what it must have been like for the cowboys of old. In the distance the clouds turned a darker shade of grey but were too far away to be any threat.

"You know, this reminds me of when I was a lad in Inniskeen. Sometimes we'd take a few slices of bread and chunks of cheese up to the fields and watch the cows graze. There's a lovely peace to this place."

I was sure that my father's childhood was much harder than he had ever shared with me.

"You know, my great-granddaddy was a cowboy," he said as he took iced tea from Stacey.

This was news to me and I wondered if he was having a senior moment.

"My great-grandfather left Monaghan in 1840 and lived in the Black Hills of Dakota. He stayed for twenty-five years and had his family here."

I could have dropped my iced tea but I was enjoying it too much.

"Which great-grandfather?" I asked.

I could see that Stacey was amazed that I didn't know something like that about my own history.

My father continued in his slow steady voice. "On my father's side. Things were tough in Monaghan in those days – even before the Famine it was impossible to make a living and there were too many people on too little land. So my great-granddaddy and his wife set off for a new life and had all four of their children in the Black Hills. My granddad decided to go back to the old sod when he was twenty-five – it was very unusual in those days, you know, to come back to Ireland because the boat trip was terrible."

I lifted my jaw which had dropped with shock.

"But your father was born in Monaghan?" I needed to know this family history that had been kept from me.

"Yes, he was, only down the road from where I grew up. But his father had been in America and used his skills whenever a cow was stuck in the river. He was able to lasso like a real cowboy. He was famous in my hometown."

So many thoughts ran through my head but the one that stuck was a question I had asked my father before I finished college. I was trying to get a work visa to go to America but, when I'd asked my father if we had any connections with family born in the United States, he was adamant that we had none. If his grandfather had been a US citizen then I suspected that I would have been entitled to apply for a visa with some advantage.

"Why didn't you tell me that when I was looking for a visa to go to the States when I finished college?"

My father looked at me with guilt in his eyes. "It's bad enough that you went off to England and left me – but America would have been too far."

I couldn't get mad with him – especially not in Stacey's company. I had always regretted not living in America before I got married but I couldn't be cross with my father at this stage in my life. It was calculating of him, but I realised that he loved me so much he wouldn't have been able to tolerate it if I lived so far away. Things had happened the way they were meant to.

A gentle breeze whipped up the warm balmy air and caressed the side of my face.

I could almost see a ring of calm around my father as he sat in a state of bliss, breathing in his surroundings.

"You know, when I was about ten years old my mother took me up to a place not too far from where we lived," he said. "It was a gentle slope like this one and she told me something that stayed with me forever. She said there would come a time when I was older that I would sit in a place like that and feel completely at one with my surroundings. She said I would feel like part of everything that was happening around me. I was so small back then that I thought she was crazy but over the years I've tried to experience what she was talking about and, do you know, I think I know what she meant now."

He rocked gently back and forward and took another bite of his sandwich.

Stacey didn't register what he was saying but the words had a huge impact on me.

"Who wants more iced tea?"Stacey said and we all took some.

There was a strange energy about this little hill that held the story of so many young lives and millions of cattle that had moved across the plains. The heat of the day enveloped us as I swatted flies away from our picnic. I ate silently and considered the tales these hills had to tell and the young men who had trod them before us with their cattle.

Later, as we drove on the next leg of our journey, I asked my father what he had meant about connecting with everything, as he sat by the monument .

"It's the next stage in our development as humans, Rosaleen, when we understand that we are all part of the energy that surrounds us. Remember when I told you about the stars back on the ranch – it was that insight that my mother gave me when I couldn't fathom where I came from. She helped me to discover all the other wonderful and marvellous mysteries in life – which are not so mysterious at all really."

I wished I had his vision. I was envious of this wonderful blind man who could see so much more than I ever could, and his lessons were resonating with me.

Chapter 19

Chickasaw Country, Oklahoma

We were sad to say goodbye to Stacey. She'd been a kind host. But, with the addition of my painted duck egg and a different perspective on the world, I was ready for Chickasaw Country. We drove along Route 7 which unveiled rugged and varied terrain as we headed south to a lush and greener prairie, not far from the border with Texas. We passed a couple of upturned armadillos along the edge of the highway, who hadn't made it across the road. Then we took a right at the picturesque town of Davis toward Turner Falls.

The falls cascaded profusely down the rocky mountainside into a natural bathing pool below. Tucked in along the route to the falls, the camper vans and holidaymakers had made their home.

It was a shame that my father wasn't a swimmer and hadn't usually swum in all the years that I'd been on holiday with him. He was even more unlikely to swim now. But, as we pulled up and the roar of the water gushing down the rocks became louder, my father surprised me by asking if he could paddle in the pool. He was wearing shorts. So I parked up and decided to join him. The water was cooler than I expected it to be as the weather was clammier and hotter than it had been in any other part of Oklahoma.

He held my hand as we edged along the gradual slope, past mothers and fathers with their young children playing and splashing in the water.

I was reminded again of the reversal in our relationship. The feelings of unsteady legs and anticipation of water creeping up my ankles was something my father was feeling now, with all the uncertainty that I had felt experiencing new things as a child. He couldn't see where he was walking but with each step I held him tightly and we walked as one.

Neither of us spoke or acknowledged the reversal of roles. It wasn't necessary. It was enough to relish the moment and enjoy the cool crisp spring water on our legs.

The short diversion was a welcome relief from the heat but over the mountain and in the distance I saw dark clouds gather and I suspected that our night would be eventful.

We pulled up at the Chickasaw Center set high in the Arbuckle Mountains about dinnertime.

My father was anxious to speak to the receptionist and I wondered what was troubling him so much. Then I heard the words that must have been swirling around his head as we travelled through the countryside.

"Is there a Catholic church nearby and, if so, would you know what time Mass is on in the morning?"

I'd completely forgotten about his request earlier in the week, being so consumed by our travels. Maybe it had something to do with meeting Michael, but I was feeling less hostile towards the Catholic Church. And I was feeling more tolerant of my father's needs. This was important to him and if it meant that we had to get up a little earlier in the morning then it was the least I could do.

"That's grand," he said as we walked to our new room. "Nine o'clock isn't too early for you, is it?"

"Nine is fine," I agreed.

There was no need for discussion; we had reached peace.

We went to our room which was illuminated by an enormous window displaying the beautiful Arbuckle Mountains, covered in pine trees and craggy rocks.

"I think I'll take a swim – is that okay with you?" I asked.

"Of course – I might put on the telly and catch up on world news. I seem to have forgotten about the rest of the world while we've been on our road trip."

The Chickasaw Center was once used as a place of retreat and the isolated setting surrounded by trees was perfect for just that. It was coming up to that time when the sun was about to slide behind the trees and there wasn't another soul in the swimming pool in the basement of the centre. I slid into the warm water and lay flat on my back. My head was full of thoughts, and Michael was at the centre of them all. I was too old to have a crush, but I couldn't think of a better way to describe how I felt. I was curious about his tattoo. I was curious to know why he became a priest. I wanted to spend more time with him because in his company I felt warm and loved. My thoughts about the Catholic Church were confused. I was curious about religion again since arriving in Oklahoma. I would take an open mind with me to church the next day.

The heavens opened that night as I tried to sleep, and an electrical storm lit up the sky from two o'clock until sunrise. The sound of thunder turned into a kind of lullaby between the flashes of light. The storm brought with it much-needed rain and I suspected that Casey Black and her family were relieved. The ground had been hard up in the red country – to the farmers, their crops and cattle this downpour would bring respite. For me it brought cleansing. A release of negative thoughts that I carried around in my head along with the respectabilities and limitations imposed on me by availed marriage. I had dreamt briefly about my life in Oxford and, as the thunder rumbled, I was reminded of the rebirth brewing deep inside me.

The atmosphere had changed as we arose on this new day and I had an impending sense of changes to come.

Fine misty rain sprinkled on us as we got into our car and started the drive into the town of Sulphur. The receptionist had given clear directions on how to get to the Catholic Church and it was easy to find. We were fifteen minutes early and I sensed my father's relief as the deacon stood at the door and welcomed us inside.

"Thank God for the rain last night," he said to each parishioner who entered as he shook their hands.

We took a seat two-thirds of the way to the back of the small wooden church. This community was close-knit and I sensed the importance of this Sunday ritual to each member. A large appliquéd banner of a white dove hung over the altar. The decor was simple with natural pine wood covering the walls.

A spindly woman with hair dyed a very dark brown came

over to us with two books in her hand. "Would y'all like the readings? Where do y'all come from?"

"We are from Ireland," my father said proudly, and took a book from her even though he had no way of reading it.

I put my copy on the seat beside me and thanked her graciously. I felt judged, as every person had inspected us on entry – acknowledging that we were strangers.

The choir mistress came over next with a copy of a hymn book for each of us. She was even less discreet.

"Are y'all visiting here for a long stay or just today?"

The pungent scent of powder and roses wafted from her skin as she leaned over the pew.

My father delighted in so much attention.

I swept my eyes over the room and figured the sense of collegiality and belonging was the biggest attraction for those in attendance. I remembered what my father had said about being part of the big 'We' and forgetting about the 'I'. It was what we all yearned for as human beings – to share our experiences and ourselves with others. This was part of Michael's world and he was a conduit between God and the people that he gave service to.

I wasn't feeling that, however. I felt more like an alien as I remembered the long and arduous Sunday Masses that I'd sat through as a child. I figured this sense of belonging was what appealed to so many people but it didn't appeal to me. I bit my lip and struggled to keep my mouth shut from comment.

The Hispanic altar boys were dressed in red and white ceremonial costume. They walked up the aisle, followed by the deacon and the parish priest who wafted pungent smoke from a censer.

"It's Pentecost Sunday," my father whispered in my ear.

In the back of my mind I recalled what that meant – it

was the day when little communicants got to wear their Communion dresses one more time. I was thrown back to my own ceremony and the painful memory of what had happened to my lovely dress that I wasn't able to wear again after my special day. My mother had cut it up in a drunken rage. How could she have done that to me and why had my father let her? It hadn't troubled me in a very long time but, sitting in this country church with all the pious people kneeling in praise of the Lord, I wondered why my mother had hated me so much.

I looked at my father who prayed trance-like as the priest commenced his introductory prayers.

I didn't feel this sense of oneness with a Great Creator that my father had spoken about in the Standing Bear Park. I didn't believe in this God that the finely preened people around us were so certain existed. I looked over my shoulder and noticed that the congregation at the very back of the church had darker skin than the rest of the parishioners. My father had no clue and stood joyously singing the first hymn as it was one that he knew.

It was time for the readings and I sat back on the hard wooden pew and decided to listen to what the deacon had to say.

I found it hard to imagine what Michael would be doing today – would he be saying Mass somewhere? I found it difficult to envisage him in the white embroidered vestments. He had said that he would probably be with his priest friend a while longer in Oklahoma. A hot priest with a tattoo and great sense of humour had made me wonder if I could be part of this institution again but sitting here today I had my doubts.

The story of Pentecost was one of the great mysteries that I did recall from those days spent at Mass with my parents. The

Holy Spirit descended on the apostles in the form of tongues of fire and they were then able to speak in different languages and with a greater understanding of the world and the divine.

For a moment I considered our picnic lunch on the rock in Duncan and that feeling of oneness my father had described. That was easier to understand than this message written as a story with hocus-pocus magic attached.

The idea of spirit wasn't completely alien to me and there had been times when I felt that a guardian angel was looking over my shoulder when things were difficult in my life. When had I stopped? Did I believe in such a force anymore? I couldn't answer this, but I did believe in gut feelings and that unity with others that my father had described. I definitely got what he had said to me about energy and the use of it to control people and to survive. I understood what Michael had said about Love being all that is needed. This time was perfect to consider what I did and didn't believe. I hadn't given myself such time to reflector years because I'd been coping with the disintegration and dismantling of my marriage.

What did I believe in at all?

When the time came to receive Holy Communion, my father stood up and beckoned to me to join him. I had to lead him to the altar so I had no choice. I hadn't been to Confession for over twenty-five years and wondered if the Church still insisted on confessing one's sins before receiving Holy Communion. The last time I had been to Confession had been an unsettling experience. The priest wanted to know about my sexual exploits and how far I '*had gone*' with my boyfriend. The stink of whiskey from his breath was off-putting and should have been a warning to get up and leave but instead I said and did nothing and took my punishment of three Hail Marys without dispute. I was sick to the core now when I thought of the clergy who had abused their roles, and not just in Ireland. But that was a different time, and the weeds were slowly being pulled out of the crop, I hoped.

Meeting Michael made me consider that things might be changing for the better.

The walk up the aisle was short, and I put out my palms to receive the tiny white host without any great emotion. But the symbolism of what we did was immense for my father, who shuffled along beside me with a bright smile.

I led him back to the pew and, as we knelt down together again, he leant over to whisper in my ear. "Thank you."

In that moment I understood how important it was for him and how little effort it had cost me to accompany him on those short steps to the altar.

I couldn't say that I felt the Holy Spirit at any point during my time in that little wooden building but I did get to see the importance of the church to the community that lived in the town of Sulphur. It was the same sense of belonging and togetherness that people were feeling in churches all around the world and I remembered Martina and what she'd said to me. This was another way of people deriving energy and it wasn't doing any harm on this level. The institution of the Church might indeed have need for a complete renewal or overhaul but wasn't that the way with all institutions of power once they became too big?

When my father and I sat back in our car I felt lighter, with a good energy that prompted me to speak again to my guardian angel in the future. Something in my gut told me that I would need an angel in the months that followed.

Chapter 20

Newcastle, Oklahoma

Michael was about to take his niece and nephew to the mall when Roz crept into his mind again. He was torn after meeting her in the Irish Bar the other evening. If he'd drunk another cocktail and stayed a little while longer, would they have ended up in her room – or in her bed?

But while the memory of her niggled inside his head he felt the need to do something. He wondered if it would do any harm to contact her before he left Oklahoma. It was a stupid thought, really, and one that could end in disaster. He pulled himself back into the present and remembered situations that he'd previously found himself in. It wasn't easy doing the job that he did. There were moments when he became weak and lonely, vulnerable too. He hated that word, but it described how he felt.

When he'd turned fifty, he'd realised that life was such a transient and short experience, remembering all the wonderful souls he'd met along the way and helped on their journey to the next life – whatever that might be. Heaven and hell were on this earth and he'd encountered both with clarity. He knew his own weaknesses well enough to realise when he was being pulled into a position that would ultimately end in disaster.

He thought that he'd handled the situation in Oklahoma City with calmness and a collected head. But sitting in the bar at the top of the swanky hotel was that piece of normality that was forbidden to him as a Catholic priest. He was so good at rising above his personal emotions that when someone pulled him into the mortal coil of real life he felt it land like a punch. He was deflated and empty since meeting Roz because again he felt the emptiness in his soul. That longing to bond with someone more deeply than his body or spirit would allow him to.

It was the feeling of living a half-life that resonated with him and the fact that he had lived more than half his time on earth.

Fifty was a milestone that had crept upon him suddenly. He was always in control of his life and his thoughts but that notion that he'd never give himself completely to another human being bothered him now in a way that it hadn't before.

Why was life like this?

Then he punched the wall so loudly it made a din and he said to God, "Each time I think I have a handle on it *You* go and throw something or someone at me in this way!"

His sister's kids came running in on hearing the noise and asked if he was okay. He wasn't sure if he was or wasn't.

"Sure. Are you ready, guys?"

They jumped into his car and he turned on the radio to fill his thoughts with music. Going to a shopping mall was way outside his comfort zone but he would enjoy playing bowling with the kids. He'd given up the opportunity to have his own, so this was the closest he would get to ever being a father. Then suddenly he realised what a coward he had been. Claudia was correct that he had hid behind his collar his entire life with a certain sense of smugness. But he didn't feel safe anymore and every time he thought of Roz he knew that he had given up so much more than he ever realised.

Chapter 21

Sulphur, Oklahoma

"Where are we going to now?" my father asked buoyantly.

My mind was somewhere else. I was still wondering how and why Michael had committed his life to God. It felt like a waste but, then, as she thought of all the years she had given to a man who never really loved her, she felt as if she also had wasted too much time.

"I thought we might check out a park. It's just past the crossroads on the same route that we took earlier."

The town of Sulphur smacked of the Old West. A fountain in the middle of the square marked the main attraction and how it got its name. In the past invalids came hoping for miracle cures from the healing powers in the sulphurous water.

I took a left turn and drove through woodland and forest rich with wildlife. Squirrels and rabbits scampered as birds flew up into the air. I parked and found a path that led to Travertine Creek.

"Apparently there's a place nearby called Little Niagara Falls – you don't mind if we check it out?"

"Not at all – you know that I'm happier in nature than in a city," my father said.

Then he held his nose up in the air and breathed in the forest scents of rich foliage and wildlife.

I loved being in nature with my father now. We were doing things that we hadn't done together in so many years. Those Sundays with my bicycle in Ardgillan Demesne didn't feel so far away. With each step that we took we trod through time. I watched out for him the way that he had watched out for me. I was him and he was now me – a father and daughter trekking through time, surrounded by nature and life and energy. As we walked there was nothing else.

"This walk is like going to Mass again, Rosaleen. Thank you for this morning – it meant a lot to me."

"It was fine – I'm glad that we went."

As I said it, I really meant it. I did feel better for sharing in something that was so important to him. A part of me felt that going to Mass had brought me be closer to Michael too.

"I wonder if meeting Michael has softened your opinion of priests?"

I was freaked –my father had read my mind again.

"I don't know what you mean."

"Don't think I'm judgemental about celibacy or that I'm caught up in the doctrines of power and the things that are wrong with the Church, but Michael's a good man and he had to give up too much to pursue his vocation. I'm grateful to men like him."

"He has given up a lot but so have I. My dream of living happily ever after with someone who loved me and making a family are destroyed forever."

"I'm genuinely sorry for your loss, Rosaleen. It is very unfair and if I could kill that bastard Keith for how he treated you I would do it. But then I wouldn't be a Christian and I think you now understand how important God is in my life." He took a sharp breath. "What I'm saying is that God is all around us. He's with us here as much as in the church."

"I think I'm more comfortable here, Dad. But I know what you mean. And, yes, maybe meeting Michael has given me a new perspective on the Church. Everyday we learn more if we are living our lives correctly."

My father just nodded.

We came to the waterfall. A father and his son sat at the edge fishing while a woman and her child walked by hand in hand. This was a special place and I felt truly connected to the land and my father and, even though I would not admit it, I also felt a connection with nature which I began to see as a reflection of God. God was something that I hadn't felt around me in a very long time.

We ate lunch in the Artesian Hotel which was built on the ashes and remains of the original building which had burnt down in the sixties. John Wayne had stayed there, and my father was fascinated that he was tracing the steps of his idol as we journeyed on our road trip.

"So where to next?" he said, wiping the remains of his lunch from his lips.

"We have to meet Pam at the Chickasaw Cultural Center and spend the afternoon learning about all things Native American!"

"Ahh, that's great," he said and put his hand on mine. "Thank you."

I had something to do first. I hadn't spoken to Thalia. I'd lost all sense of England and my home and felt more part of the road now than the person I'd left behind.

Thalia's phone rang out. I left a message for her and went back to my father who was deep in conversation with the female security guard at the door. A notice caught my eye: '**NO FIREARMS**.' It sent a shiver up my spine.

"Howdy, your pa's been keepin' me comp'ny!" The security guard wasn't tall but she was stocky and strong and had a hearty laugh.

"Has he been giving you trouble?" I teased.

"No, he's been tellin' me all 'bout his stay at the ranch. Quite the cowboy!" she said with a flirty wink. "You've gotta look of Clint Eastwood – anyone ever tell y'that?"

"He's been called worse," I agreed.

The security guard had no idea how powerfully her words fell. My father pulled his shoulders back and stood tall with pride. "Now that you come to mention it . . . once or twice!"

He was beaming when we sat back inside the car.

"What nice people," he said.

"They seem to be but there was a sign on the door back there, saying 'No firearms' which implies some people try to enter with them."

My father nodded. "Which reminds me of when you were little, Rosaleen. Do you remember that story I told Michael at the airport?"

I couldn't remember – I was smitten at the time.

"You must have been about six at the time. I was out in the garden doing jobs and you ran out to tell me that you had solved the problem of wars. When you grew up you would become the president and ban all soldiers. You said that if there were no soldiers there wouldn't be wars because there would be nobody to fight them."

I laughed. I remembered now but I still found it easier to believe that Michael was a soldier than a priest. I was always trying to solve situations and problems when I was small – they involved my mother mostly.

"Did I really say that?"

"You did," he paused. "And, do you know, I actually think that you were right. The people who fight the battles are only doing what the men in power who cause the wars are telling them to do. That goes for the outlaws too – the really bad guys rule with fear and get others to do their dirty work for them. There's a scene in *The Grapes of Wrath* where the Okies in the cavalry are told to shoot an Indian who wouldn't move. I can see it in my mind's eye as clear as if I had my sight back. The young warrior stood proud and tall on a peak – afraid of nothing – a beautiful proud man. On the instructions the soldiers had to kill him. None of them wanted to do it. Who really wants to kill and to maim another human being? We aren't put on this earth to kill. We are meant to be kind and love one another. But war is a way of bringing out the very worst in the human spirit and fear is the way to control people to take part in it." He sighed. "What allows evil to rise is when good men stand by and do nothing. The Jewish Holocaust could not have happened only for the ordinary people who went about their jobs in the camps allowing it to happen. There comes a time when you see that by doing nothing you are as much responsible for allowing bad things to happen as those perpetrating the evil."

I felt his words heavily on my ears. I realised that he was right. To live with pain and be in pain was something I had spent so long numbing my spirit against, until I realised that I didn't feel anymore. Maybe it was my coping mechanism. My father was right. I used to have a conscience and a sincere desire to make the world a better place when I was a child. But what had I done with my talents? I had a mediocre job in a newspaper and I'd brought a beautiful child into the world. I hadn't achieved anything great – I hadn't helped my father when things became very difficult for him. I'd coasted along as an observer of life rather than someone who actively did something for those in the world with whom I shared it.

"Are you all right, love?" my father asked later as we sat in the car on our way to the next stop.

"Yes, I'm just trying to figure out where this place is – it's not on the GPS," I lied.

Truth was, I needed to sit with my thoughts because a gnawing in my stomach told me that the place we were about to visit was possibly going to teach me another of my father's lessons.

Pam was a short woman with long, thick black hair and a wide gentle smile. She stood outside the main entrance to the Chickasaw Cultural Center with two other guides who were waiting to meet their guests. The driveway was long and serpentine, following the rim of a tranquil man-made lake. The centre itself sprawled over a huge distance and was landscaped with sandstone and wild prairie flora.

A tall bronze statue of a warrior marked the greeting spot,

and each section of the centre was signposted by a marker carved from wood. Every detail of this place was subtle and planned in a curvilinear shape, from the footpaths to the walls.

Pam walked over to us with her hand held out warmly. "Y'all must be Roz and Patrick from England."

My father's white stick was a wonderful prop.

"Yes, we're both Irish actually but I work for a newspaper in England," I said. "And you must be Pam?"

She started to walk slowly as we followed a crowd of tourists from another part of the States.

"Come on over this way," she said, beckoning us to a small amphitheatre in the centre of the park. "I wan' a show you sumthing."

As we walked, she talked.

"This here's a place that the elders fought to create for a long time, a place where we celebrate our culture and teach our children about our tribe. My father told me many years ago when he heard they were building this that it would be a good place to work and he was right."

"It's beautifully landscaped," I said and described some of the details to my father.

Pam didn't interrupt but when I finished talking she clarified the reasons for the patterns in the landscaping.

"The elders planned the layout in circles because life happens in a circle. They didn't use hard lines or edges to shape the paths like the way the roads are built in towns. They made sure that this place resembles all that the Chickasaw tribe represents."

"I've heard of lots of tribes mentioned in movies but you don't hear much about the Chickasaws," my father said.

Pam explained. "The Chickasaw were one of what the

early European invaders called the Five Civilised Tribes. The Choctaws, Chickasaws, Creek, Seminole and Cherokees all lived in the south-eastern woodlands of Mississippi, Alabama and Tennessee, in settled agrarian communities. They traded and worked with the white man – many went to school and college and all was peaceful . . . until the settlers in the east needed more land. They were moved from their homelands in Alabama and Tennessee after the Indian Removal Act in 1830."

"That's what happened to the Irish in the seventeenth century. To hell or to Connaught, the English said to us," my father declared like a rebel. "Those they didn't murder, they drove westward over the River Shannon and took our lands."

"So you understand what happened to our people," Pam continued. "We were tricked by treaties and told to move to Indian country but the removal was slow and painful and many perished on the way."

"That is what happened to our people during the Great Irish Famine," my father said. "Many were pushed off the land while food was leaving the country in big ships for England."

He knew his history well but he surprised me with his next piece of knowledge. "I heard a story that the Choctaws gathered together the money they had on their reservation after they settled here and it came to 170 dollars. They then sent it to the victims of the Irish famine."

Pam nodded. "Yes, that is true. Our people share a lot of sadness."

"Roz, I've heard that 170 dollars then was the equivalent of around 4000 Euros nowadays. And some calculate it was a lot more."

"That's incredible," I said. "What amazing generosity."

We ascended along a footpath that led to eight figurative

statues. The tallest figure stood nine feet tall and around him were all generations of his family.

"This statue is called 'The Arrival' and it marks the end of the 'Trail of Tears' that our ancestors endured before arriving in Oklahoma," Pam explained."This is pretty much how they would have looked when they got here. There were no provisions for them and 500 of our tribe died of smallpox when we were given contaminated blankets to keep warm."

I'd heard this story before but Pam was divulging a personal message that made it seem more real.

"I suppose it's not very different to what's going on in the Middle East and Syria, especially at the moment," my father commented.

He struck a chord with me and I felt guilt again for resting on my laurels and not developing my craft as a journalist. He was correct. There was a pattern of greed in humanity that hadn't dissipated with time. The lust for land – for other people's territory – and the entitlement to destroy the lives of those considered less important.

"I didn't realise that all the tribes were so different. When you say 'civilised', in what way were they different to the Apaches or the Sioux?" I asked.

"The tribes in the west were nomadic and moved on the plains following the buffalo. Long before the French and English came to America the Five Civilised Tribes lived in towns and communities. We had religious ceremonies and schools and we traded with each other. We were farmers and made wooden houses and community halls for powwows." She beckoned for us to follow her. "Come this way and I'll show you our living village."

We followed her under the warm sunshine along a raised

bridge. It stopped at a vista forty feet above the ground. There we had a stunning view of the replica Chickasaw village below.

"This is what our homeland was like in Alabama before we had to leave."

An impressive set of structures dotted the landscape, set within a fortress-like surrounding and manicured to impeccable detail. In the distance I recognised a mound shape not unlike Newgrange, the prehistoric passage grave back home in County Meath.

"What was that used for – the mound?" I asked.

"That's where we buried our dead."

I shook my head in amazement. "It's remarkably similar to the burial chambers in ancient Ireland."

"Really? Would you'all like to go down and see the houses?"

We followed her to a circular area covered by a pergola.

"This is where we perform the Stomp Dance – it's our religious ceremony."

"We saw tribal dancing at the Red Earth Festival, didn't we, Rosaleen?" my father said enthusiastically.

"So this is how your tribe prays?" I said.

Pam nodded. "Yes, ma'am, we dance and there are some who won't do it in the centre in front of tourists. It's a personal way to connect with Spirit."

I wondered how much Pam could tell us about her culture and how much she pared down for the people that she showed around the centre.

"Do you mind telling me more about the spirituality of your people?" The fact that we were in this place on Pentecost Sunday made me wonder about her peoples' beliefs and connection with the Holy Spirit. Maybe theirs and ours were one and the same.

"The Great Spirit is all around us and in everything," she continued.

"That's exactly like our God – sure it's the same God," my father butted in.

"For many years we had to hide our religion and our beliefs – it's how we have survived as a tribe and stayed strong. We went to the white man's church and played along with their rules. Then we met secretly after to do the Stomp Dance and pray to the Great Spirit in our own way. You must understand that the government did all they could to destroy our culture and for many tribes they succeeded but they did not succeed with the Chickasaw. We have kept our culture strong and passed our wisdom down from generation to generation."

My father was entranced by Pam and so was I.

"How did you do that?" I asked.

"When I was a little girl most evenings my father would sit all us children down on the porch and light up his pipe. He'd tell us the stories of his people from the time before they left Alabama . . ." She paused as if in pain. "But whenever he told me about the journey his ancestors made on the Trail of Tears, my feet would become very heavy and very cold. And, as I looked at him through the smoke, I could see my forefathers walking in the wet and heavy forests on the way to this new land."

We understood. There was a truth and spirituality about the way she spoke.

"Our ancestors had strong communities that worked well with the white man. They had slaves, you know, but my family gave our slave a choice to stay or to leave and head north after we were settled in Oklahoma."

"African slaves?" my father asked in surprise.

"Yes – the Civilised Tribes were on the Confederate side

during the Civil War. We were part of the Deep South and how it was made. We were like the white settlers, so it hurt bad when they decided to make us leave. We didn't fight – we weren't like that. We just left when we were asked. But the land in Oklahoma was good and we were happy when we made our communities here again. My father studied agriculture in school and used it to farm the land."

And, as we trod the paths around the wooden dwellings, I observed the history of the community of civilised agrarians.

"You know, Pam, this community reminds me of the one where I grew up," my father said. "What crops did the Chickasaw grow?"

"The 'Three Sisters' – right over here," Pam said as she directed us to a vegetable patch. "The three staples of beans, corn and squash."

We continued to walk and entered a house painted white and made in wattle and daub.

"This here is our winter house," she explained as we walked into the spiral dwelling.

A hole in the roof let smoke out from the fire in the centre. Animal skins covered the wooden beds and chairs and utensils made of pottery were scattered around the fireside.

I took my father's hand and led him around the building, explaining what each texture was as he touched it.

"Is that a goat skin?" he asked, as his hand ran over a hide on the wall.

"Yes, we kept goats and cows – and chickens of course."

We walked through the buildings – each building had an important function in the overall community.

I was curious about their healers as I'd read about them in the past.

"Pam, would you mind if I asked you a question about

your medicine men?" I said. "How does it work and do you still have them in your tribe?"

She paused – as if unsure whether she could trust me.

I understood why. Much of history had mocked native traditions.

"It's okay," I said. "I really want to know how they heal."

She looked over her shoulder and drew my father and me closer.

"We have a medicine man in our town, and we go see him when we are feeling poorly but, you see, it's not like a normal doctor because he's not just gonna fix your body."

"I bet he doesn't charge much?" my father said.

"You're right. You bring some plug tobacco and then he'll smoke it while you're there and pray over it – then sometimes he'll send you home and tell you to sleep with a bit of the treated tobacco under your pillow."

"That's feckin' brilliant," my father said. "And I bet none of the medicine men ever get cancer."

"No, sir." Pam shook her head. "They smoke pure tobacco."

"They mustn't have much money?" I said.

"People bring them things to live by – they don't need much. Everybody provides for them."

"Reminds me of when I was a lad," my father said. "People lived in small communities and we worked hard and lived off the land – I remember my mother paying the doctor with a dozen eggs."

"That's kinda like the motto of Oklahoma state – have you seen the seal?" Pam asked. "It carries the words *Labor Omnia Vincit.*"

"Work conquers all," my father said. "It's Virgil, from his poem inspiring people to go out to the land and live off it."

"That's what we're all about here in Oklahoma. When the government didn't want this land, they called it 'Indian Territory', but then came the official 'Land Rush' of 1889 and new settlers took even more land from us. But the Chickasaw Nation is an independent state now and we have our own governor – we haven't had a recession like the rest of the United States because our governor planned for the future and invested in industries that have brought us good fortune."

"So you don't have unemployment?" I asked.

"Heck no, we don't have enough people in our tribe for our industries so we employ others."

"They could learn from your tribe in the White House!" my father said.

Pam shrugged. "It's the way we are. The elders think of the entire tribe when they make plans and plan always for the future, investing in our youth. We have good education. Everybody goes to college and we support artists and continue to develop our cultural centres. Would you like to go to the centre and see the exhibits?"

My father was fascinated. "Do you see this, Rosaleen? You need to write about this and tell the rest of the world how to improve their communities. This is a wonderful success story."

Pam started to walk us in the direction of the centre. "It wasn't so easy at first because the US government did everything they could to try to kill our traditions but it just made us stronger and more determined to keep our language and continue with our ways. My father was sent to boarding school by the government, with all the other young Chickasaws. They did this until only a couple of decades ago. But the Chickasaws used these opportunities to go to university and learn business and accountancy and law and we use this to our advantage now."

"We could do with somebody like your governor in Ireland," my father said.

"And it's a pity your governor isn't in the White House," I agreed.

Then my phone rang.

I asked to be excused and found a quiet corner to take the call. I was glad that I had because Keith was yelling down the phone.

"*You stupid woman, this is the last straw!*"

He hadn't used this tone with me for a long time. Whenever he'd done it before, it sent a shockwave through my body and I was completely unprepared for this outburst.

"I told you before not to talk to me like that," I said. A little voice in my ear said, *He's only trying to control you – get energy from you.* And I was reminded of our meeting with Martina and Norman. It wasn't a normal disagreement between us anymore. I understood the motivation and intimidation and I tried to defend my energy as I let him continue.

"I can't believe that you gave Thalia permission to go to that party. I've just met Tom Stevens at the golf club, and I had to be told by him what my daughter was up to."

Emma's father was a talkative man who loved to show off. How could I get out of this situation? I remained firm inside. I needed to warn Thalia.

"So I'm taking her back to my apartment where she should be. I'm going to have to cancel my meetings tomorrow, but she is staying with me until after you get back."

My heart raced. My poor daughter would be traumatised if Keith showed up and embarrassed her. She had exams coming up and this could send her over the edge.

"Listen, Keith, she's a good kid and studying hard. Please leave her. She doesn't ask for much."

"I'm her father and the only person in this country responsible for looking after her. I'm calling around first thing in the morning and taking her home."

With that he slammed down the telephone and I thought I was going to throw up. I would be in Oklahoma for two more days. All he had to do was leave her be for two days. I took deep breaths and tried to focus on what had happened and deal with the situation in a constructive way from what I'd learned.

I dialled Thalia's number and waited for three rings before she answered.

"Hi, Mum."

"Thalia, darling, how are you? I know it's late to be calling but are you okay?"

"Yes, I'm fine . . ."

I could tell that she wasn't. "What are you doing?"

"I'm studying."

"Is Emma's dad there?"

"He's just come in – said he was at the golf club."

"Thalia, he met your dad and told him that you were at the party."

Silence at the other end of the line and I hoped that my daughter was all right.

"Put Emma's mum onto me."

"I can't. She's out."

"Can you ring Mrs Higgins and go stay with her? I don't want a scene at the Stevens' house."

"Okay, I'll stay with Mrs Higgins. Oh Mum, he'll kill me!"

"No, he won't, darling, but I just want you to be safe and happy. Your friend and her parents don't need to see your dad at his worst. I'll text Mrs Higgins too. I love you."

"I love you too, Mum."

And I wished I was at home with her and sorting out my own little world instead of trying to figure out everything else. But I understood Keith a little better now, and the way he'd tried to control me for so long. Even since we'd divorced, he was still doing it. I also realised that I was gaining confidence with useful knowledge from this trip that would help me in the future.

Chapter 22

Pam and my father sat inside the main door of the centre, completely at ease with each other. It was more than four thousand miles away from my life in Oxford – it was another world. I could do nothing for the moment to help Thalia and I had to try and focus on the here and now – but it would be difficult.

This time was for my father and me. I relished his inquisitiveness and joy as we explored this inviting place. Pam was inclusive and caring towards my father and the way she brought her own father into the conversation on so many occasions during the course of the afternoon confirmed for me how close they were.

"Is everything all right at home?" my father asked.

"It's Thalia and Keith. Just a misunderstanding – they'll be fine."

My father turned to Pam to explain."My granddaughter has a terrible relationship with her father – he never listens to her – he doesn't treat her with respect – spends no time at all with her."

I was uncomfortable that he divulged so much to a stranger. And I hated to hear him speak this way . . . because it was true.

Pam sensed my unease. "It's the way sometimes – not everyone can be fortunate like us, eh?" She looked up at me with her piercing brown eyes. We understood each other.

"When my father passed to the other side, I thought I was going to die too," she said."I couldn't stand to live without him. But he told me to always have faith that he was around and he would give me signs to tell me that he was here."

"And did he?" My father was more than curious.

She nodded her head. "There've been times when I've felt him with me. I know that his spirit is still alive because he's so strong in my memory and while somebody thinks of you then you'll never be dead."

It wasn't enough to convince me that there was life after death, but I wanted to believe Pam. I wanted to believe in the Holy Spirit and the Great Spirit, but something inside stopped me.

"Come and I'll show you the Spirit Forest," she said, rising and beckoning to us.

My father and I followed her along a path with sculpted trees and animals. It didn't have the same atmosphere as our walk through the real woods earlier, but we followed and let her tell us about her people.

We walked with her through displays of native instruments and utensils until we came to the Trail of Tears corridor. It was simply decorated, about thirty feet long with paintings and sculptures of cavalry and Chickasaws trekking through the forest.

Pam paused before entering. "You know, when they were building this, I couldn't walk this way . . . sometimes things would move . . . or there'd be a sense of heaviness like death hanging in the air." She turned and looked at us earnestly. "One evening I had to come back this way and in the shadows at the end of the corridor I saw two spectres of Chickasaw ancestors walking towards me and they were followed by a coldness that passed through me where I stood."

I felt a shiver up my spine as she told her story. My father was silent and held on to my elbow gently as we stood and waited for her to continue.

"My friend came by the next night and saw something similar and she too had the same feeling of coldness pass through her."

"Are you okay to walk this way now?" I asked.

Pam nodded unsurely. We took small slow steps and when we got to the end I could sense relief from her.

"I try not to come in here – I prefer taking folks through the village outside."

We understood – even though we didn't really know what it must have been like for her family in the same way that she did.

But we were coming to the end of our tour. I felt privileged to have met Pam, who'd taken my father and me into her confidence.

"Thanks so much for showing us around, Pam – you've been so kind in sharing so much of your private experiences with us," I said.

"Hey, that's fine . . . but, you know, if you like I can take you to the archives. We don't usually show them to people, but I think they might be of interest to you."

I looked at my father who appeared tired, but he nodded his head vehemently.

"Yes, you see all that you can," he said to me. "Don't worry about me."

"Okay then, thanks, Pam," I said, and we followed her to the low-rise building on the edge of the campus.

"It feels like it could rain again," my father said.

"Yes, sir, I think it might," Pam said, as we stopped at its door. "In here is every book that mentions our tribe and documents accounting for almost every member of our tribe since our records began."

We entered what looked like a massive library and followed her over to meet the curator. He was a tall man who didn't look Native American at all but assured us that he was half Chickasaw.

"My name's Mike," he said and offered us his hand.

"Pam's been showing us around all afternoon and we've been given great insights into the tribe," I said.

I was tired but I felt a niggling in my ear like there was a reason why we were here. It wasn't going to be of any particular use to my article and Dad and I were tired, with a long drive back to Oklahoma City ahead of us. Still, I smiled and followed Mike in through the shelves of books and folders as he showed us pictures of the distinguished members of his tribe.

"And you've documents for every tribe member?" I asked.

"We have for most . . . the yearbooks from the state boarding schools documented most."

"You know, I've tried to find a picture of my father but his name hasn't cropped up in any of the records," Pam said.

"Which college was he in?" Mike asked.

"Chilocco," she replied.

Mike winced. His reaction told me more about this school's reputation than any words.

Pam nodded. "It had a bad reputation but my father said he got on alrigh' there. He was in charge of the goats and he liked being out in the fields all day."

Mike led us through a passageway and a locked door.

"Come this way," he said, and we followed him to a room piled high to the ceiling with files.

"This is where we keep our fragile records – and yearbooks," he said and raised his hand to the shelf with folders labelled *Chilocco*. "What year did he leave?" he asked.

Pam shrugged. "He was born in '32."

"So he probably finished in '48 or thereabouts," Mike said as he fingered through the pages. "What was his name?"

"Benjamin Allen. I've asked about him several times and others have looked up the files but nobody's ever found a picture of him," she said.

We started the search at 1945 to be sure not to miss him. Every candidate was scrutinised and the pages flicked to '46. More years were surveyed: '47, '48, '49 and '50.

Pam nodded in acceptance. "We've looked many times and there's no sign of my father."

Mike led her over to another folder and they searched some more through group photos.

"But I've no photographs of my father when he was a young man so I wouldn't recognise him – there would need to be captions giving names," she said.

Suddenly I felt my inner voice urging me to look back at the discarded folder. Shivers ran up my spine as I turned the page and scanned the portraits of all the young people who had been incarcerated in Chilocco.

"What did you say was your daddy's name, Pam?" I asked.

"Benjamin."

My heart thumped as a strong handsome youth looked out from the page and I knew instantly that it was Pam's father.

"Allen?" I asked.

Pam rushed over. "Yes, Benjamin Allen. What did you find?"

I pointed at his image and Pam cupped her hands up to cover her mouth.

"Is that him?" I asked.

She nodded, her hands still over her mouth. She picked the book up and scrutinised it closely, and as she looked a tear trickled down her cheek. She handed the book to me then and asked to be excused.

Mike turned to me in amazement. "We'll give you a job here if you like."

"Did you really find him?" my father asked, who couldn't make out the small passport photograph-sized image.

"Yes, and he looked like Pam," I replied.

"Ah, God love her," he said. "She must be very upset to see that picture. And she'd never seen it before – to think it was here all that time!"

Mike was the epitome of restraint in his manner but even he was moved by Pam's reaction. "It took a stranger to come and help Pam to find her father. I'm glad that you came here today – that will mean a lot to Pam and her family."

We put the file away and went out to where Pam was wiping her eyes with a paper tissue.

"I'm sorry," she said.

"Please don't apologise – I can imagine how emotional you must be feeling," I said.

"It's just, it's just – I ain't never seen that picture before and I felt him here with me. I've been feeling him around me all day. It's been so nice with you and your paw an' all."

"I think I understand. There's a special bond between father and daughter that isn't like any other," my father said gently.

She nodded in agreement and put her hand on my father's forearm.

"I'm really glad to meet y'all today – it's been kinda special," Pam said.

"For us too," my father replied. "And I feel like we know your father now."

Pam was still shaken. She bit her lip and nodded in agreement.

"Y'all better keep in touch now and tell me when you print that article."

"Of course," I assured her.

We hugged our goodbyes like long-lost friends.

We'd bonded in a special way that was different to what I'd felt for any other person I'd met on our trip.

As my father and I made our way back to the car, I felt elated. I'd forgotten about my traumas back in Oxford. What happened in Oklahoma was meant to be and the timing had been perfect. Maybe it was all part of a greater plan and the incident with Thalia and her father would lead to something better for all of us. I had to believe that because I was feeling helpless and very far away from her.

"Well, wasn't that a lovely experience? She was a marvellous lady," my father said as we sat into the car. Then he sensed my concern. "Is everything okay?"

"Sure – just the usual father-and-daughter trauma back in Oxford."

My father put a hand gently on my thigh.

We smiled at each other and set off on the road again. He didn't need to preach a lesson – we'd learnt a lot together from Pam and the spiritual visit we made to her tribe's special place. And I'd learned about the nature of spirit first-hand. I was convinced that Pam's father had walked with us earlier in the same way as she'd described her ancestors did. This trip had a sense of predestination about it and we were meeting the perfect people on each leg of our journey to discover more about ourselves and those in the world that we shared.

Chapter 23

Oklahoma City

"Who's ready for McDonald's?" Michael asked his nephew and niece.

"*Yay!*" they said together.

Michael had enjoyed the company of seven-year-old Billy and nine-year-old Caitlin more than he'd suspected he would.

The movie they'd watched was *Finding Dory* and he wondered if he could be compared to a fish lost at sea – or perhaps one swimming around and around in a fishbowl, only looking out and observing life but never truly living it himself.

"What will you have?" he asked the children.

Both had tremendous appetites and enthusiastically ordered adult-sized meals.

Michael wondered what sort of a parent he'd have made. He had the patience alright for fun activities and days out, but he wondered how parents coped with bringing up children in today's world where technology had such a hold on young people's minds. When he was growing up, he didn't have the pressure of online popularity contests like so many kids had today. He had always found it easy to get on with friends and with the opposite sex. It was one reason why his mother found it strange when he announced that he was going into the priesthood.

Yet for Michael it was the easiest call to make. He had always yearned to have his spirit filled and his soul connected to the omnipresence of God. As the years passed that omnipotent master and leader had blended with the souls of every person that he had met in the many walks of life that he'd followed. God had merged with the trees that he walked past and the animals that he saw in fields or walking on the road with their masters. God was in his thoughts and manifested in ways that he could never have imagined back in those early days when he took his vows of poverty, chastity and obedience.

Michael didn't believe anyone should have to live in poverty or chastity and the only sort of obedience that mattered was to do right by your fellow man – not just do what society said you should do to fit in. Obedience to Michael was ensuring that you didn't hurt another soul no matter what trauma or mental state they were in.

Billy and Caitlin were almost finished the last of their fries and ready to engage with him again.

"Did you like that?" he asked.

"Sure was good, Uncle Michael," Caitlin said. "We like it when you stay because Momma isn't so sad. There's too much shouting in our house."

"Yeah," Billy said. "I'm going to camp and can't wait to stay with my friends."

"Where's that, Billy?"

"It's down Chickasaw Country. We're going to do biking and sleeping out in a tent."

"Will you be going away too, Caitlin?" Michael asked.

"I'm going to Texas with my friend Fiona and her family – she's got an Irish granny too – like me. Well, maybe it's her great-granny!"

Michael smiled at the two small souls in front of him. If their parents divorced it would make their tiny lives so much more unstable and vulnerable. Poverty and scarcity usually followed for one parent and in his sister's difficult position it would be horribly difficult to survive.

With marriage break-ups becoming so common these days, it seemed as if half the world was in a mixed or blended family. Life was made harder for everyone but especially the children. He may have saved himself such loss by not having his own offspring but there was always a cost. What if he had missed out on the greatest gift of all? Everyone he seemed to speak to who had become a parent had sworn that their children made life worth living – so how could he compare?

Since arriving in Oklahoma he was doubting and questioning his own tidy compartmentalised views of the world. He was wondering how his life might have turned out having someone to share it with – a soulmate. Then Roz appeared in his mind's eye.

Chapter 24

As we reached Davis I started to think of food.

"Are you hungry, Daddy?"

"Do you know, I wouldn't mind a bite to eat," he said. "All that excitement with Pam has me peckish."

We still had a two-hour drive ahead of us. It would be best to have some food before beginning our journey. My itinerary suggested that we eat at Smoking Joe's Rib Ranch BBQ and I thought it was worth trying. My father was an easy companion to satisfy and always ate whatever was put in front of him. He put it down to the fact that he was the youngest and had no say in what he would like to eat.

The parking lot was full of trucks and jeeps and there were even a few motorcycles.

This restaurant had a busy trade as the queue was long and every table full.

"What's that smell?" my father asked.

"Lots of meat, I think. Maybe this isn't a great idea – the menu seems to be quantity rather than quality and there's no veg or salad on it. What would you like?"

"I'll be happy with chicken and chips," he said.

A T-shirt hung on the wall saying, *'I Like Pig Butts'*. It was printed on a billboard in the window also, alongside a cartoon of a pig with knife and fork in hand and the caption *'Get Your Grub On'*.

I wasn't a fussy eater but I did like variety in my diet.

I scanned the menu and half a chicken was an option – no smaller size on offer. I felt less like eating the further I got to the top of the queue as enormous chunks of meat piled high on top of each other were passed out on trays. The sight of so much food was repulsive.

Finally it was my turn.

"Can I have a chicken dinner and chips and a small portion of BBQ ribs."

The waitress looked at me as if I'd ordered for a small child.

Her mouth gawped open. "That all? No coleslaw or nothin'?"

What was it with coleslaw? There were other salad options and right then I'd have given anything for a tomato or a few peppers chopped up.

"Do you have Caesar Salad?" I asked hopefully.

"Yep, we go' Caesar dressing."

"No, that's okay, thanks, and can I have water, please?"

The cups came in three sizes, huge, enormous or bucket-size and you could fill your cup with fizzy soft drinks or root beer as many times as you liked. I wondered how many animals were slaughtered to produce the enormous quantities of meat, as I looked at the piles of food coming from the hatch behind the counter.

Finally a tray arrived with the ribs, a huge half-chicken, a mountain of chips and a pot of sandy-grey beans on the side. I lifted it, and with my father following closely behind we went and took a table at the window.

"If you'll sit here, I'll go get our drinks."

When I got back to the table my father was squinting down at the tray. He put a finger out to touch the chicken.

"That's a flippin' ostrich not a chicken!" he declared.

"You should see the ribs – they're as black as coal – I'm not sure we can eat any of this."

"We'll have a few chips at least."

"You should see the size of the plates these people are bringing down to the tables – there's half a beast on every tray."

I was mentally bloated as I picked at the carcass with my fork.

"I remember the pig kills when we were young – my mother would make great use out of it – feed the whole family for weeks. I couldn't imagine a pig lasting long around here."

I was reminded of a movie I'd seen which showed the mass production of animals for consumption and the way they were kept in cages and fattened up to be slaughtered, having had no quality of life. *Samsara* it was called, and someone had posted it on Facebook. It was Thalia who drew my attention to it when she was trying to convince me to let her be a vegetarian. I was put completely off the ribs and I picked at a couple of chips instead.

"I feel guilty that some poor pig had to die and now it's not even edible. What have we become?"

"It's difficult to stomach alright," my father said as he tried to remove the chicken thigh from the bird.

"Thalia hasn't eaten meat for some time," I mused. "Looking around me here, I think she has a point."

"We eat too much. It's not right the way food's produced

nowadays. You know, when I was a kid we only ate tomatoes when my mother grew them. And they had a taste and flavour completely different to the way they are nowadays." He huffed. "That's why I insisted on supplying organic fruit and vegetable at my market. It's probably all those chemicals and pesticides that's giving everyone cancer."

"I wrote about this in the paper actually when I was covering a feature about organic farmers in Oxford."

"Did you?" My father sat up. "Good girl. If the food chain wasn't in the terrible state that it's in, there wouldn't be so many sick people."

"I've been thinking that too – and, if the fruit and veg chain is this corrupted, can you imagine what the animal food chain is like?"

"Absolutely – a fella was telling me that the big department stores freeze fruit and veg with nitrogen and stockpile it in containers for up to four years and only then is it released when the supermarket needs it. Can you imagine? There must be no good at all in it by the time it's cut up and put on the table."

My father kept an interest in everything, despite the fact that he hadn't worked in the market for so long.

"This is an issue that has been written about quite a lot," I said.

"But is anyone doing anything about it? Instead of growing onions and sending them off to Spain we should be eating them ourselves, but we are buying-in Spanish onions while ours go out. The whole world has gone mad. I don't know where it will all end."

I turned my ribs over and decided that if I put the meat up to my lips I'd be sick. It was the wrong time for the conversation – or maybe it was the right time. We are all flesh and blood.

"Remember to try and fill yourself with live food – and if you do eat make sure that it's not well done. Plenty of live food to fill the soul," my father said. "It sounds like my grand-daughter is enlightened in her tastes. I hope that you don't think I'm crazy when I talk to you about the energy in all things."

"Of course I don't. I believe you." I really did.

"Well, there is none more important than the energy we get from live food. I eat simply when I'm alone and I've got used to it," he said with a smile. "You know it's like when we were in that lovely forest after Mass and we felt at one with nature – or yesterday when we were up at the lookout point. There is so much to be grateful for in life."

Although he didn't say it, this was one of his lessons, I knew that it was. I needed to support my daughter in minding her health and I'd have to start by doing it myself. I wasn't sure when or if I'd eat meat again.

"Are you ready to hit the road and go back to Oklahoma City?" I asked and smiled to myself as I realised I was begin-ning to speak like my father.

He nodded.

We drove to the strains of Neil Young's 'Alabama' and the mood fitted ours as the car took a straight route along Highway 35.

I wondered would Mr Young have sung a different song if the Chickasaws had been allowed to stay in their home state of Alabama. Had I been filled with the Holy Spirit or a force of nature? I wasn't sure. But I did feel different after the day's events. Pam was someone that I was meant to meet my entire life and she'd been waiting to meet me. This trip with my father brought a circular conclusion to the journey Pam had taken with hers. I felt sure that we'd remain friends or stay in touch at the very least.

It was the end of the day when we arrived in Bricktown, Oklahoma City, underneath the gaze of the Chickasaw stadium and the Devon Tower.

My father and I checked into our hotel.

We took the lift up to our rooms.

"Meet in the bar for a nightcap?" I asked.

"Sure – but I'm going to have a shower first."

"Me too."

But when I slipped into the bathroom, I decided to run a bath instead. As Michael came to my mind, I wanted to be alone with my thoughts and savour each and every one – it had been long day.

Michael was eating dinner with his sister when Roz came into his head again. He wanted to see her and was becoming impatient. All he needed was an excuse to call her up and see if she was free. He wasn't looking forward to sitting in all night in front of the TV with Claudia – and Ben who could barely stand him. Then a thought occurred to him that he and Claudia could go out for a drink and it might be a good antidote to the evening if he invited Roz and her father along. He went into the kitchen where his sister was getting the children ready for their trips away next day.

"Do you think we could go out for a drink in the city – I won't be here much longer?"

"I'm not sure Ben will want to mind the kids."

"They're his kids, Claudia – you don't mind your own kids."

Claudia bit her lip. "Give me a minute," she said and went into the TV room where Ben was sitting. They exchanged a few words and she came back looking a little lighter.

"Okay then. That'll be nice."

Michael had a dilemma. His plan was backfiring because he wanted to see Roz but he didn't have her number. He went onto his phone and searched for her on Facebook. Roz Waters: there were only two. Her picture was pretty. She reminded him of someone from his past. Maybe it was a past life, he thought. He was letting himself be carried away but deep down he believed that we continued to meet our loved ones on our journey in different ways. Reincarnation made sense on many levels and explained why we did certain things as a species over and over. It was part of the reason why he had gone over to her when he saw her at the airport on that first day.

He was potentially playing with fire but with such strong feelings he had to see her. His gut never sent him in the wrong direction, and he'd met enough soulmates in various guises to know when he'd found another.

Roz was like a wounded bird that only needed a little care to heal her wings and take flight.

He wanted to be the one to release her from her shackles or the weight that she carried around on her pretty shoulders. He was mindful too that she was like his sister in many ways. Perhaps if they all met, there could be some sort of epiphany. Both women had been drained and dragged down to a lower level by men who didn't treat them right.

He had to be clear in his head that his need to connect with her wasn't only for his own selfish reason: the desire to be loved on an intimate level which he hadn't experienced for some time. But he knew that his reasons were selfish. He wanted to be with her intimately.

Meeting Roz was his destiny and he had to carry out the part that he'd agreed to play in it before they'd ever met. He firmly believed that there were pivotal people on life's journey that everyone has to connect with for whatever reason. Either to be a blessing or to teach a lesson; and he wondered which Roz was.

He typed a message on her Facebook page and prayed she'd see it. He'd made the next move.

~

I tapped on my father's bedroom door.

"Are you ready, Daddy?"

"I'll be out in two minutes," he said.

I took the time to check my phone for messages and got quite a thrill when I saw one from Michael on Messenger. He would be in Oklahoma City at eight o'clock with his sister and wanted to know where I was staying. I replied immediately and told him that Dad and I would be in the main bar at the Hampton Suites in Bricktown.

My father came out of his room.

"I'm ready now," he said.

"I've just had a message from Michael – he's going to meet us in the bar."

Dad perked up and smiled. "That's great news, always a pleasure to see that good man."

Butterflies started to flit around my stomach and I suddenly didn't feel like I looked good enough to see Michael.

"I'm just going back to my room to get something," I said.

My father waited patiently outside the room while I ran into the bathroom. I put some liner along the rim of my eyelid and put some blush on my cheeks, I touched up my mascara and frowned at the lines running along my forehead. There was nothing more could be done. I was the age that I was and anyway I knew from Michael that for him beauty wasn't skin-deep. It was nice to make an effort, however, to want to look good for someone else. I stared at my reflection and delusional thoughts were filling my head. Michael was a priest – he was celibate – he was unattainable. But it didn't stop me from wanting him.

~

"I'll drive," Michael said.

Claudia threw the keys of the jeep at him and they took Interstate 35 into Bricktown.

"I've been taking on board what you've been saying, Michael."

Michael felt bad for criticising Claudia and her life – he really had no clue what it was like for her living in this country and where she was going.

"I'm sorry if I haven't helped. I really did come over to do whatever I could to help."

Claudia nodded. "You can't help me, nobody can. I'm the only person that can help me." She turned and put her hand on her brother's arm. "I'm sorry for all the things that I said the other night. I know you only have my best interests at heart."

Michael smiled. "I do. I really do want you to be happy and I'm worried for America because it isn't the country that I came over to at the end of the last century."

"Nowhere is," Claudia said. "Every country is in a constant state of change and none of us realise it while we are living in it."

Michael agreed. He knew better than anybody the impact of war and destruction on the places where he had been on tour – in the Middle East especially.

"Have you a plan for what you're going to do?"

"No," Claudia replied. "But I intend to make a plan and that's a start. You know, Michael, America is a very different country to live in from the one that you come to visit. Every-body thinks that they know America when they go shopping for a weekend in New York or if they spend two weeks in Disney World in Florida."

"I can understand that."

"Can you, Michael, really? I told you already this isn't the Land of the Free and the Home of the Brave . . . we are all slaves to the dollar and the banks and that's not enough for me anymore. I will make a change and I will fix my life."

That was good enough for Michael. "I'm here for you, that's all I can say."

"And that's enough," Claudia said.

They drove in silence along Interstate 35 for the next ten minutes until they arrived at Bricktown.

"Which hotel is your friend staying in?" Claudia asked.

"The Hampton Suites."

"I don't think they have a bar. But don't worry, there's plenty of places beside it. Park at the drop-off and we can ask them where they'd like to go."

∾

My father took the crook of my arm as we went to find the lift. The lobby was huge and open-plan and the sitting area didn't have a bar. So we sat down near the front door and in a matter of seconds Michael walked through the front door. I was trembling inside and berating myself too.

I stood as he walked straight over to us and this time he openly gave me a hug.

My father put out his hand and shook Michael's hand heartily.

"Great to see you guys! Do you want to go across the road for a drink?" Michael said. "I brought my sister along and she says there are plenty of bars."

"Sure, she knows the town best," I said.

"Come on – the car's outside – we can drive over and park outside."

"I love the way you can park your car in the middle of the city over here," my dad said.

Sitting in the passenger seat was a woman with auburn hair.

"Hi there! I'm Claudia. Pleased to meet you."

She resembled Michael slightly in her expression and had the same teeth and smile.

I shook her hand. "Pleased to meet you." I was nervous meeting Michael's sister. I wanted her to like me. I felt very dowdy next to her – she had lived in America for some time and seemed to have gained a confidence from living here.

We climbed into the back as Michael got into the driver's seat.

"Welcome to Oklahoma City, Patrick," said Claudia as we drove off. "Although Michael tells me that you're on your way home, is that right?"

"Yes," he replied. "We've had a remarkable time."

"There's so much of America to explore – I feel like we've barely seen the tip of the iceberg," I added.

"There sure is," Claudia agreed. "Most Americans don't leave the USA ever – and why would they when they have the most incredible natural landscapes here? We used to go skiing in Colorado before we had kids. Then not too far away you have the Gulf Coast which is warm year round."

"You're right, Claudia. I'd been to a few coastal states before but coming to Oklahoma is a good place to find the real heartland," I said.

"There's good and bad wherever you go. But things are getting really tough for people here and there's a whole way of life dying out," Claudia said. "I've seen a drip-drain of small businesses and rural communities for some time. It won't be long before we're all swept up and moved to big cities."

This was quite heavy conversation for our first meeting but, if Claudia was anything like her brother, I imagined she had a deep insight into life and people.

"Indeed," I replied. "Michael said you're a teacher, Claudia?"

"Yes – science. And you've got probably the best job in the world."

I giggled. It was something many people had said to me. "I only do travel-writing now and again. This was an unusual gig and I felt it was one I just couldn't turn down."

"I'm glad you didn't turn it down," Michael said, looking in the rearview mirror at me and making me blush.

We only drove a few more feet before Michael parked up outside a bar and we all got out.

"Well, that must be the shortest drive I've ever taken," said Dad.

Michael helped my father out of the Jeep and we went

into a bar with live music playing in the corner. It was quiet and perfect for our small gathering.

Michael ordered our drinks and I sensed that he was desperate to make his sister feel comfortable but that he wanted to talk to me. The flirtatious glances felt so alien to me at first but I gradually learned to respond until we were communicating with our own silent language.

Dad started his interrogation of Claudia but she didn't seem to mind.

"How many children do you have, Claudia?" he asked.

"Just the two, Billy and Caitlin – they are quite the handful but great kids."

"Rosaleen has just her brother too. I think two kids is enough in this day and age. You know, there are too many kids in this world left to fend for themselves, with parents deserting them."

Claudia nodded. "I agree, Patrick. The world has enough mouths to feed. If every couple only had two children then we would see a stalling of the population immediately – a reduction even."

A waiter came down with a large pitcher of beer and four glasses.

Michael glanced at me as he poured into one of the glasses.

"I know it's different in third-world countries," Dad continued, "but there must be some sort of plan to make the quality of life better for everyone. I've been trying to figure it out."

Claudia laughed. "That would be quite the achievement, Patrick – it hasn't been done yet."

Michael interrupted. "Well, if it's any use to the planet, I haven't reproduced so that surely is a contribution?"

"And I've only had one child," I said. "Mind you, I wouldn't put it past my ex to have another. His new partner is a good deal younger than I am."

"Well, there is plenty of food and resources to go around the planet if there wasn't so much greed or control of the masses," my father said.

"I think you could be right there, Patrick," Michael agreed. "If there was a fairer distribution of wealth to go around then we could see the world's population sort itself out."

"We are getting very serious for our last night in Oklahoma aren't we?" I said. "Tell us more about life here, Claudia."

"You've probably seen most of what there is to see in Oklahoma," said Claudia. "We are simple folk here and still very much connected to the land."

"I like that," my father said. "I've been reminded of Monaghan on many occasions during our road trip. I've said that, haven't I, Rosaleen?"

"Yes, Dad, you have indeed."

Michael was remaining quiet but looking at my expressions and reactions and I felt a little thrilled each time I saw him look at me.

"Connection to the land is good," he said then. "I think we've lost a lot of that connection in Ireland."

"We have indeed, Father," Dad said.

It made me feel more than a little uncomfortable to hear my father call him that and I couldn't help but wonder whether he had done so deliberately. After all, he had never addressed him as "Father" before. Had he noticed that I was attracted to Michael? Was he sending me a warning signal? I had largely blocked the fact that Michael was a man of the cloth from my mind. To me he was a man who made me feel good about myself, whether I was just thinking about him or just sitting by his side and I was eased when I looked into his eyes.

"Is anyone hungry?" Michael asked. "I'll get a couple of menus if you like?"

"Good man, I'm feeling peckish alright," my father said.

Michael got up and walked up to the bar and I followed him with the excuse that I was going to the restrooms.

We were finally alone and I was in a daze.

"How has the trip been?" he asked.

"Incredible. Amazing. I can think of lots more superlatives."

"I've been thinking of you two driving on this great adventure and I have to say how much I admire what you're doing. How many people take time out of their lives to do something like this with a parent – or a child?"

I nodded. "I had no idea before we set off what a life-changing and transforming process this road trip would turn out to be. And I don't want to sound corny but meeting you has been a highlight."

Michael turned red and smiled widely with a shake of his head.

"I've been given food for thought too on this trip. It's painful to see Claudia unhappy in her relationship and I hope she'll get the courage to do what's best for herself and her family."

"A marriage break-up is the hardest option– losing that comfort and security that goes with the family unit. But I think that it is a blessing that I've been given a second chance to find myself and who knows maybe even to find love in the future?"

We both paused and looked at each other intently.

I spoke first. "You'd better get those menus before the others think we've dumped them."

I swiftly turned on my heel and headed for the restrooms. I was feeling flushed and excited because I hadn't lied. I had spoken the truth. My life was better for being bold and taking life by the scruff of the neck and just living.

When I returned to the table my father was ordering some chicken wings and Claudia said that she would have some fries.

Michael ordered a burger.

I wasn't hungry.

I listened to the ping-pong conversation between my father, Claudia and Michael and felt so comfortable. I couldn't remember the last time that I'd been so happy sitting with a group of people. I was truly being myself.

Eventually my father's energy faded and he called for his bedtime.

"It's been a lovely evening," Claudia said. "It's so different being with just Irish people. You know, I'm going to take you up on your offer to go home and see Mam and Dad, Michael."

Michael's eyes lit up. "Wonderful!'

We all stood up and Claudia gave my dad a warm hug. Then she did the same with me.

"Let me walk these folk across the road," Michael said to her.

"I'll go to the restroom and see you at the car," Claudia said.

Then my father and Michael set off together and I walked a couple of steps behind, looking at their frames and noticing the similarities in the way they moved, albeit one years older than the other.

When we reached the lobby, my father turned to Michael.

"It's been a great evening. Thank you for your company, and it was a pleasure to meet your lovely sister."

I was about to say goodbye to Michael when I realised that I'd left my jacket on the back of my chair in the bar.

"Oh, Dad, I have to go back to the bar. I left my jacket behind. Michael, could you take him upstairs?"

"No, no," said my father, "No need for that. You go with her, Michael. I'm grand here now that I'm in the hotel – I can find the lift no bother."

My father shooed us away, so we left him to it.

We both walked more slowly this time and stopped outside the entrance to the bar, beside Claudia's car. It was like we didn't need words. We both instinctively knew what we had to do. It was as if we were moving in another dimension and floating together like two magnets connecting without resistance. It was perfect. Under the bright lights of Bricktown, he touched the side of my face with the palm of his hand and leaned forward. We fused into a lingering kiss. His lips were the softest and sweetest I had ever tasted.

"Don't judge me," he said.

"What do you mean?"

"I am who I am, a human being. No more and no less."

"How could you say that?"

"Because you see me as a priest. Don't lie, I can tell."

"I see you as a man first. You can't read my mind."

"I felt it in your kiss."

Was he correct, I wondered? Did our kiss taste sweeter because it was forbidden?

I'm not sure how long we were in this gentle embrace, but we didn't hear Claudia until she coughed loudly.

We abruptly stepped away from each other and saw her standing there with my jacket in her hand.

Chapter 25

I tossed and turned as the first rays of sunlight slipped through my window, announcing the new day. I'd had one of the most restless nights ever. My head was exploding with the memory of the kiss Michael had left on my lips. I was sixteen again and really needed to pull myself together. Michael had made me think – was our kiss sweeter because it was forbidden? I hoped my dad hadn't noticed our attraction and little innuendos. I wondered what Claudia had said to him later. She seemed to be amused at us and I hoped she didn't think badly of what I had done with her brother. I didn't know her well enough to read her reaction.

But, for all the excitement and positive energy I was getting from Michael, something was troubling me – I was concerned about Thalia. I checked my watch and decided to ring and see if Keith had carried through on his threats.

"Hi, Mum."

"Thalia, are you okay? Did Dad call by?"

"No, he rang me and said I wasn't to go to anymore parties – he was fine really. In fact, he was in a good mood."

I was puzzled. Why all the drama the night before? Was he trying to play mind games with me because I was so far from home? It certainly seemed that way.

"So he didn't say anything about staying with Emma?"

"He just asked if I'd enough money and if I was okay here until you got back."

A part of me was hugely relieved. Another part was absolutely furious at the way Keith had threatened me and been so awful the night before. He'd probably just wanted to disrupt my trip and time with my father.

"I'm glad that's sorted out," I said. "I don't know what I'm going to do with your father."

"Stop letting him play with your head, Mum! He knows exactly what buttons to press to get you going. He's been doing it to you for years – I could see it even when I was a little kid. He's moved on and it's time that you did. Don't let him spoil this time you have with Granddad. Men can be such bastards!"

I was shocked by her outburst and use of language. She had been burdened by the irresponsible behaviour of the adults around her for most of her life. But she was reacting more forcefully than usual, talking about her father.

"I'm having a lovely time with Granddad," I said. "Keep safe and happy until I return."

"I will." She paused. "Got to go now, Mum – Emma's mum is taking us shopping."

"Okay, I'll call you later."

"There's no need. I'll be seeing you in two days, won't I?"

"Yes, darling, I'll see you then."

But she had hung up before I finished.

My mother's intuition wasn't convinced. What if everything wasn't okay with Emma? I suddenly felt very far away from Tally. I wished I could be with her because she was speaking with a different voice. She had been so right about my relationship with her father and I hadn't set a good example for her by staying in such a toxic relationship for longer than I should. I had been a complete lightweight mother – a wimp. I felt emotions inside that had been waiting for years to escape and with them came a torrent of tears. I almost choked on them as they poured down my cheeks. I was sick of being toyed with like a child. Keith had tormented me for the last time. I wouldn't allow him to control me with his intimidation anymore.

I'd learnt from Martina and my father how to use my energy wisely. And last night I'd experienced an awakening of truly magical proportions when Michael and I had kissed. It wasn't ideal, it wasn't proper but it felt so right. Michael had really opened my eyes to the new way that I had to live. But something jarred inside. Why did the man I had finally found and connected with have to be completely unattainable?

The universe had a funny way of working. Or maybe it was God. But why would God send me someone that I couldn't actually have for myself? Meeting Michael was like finding a missing piece in the jigsaw puzzle of my life. It was like waking up for the first time.

Nobody understood my inner turmoil except me. Perhaps my father did, and I hadn't realised it. These past days had been like an awakening of all the wisdom he passed on to me as a little girl and now as a woman I was finally ready to listen. But just as happiness was within my reach, it was already slipping through my fingers because Michael was already taken and, although it had been wonderful finding him, he wasn't available and realistically could never be mine.

~

My father knocked gently on the door. I wiped the tears from my eyes and hoped that he wouldn't realise that I'd been crying.

"Morning," I said, making sure to appear upbeat. I sat down on the bed.

"I couldn't sleep at all last night," he said. "I was wriggling around the bed until three."

"I had a restless night myself."

He sat down on the bed beside me. "You know, I've been thinking about these last few days and they've been marvellous – truly magic. Thank you for bringing me here."

His eyes were wide with brightness and joy, so bright I could almost see into his soul.

"It's been special," I said. "I've had a chance to get to know you again."

"For me it's wonderful to be alive, to be able to do this." Then he paused. "But I've a confession to make."

"What have you done now?" I poked him in the ribs playfully.

"I never sat you down to discuss your mission," he said and shook his head as if he had failed in some examination.

"My what?"

"When I was a lad my mother took me aside and asked me what I was put on this earth to do with myself and how I was going to serve others. I let you go through college and, before I knew it, you were gone from me to England."

I put my hand on his shoulder. "You always did your best for me. What's this talk about missions? Getting through life is one big mission from what I can see."

My father nodded. "Exactly, and I understand that now

after spending these past few days with you on our own. But it shouldn't be that way. Life is an adventure to be enjoyed and explored and relished. I can't help feeling that you're walking around as if you're in a daze."

"What do you mean?"He was unnerving. It was as if he'd read my mind through the hotel-room wall the night before.

"You're asleep, Rosaleen. Don't take offence – I was asleep for years. I had to lose my sight to really see the world around me. I sometimes think that's why I lost it. I didn't *see* . . . get it? I wasn't living because I didn't *see* what was going on in the world."

"I'm perfectly fine," I said defensively. "My life in Oxford is fine."

"You know, Rosaleen, for someone with their sight, you have difficulty seeing sometimes."

I took a deep breath. I couldn't answer that. I didn't have the words. Was I happy? I wasn't even sure what happiness was anymore. I survived.

"I'm doing my best to rectify that, truly I am," I said.

I didn't have many people in my life that really mattered to me. I'd many acquaintances in work and at home in Oxford but very little in my life was important to me.

"As someone who lived with an alcoholic for so many years, I know what 'fine' is and you are not the wonderfully capable woman that you were born to be at this moment in time. But you can be. Don't take as long to see as I did."

I was speechless. I didn't have a mission. I wasn't meant to be anything – I wasn't anyone special. And then I remembered my conversation with Thalia, and I burst into tears. Unguarded this time, my head fell onto my father's shoulder and he wrapped his arms around me.

"There, there, go on. I've been waiting for you to tell me

the truth since we got here. It's okay to be unhappy – it means that you are alive, connecting to yourself. Christ, if I had a dollar for every time I cried over the years we'd be very rich!"

I sniffled into his sleeve but was too caught up in myself and my feelings to answer. I was tired of living a lie. I needed to fill my soul. Traipsing through Chickasaw country had helped me to realise it. Going to church had made me realise the spiritual void inside. Meeting Michael had made me see that there were people that I could love. There had to be more to my life than the way I was living it.

"Come on now and dry your eyes," my father said as he gently stroked my hair away from my clammy cheek.

"Thanks, Dad."

"And let's get on with enjoying our last day together – what?"

I nodded and pulled away from his grasp.

"So," he said jovially. "Where are you taking me today?"

"I think we're going to a stockyard and cattle auction."

"Well, be the hokey!" he said with a smile. "That sounds fantastic."

It was fitting that the last part of our adventure was set on cowboy terrain once again as it had been at the start of our journey. We were more comfortable together as father and daughter after traipsing through such varied experiences. The familiarity of knowing each other better meant that we were in a new zone.

We pulled up to Stockyards City at a crossroads marked by a large bronze effigy of a cowboy on his horse – lassoing a Longhorn steer. From a distance the aroma of heat, sweat and animals wafted down the long wide thoroughfare and I felt as if we had stepped back in time. The Cattleman's Cafe was built more than a century ago and within this simple box-shaped structure lay thousands of stories told of the lives of farmers and cowmen. The simple booths of pressed burgundy leather, with menu cards and condiments stacked neatly on the metal-trimmed tabletops, transported me to a different time.

My father's curiosity led him over to a glass cabinet.

"What's inside this?" he said, tapping his stick against the glass.

I described the vintage memorabilia display which included cowboy belt-buckles, menus from the fifties, steak knives and mugs – and the photographs in mahogany frames that lined the walls, documenting the slow transition of time in this complete cowman's world.

We passed a couple of booths, each occupied by a single man and every one of them smiled warmly at us. I needed to find Seth from the Visitors Convention Bureau, who would take us around the cattle market. Then a fine-featured man jumped to his feet on seeing us and held out his hand.

"You must be Roz," he said.

He was tall and lean with thin-rimmed spectacles and didn't look like a cowboy or Oklahoman – apart from his cowboy boots. I'd noticed since arriving in Oklahoma that everyone wore cowboy boots, from shop assistants to office workers.

"Yes," I said, "and this is my father Patrick."

"Good to meet you, Patrick – I hope you guys are having a good time."

"It's been marvellous," my father said. "We stayed on a ranch and went down to Chickasaw Country."

"Yes, I got a copy of your itinerary. Will you have some breakfast?"

He ushered us into the booth where he was sitting and a busy waitress wearing a wine-coloured apron came over to take our order.

"What'll y'all have fur breakfast?"

Seth ordered pancakes, eggs with sunny-side up and some bacon with coffee. This was an authentic experience of a way of life that had existed for so many years and a welcome release from my thoughts of Oxford and concern for Thalia.

Our food arrived so we ate and talked of this strange place that didn't need to be quantified by time.

"Cattlemen've been comin' here for over a century and they're jus' the same as they've always been," Seth said as he supped his coffee.

"I can feel it in the atmosphere – I wish I could see it all," my father said, picking up and squinting at the glass sugar jar.

The waitress returned with three large plates covered with more food than we could possibly eat.

"Folks come here and talk before decidin' on business in the market," Seth said. "We're lucky today because it's rained – the smell's mighty strong otherwise."

I didn't want to say that it was strong regardless.

"Reminds me of my hometown," my father said. "We kept cattle when I was a lad, and you'd smell the manure for miles down the track before you got to the cowhouse. I used to go to the market sometimes if my brothers would let me and I loved the excitement."

"I'll be interested to see what you think of our stockyard – it's one of the biggest in the country and y'all gonna see plenty of cattle." Then he paused, aware of what he'd said and looked down at my father's white stick. He didn't know how to back-track.

I put him at ease. "It's okay – my father is going to see it in his way – he'll be noticing things that you haven't by the time we're finished."

My father chuckled. "She makes me sound like a clairvoy-ant, which I most certainly am not, but I've found that since I've lost my vision I can tell you things that you might miss because you're only using your eyes as your main sense."

Seth followed close to my father as we left the Cattlemen's Cafe. Dad had found a kindred spirit yet again.

I, on the other hand, felt like an intruder in this old estab-lished world. It was remarkable to find a slice of rural life in a big city only a ten-minute drive from downtown. I wasn't sure how I would feel about seeing all the living merchandise penned-in, waiting for delivery to their new owners. I didn't have long to wait because Seth led us to his pickup and drove us the few hundred metres down Exchange Avenue through the entrance pillars to Oklahoma National Stockyards and the cattle market.

The fumes became stronger as the heat of day rose by a few degrees and I was glad that we hadn't come at the height of summer.

Seth directed us towards a walkway in the sky that crossed over hundreds of pens packed with livestock, monitored by patrolling guards on horseback and security guards constantly counting. It was a world I had never considered existed.

But it was very real. These were probably similar to the beasts that would end up in the BBQ house we'd been to. Their captors urged them on with long swatting sticks that slapped off the beasts' backs and rumps. The men laughed and joked and waved to each other as if this was a good day and I understood how unbearable this place must be to operate on a hot or wet day. The animals pulled their hooves laboriously through the thick, muddy faeces that covered the brick-layered ground.

"How long will they have to stay in the pens?" I asked.

"They don't usually stay longer than twenty-four hours before gettin' taken to their new home by train or trailer," Seth said.

"This brings me back – I can remember the smell so well," my father said with a shake of his head. "I only wish I could see down to the livestock."

I didn't like the use of words like that – they were animals, cattle. Living creatures being bought to fatten up or slaughter and sold in a restaurant or supermarket and I needed no more convincing that it was time I turned vegetarian. I'd never really thought about what I was eating when I'd ordered steak in a restaurant or made a Stroganoff for dinner in my home. I was oblivious to the world outside my own and wrapped up in the concerns that I dealt with in my small circle. I felt now that my eyes were closed. It was as my father had said earlier. I didn't take much notice of the world around me and I certainly hadn't looked inside myself for many years. It was time that I assessed who I was and what I wanted to do with my life because I couldn't go back to the way things were in Oxford. I needed to offer my daughter a different option, a newer and better way to live, even though I didn't know yet what that would be.

The market was set out like an arena, with the auctioneer sitting behind a stall underneath the words *Oklahoma National*

Stockyards – Serving our producers for over 100 Years. He wore a summer Stetson made of grass fibres which was a dirty creamy shade, discoloured by the dust and dankness rising from the cattle's steaming hides. Two men guided each lot of cattle into the stalls with swatting sticks and attitude, their checked shirts cut off at the shoulders and tattoos peeping out from underneath.

Numbers poured from the auctioneer's lips in an unintelligible wave of mumbles. But the board on the wall flashed with digits changing rapidly to indicate the price per pound of the cattle. Sitting on the faux-leather seats in curved rows facing the auctioneer, the bidders raised their arms and nodded to make their bids.

"That's some speed he's talkin' there," my father said to Seth.

"I find it difficult to understand him myself," Seth said. He sat back in his seat and watched my father's expression with a curious amusement. "How does it rate compared with your cattle markets in Ireland, Patrick?"

"They're very similar – we didn't have phones on our seats like you have here, mind you." My father grappled with the handset in the arm of his seat.

"Oh, they're never used, not now that everyone has a cell phone," Seth said. "But there was a time when this was a state-of-the-art venue."

It was a rough and crude place now but also a historical site. I dreamed of a future where livestock wouldn't be sold in this cruel and mercenary way. I hadn't touched the bacon at the Cattleman's Cafe and wouldn't miss eating meat in the future. It was another part of my life that I was done with. There was strong change coming down the track – stronger even than the stench coming from the crowded pens outside.

"We'll have to get your father a Stetson," Seth whispered in my ear.

"I heard that," Daddy said, and we all laughed.

I was happy to leave the animals and men who plied their wares through the narrow lanes of the stockyard. Seth brought us to Langston's Store, a supplier of cowboy clothing and essentials which included knives, boots and anything else that a cowboy might need in the course of his day.

I watched my father run his hands along all the different hats and consider the different textures and shapes.

"I think I like this one," he said, holding up a summer hat, not unlike the one Joel wore at the Black's ranch. I thought it a nice coincidence, considering he hadn't had a good look at Joel's Stetson.

"That there's a summer hat," Seth explained. "Now all you need's a shirt to go with that."

I searched through the rails until we came upon a rust and navy shirt with pearl-studded buttons. It leapt off the hanger and I led my father to the changing room to try it on.

"You're gonna have to get that, Patrick," Seth said. "Or should I say Clint?"

"Here, give it to me," I said and took the label over to the counter. I hoped that he'd wear the shirt when he returned to Dublin. It would be a good reminder of our time together.

"Are you going to get some boots?" Seth asked me.

"They look great on people in Oklahoma but honestly I don't think they'd go down well in Dublin or Oxford where I live."

"I'd love a pair," my father said.

I laughed aloud until I realised that he wasn't joking.

The range was huge with every colour imaginable. He decided on a rusty-brown pair with embroidered triskeles and leaf designs that he felt under his fingertips.

The shop assistant measured his feet and returned with a pair that cost $350. I thought he'd go off the idea once he heard the price but there was no deterring him from his purchase. He stood tall in his new boots and paraded them up and down the store with a pride and confidence that made me smile. They suited him. The entire outfit was coming together and when the assistant told him that he looked like Clint Eastwood the deal was sealed and we left the store with almost his entire body covered with the new clothes.

"Maybe we can get you a saddle now," Seth said with his tongue in cheek. "So where are you going after here?"

"To the cowboy museum," my father said.

"That's a great spot – you know John Wayne opened that in the sixties?"

I'd read that on my itinerary but let Seth tell us more. He knew so much about Oklahoma that he reminded me of our journey with Pam in Chickasaw. Such lovely people were filling our path and I was content to go along with whatever was on offer.

"Are you going to a baseball game?" Seth asked. "The Red Hawks are playing tonight."

"That's serendipitous," I said. "Would you like that, Dad?"

"It'd be a bit of craic all right," my father agreed.

Seth took out his cell phone and started tapping letters into it. "I can organise them for y'all."

"Really, that would be great, thank you."

"Hey, that's not a problem. It's good that you're in town on a game night – it's right beside your hotel."

My father beamed at the prospect. "That's great news — thanks so much, son," he said and he patted Seth on the back.

"Thank you, Seth," I said. "We've had a terrific morning."

Each place we visited had been cherry-picked as the ideal location to explore a different side of Oklahoma and what I found strikingly unusual was the fact that life was the same wherever we travelled on this journey. Cowboy, farmer or cowgirl, it didn't matter — what mattered was living life to the fullest and learning and helping people along the way.

Chapter 26

We said goodbye to Seth. He recommended that we take a trip to Ann's Chicken Fry House on Route 66. It was *en route* to the cowboy museum, he said, with vintage automobiles from the fifties in the parking lot.

"Isn't Seth a grand lad!" my father said.

The road took us up Meridian on our way to the Will Rogers Highway aka Route 66. With his Stetson planted on his head, my father grinned like the Cheshire Cat.

"It was nice of him to offer the baseball tickets," I said.

"I think we've been very lucky the way everything has worked out on this trip – but I have to let you into a little secret before we go home. It's something I wish I'd found years ago. In some ways I'd an idea of it subconsciously but it was only after I spoke to Leo in Manchester and he'd read a book about it that I realised I'd been doing it most of my life."

"Daddy, what are you talking about?"

"We can chat about it later – there's too much to see and focus on here right now – the plane will be the perfect time to talk it through."

It was my cue to leave the topic, but I had to return to it because I knew my lessons were not over yet.

Ann's Chicken Fry House was set in amongst an array of large stores and malls that lined the new Route 66. Outside, an old Police Pontiac and pink Chevy were parked next to a rusty Texaco gas pump.

"Are you hungry?" I asked.

"Do you know, I couldn't eat a thing, but these cars are amazing." He ran his palm along the frame of the Pontiac.

I took a photograph with his iPad and we moved into the diner for a cup of coffee.

Neither of us spoke much as the day was hot outside and after our visit to Stockyards City I was overwhelmed.

"So do you think you'll wear those boots when you get home?"

"I haven't a clue but I'll definitely put them on for the game tonight."

I poured a spoon of sugar into my cup and stirred slowly. I was transported to a scene in the Disney film *Cars* as I looked out at the old vehicles through the window. I'd taken Thalia to see it in the cinema with her friends from school a few years back. Soon she'd be going to college. It was a fast world that teenagers lived in these days. The world had become smaller and in the fifties this diner was very different to any place in Ireland. Nowadays there was something generic about most cities. They all had a Starbucks, McDonald's, department stores that sold the same clothes in London, New York, Rome or Barcelona. Our planet had shrunk and people were doing the same things all over it.

I recalled a chance meeting with a nurse in Gatwick Airport on my last press trip. She said that when she got the Tube to work in the mornings, she always thought that the tunnels, with the people in trains rushing along them, were like the veins and arteries rushing with blood that she observed during operations in theatre.

It was easy to get caught up in the rush and fuss of daily routines but nice to just stop in a diner like this that was still deeply rooted in the past. I could tell by my father's expression that he was enjoying this throwback in time. He lifted his cup to his lips and took a sip.

"I usually love my cup of tea at home but it's nice to drink coffee in a place like this," he said.

He was mindful of the way he lifted his cup and put it back down on the table.

When we'd finished, we walked slowly out to the car. I couldn't help but appreciate the mindful way that my father enjoyed every step of our trip. The more I watched his behaviour, the more I realised that it was a way of being that I too had the choice of enjoying.

It was a ten-minute ride to the Museum of the Cowboy. I wasn't sure what was in store but felt that after this part of the trip we would both be ready to make our way home. In twenty-four hours we would be en route to Chicago on the last leg of our voyage. I'd also get to see Michael again, which was something constantly in the back of my mind.

Time had moved at a rapid pace, yet a part of me felt as if I hadn't seen my daughter in months. I'd changed in the course of this journey and I had to be strong. Thalia was right – it was my turn to move on.

The first exhibit was only a few feet away from where we parked: a sculpture of two cowboys sitting on horseback with their arms stretched out in a firm handshake. Underneath were the words *'The Code of the West'*.

It was difficult for my father to see the large edifice in direct sunlight so I described it and read out the words on the plaque. It was a symbol of the best of the West and the hardships endured by the pioneers. My father listened carefully to the words.

"I'd love to have been a cowboy," he admitted.

"I know, and sure maybe you were in a past life," I teased. On my spiritual journey through America I was warming to the concept of reincarnation and I had a sense that there was much more in the world that I hadn't considered before.

"I wouldn't be at all surprised," he said with a nod. "Now show me the way."

We entered the lobby, surrounded by large stone pillars and an impressive atrium next to the information desk. Our host was a tall lean woman dressed in a denim skirt with the quintessential cowboy boots.

With his Stetson now firmly placed on his head my father was truly prepared for this excursion.

"My name is Joy and I'm delighted to meet you both."

From her accent I could tell that she wasn't from Oklahoma. She went on to say that she came from Maine and was brought to this state by her husband when she was in her twenties. Although she didn't appear to have Native American origins, she assured me that she was quarter Abenaki. I'd noticed that most people had some connection to Native

Americans in Oklahoma – something I hadn't considered before, during all the times that I'd travelled to America.

"Let me show you our exhibition – you guys are in perfect time to see the Prix de West." She went on to explain about the annual exhibition of the finest Cowboy and Indian art in the country.

I was overwhelmed by the pictures. My poor father's eyes hadn't adjusted after coming indoors from the sunlight. I'd put his iPad in my bag in anticipation of him needing it and he seemed relieved when I told him that I'd record the finest pieces on exhibit.

We trekked through many rooms of outstanding work and after a few minutes my father could make out some shapes. The first one that he stopped at was a picture of a chief and his daughter. He moved in closer to inspect. "I can see a young woman on a horse, is that right?" he said, squinting, and smiled.

"That painting is titled *Father and Daughter at Crow Fair*," Joy told us. "The daughter's tunic is special and the decoration was made by sewing on hundreds of moose teeth, showing how brave and accomplished her father was by acquiring the teeth to give to his daughter to wear."

The image resonated with me. The proud family setting off for the day in ceremonial dress and the closeness of the two sitting tall on their horses reminded me of a few days earlier as my father and I had roamed the ranch on our horses. The tension in the composition was echoed in their expressions: he with his long feathered headdress and her face with all the anticipation of a debutante. It was a similar ceremony to a coming-of-age event in any tribe or society. We were all the same at the end of the day as my father had pointed out. There is only one great big *WE* and whether we are Hindu, Catholic,

Muslim or Jew we are all people going through the similar rigours and rites of passage.

"I think you'll like this next room," Joy said, stepping slowly and carefully into the next part of the exhibit.

It was the museum of movies. Behind the glass cabinets lay vast arrays of memorabilia, posters and costumes from every major Western movie that was ever made. There were interactive screens to quiz my father on the names of actors and characters and even their horses. Joy read out the questions and laughed and teased him about his huge knowledge as together they took a trip down Memory Lane. I'd watched many of the movies as a child on our black-and-white TV that was perched high in the corner of our sitting room. My father put it up high so that it would be a safe distance away from my mother – she was such a hazard and risk to have around the house.

Thinking about her now, I realised that something had happened since I came to Oklahoma. I no longer resented my mother the way that I did before. I had the same memories of my childhood but somehow I understood my father's position and place in the scheme of events. I realised that he did the very best he could with his lot, did his best for me and my brother. I watched now as an observer of my past and it gave me the foresight to face up to the way I was living my life.

And the greatest lesson of all was the one that Michael had shown me: the possibility of connecting to another soul and learning to love a man again.

Chapter 27

Michael was eating lunch with his sister when Roz came into his head again. That kiss was still on his lips and he knew that he had crossed a line but couldn't do anything to change how he felt. As each hour ticked by he was looking forward to the flight home more and more.

"You took some time to say goodnight to Roz last night," Claudia commented. "I didn't want to say anything at the time because I hoped you'd bring it up."

Michael fumbled for words. He didn't want to admit to his sister that he had feelings for Roz. But he couldn't deny it because she had seen them.

"You can't lie to me, you know," she continued. "I know lust when I see it and, Michael, you can't hide that you are infatuated with that woman."

"I'm not – she is a good soul and deserves more from life. She's been in an abusive relationship and she's trying to get herself together."

Claudia laughed out loud. "Please, Michael, you're a hopeless liar. She's stronger than you think. Most women are stronger than they realise. She's nice though – I'm glad I met her."

Michael got up to get another beer out of the fridge.

"She's certainly keen on you," she added.

Michael laughed. "What makes you say that?"

"It's an intuition-thing women just have. You know, Michael, it's never too late to fix your life."

Michael wasn't impressed. "What the hell do you mean – fix my life? I've a vocation and I'm living the best life I can."

"Come on, Michael," Claudia teased. "You can't fool me. All this concern over me and the life I'm living and you are living a bigger lie. It's not natural. We all need to love and connect with another human being. Ben and I have got old and stale – the love has gone but it's never too late to find new love."

Michael didn't want to admit to his sister that he was thinking the same thoughts. It was easier to try and solve other people's problems than face up to his own.

My father opted for a lie-down before we went to the baseball game. I spent the time trawling through Michael's Facebook page. I was a voyeur on every aspect of his life for the eight years since he'd joined. I had flicked through all his rugby photos, army photos and even some of him in ceremonial costume saying Mass. It jarred with me that he was a priest and yet I couldn't help seeing him as a man, wanting to be himself, instead of being split up into several pieces, giving up his time and doing deeds for everyone else.

At least I would see him the next day and the time was

right to be going home. I missed Thalia and would be happy when my concerns about her were laid to rest.

I dialled her number to say goodnight, but her phone was already switched off. I lay on the bed and wondered what I'd do when I returned and what part of my life I should tackle first. Then the phone beside my bed rang.

"Rosaleen, I'm ready," my father said.

And we were off on our final excursion.

The Chickasaw Baseball Stadium was spaciously arranged and that made our access easy. We strolled past the busts of Wilber Joe Rogan and Lloyd James Waner and other names that would be etched in the memories of Oklahoman baseball fans. The rumbling from the crowd was echoed in my father's expression. He was childlike in anticipation of the big event.

"This reminds me of the semi-final at Croke Park last year."

"Ahh yes, I remember you telling me about that." I was pleased at the time when he told me that he'd organised tickets for himself. The GAA provided extra availability for people with special needs.

"I had a really grand seat and I could hear the commentary on the radio in my ear with those little earphones that you sent me. I could even make out a bit of what was happening on the big screen."

"I admire your get-up-and-go, Dad. How do you keep on going? If I was living in Dublin, I wouldn't have the interest or inclination."

He stopped and turned to me as if he could see very clearly again.

"Because I'm alive, Rosaleen. Don't ever forget that while you're breathing and can get around you can basically do anything. Self-belief and interest in the world has kept me living so long. It's just a choice."

"What do you mean choice?"

"We constantly make choices in this life – whether to be happy or miserable – successful or a failure."

I didn't completely agree. But if I got into a debate he would surely convince me otherwise.

He began to explain.

"We are going to a game and we'll sit and listen to the score and wonder who will win but in the process we must be careful not to miss out on the experience. I don't mind that I cannot see the players or the bats or the balls. I can feel the crowd, sense the excitement, and be at one with the experience of simply being. In doing this I've found the greatest joy in the simplest of things, and in a way I'm just like a child again. I choose to be happy – it's my choice."

He put it all so beautifully. I slipped my hand into the crook of his arm and led him slowly and gently to our seats as the frantic fans rushed past with trays of beer and hotdogs.

In the background the music played. I recognized it instantly: Thin Lizzy's song 'The Boys Are Back in Town'.

"And there's no such thing as a coincidence either?" I said, tongue in cheek.

He laughed. "None at all – they knew the Irish were going to be in the crowd tonight."

And I was beginning to really understand about the connectedness of everyone on the planet. It didn't matter if we were in Croke Park or Wembley Stadium or a baseball park in Oklahoma – we were all gathering to partake in this game and share with the other spectators. I would have an open mind and allow the experience of the game to just be and wash over me in the same way as my father described his way of living with contentment.

There were more breaks than minutes of play and, after sitting through the game for one hour, I suggested we go for something to eat.

"I've had enough too but I'm so glad that we came," he said. "These blasted steps are a curse – why can't they just paint them yellow and be done with it."

The answer was easy – most architects aren't blind. Nor do they have any idea what it is like to be limited with a disability the way my father was. Everyone sees the world from their own perspective alone, my father was right about that.

"There's a place across the road called Mickey Mantle's – apparently he was a famous baseball player and put his name to a chain of restaurants. It has a bar."

"I'm ready for a pint of something all right."

We walked across the road and, when we were settled at the bar, I ordered a lager for Dad and a glass of wine for myself. I hoped he'd be alright for a few minutes on his own.

"I have to go to the bathroom," I said.

"I'll be fine here – don't worry about me."

I didn't need to worry. He was chatting to someone by the time I got back.

The woman was probably only five years older than me but she was flirting overtly as my father ordered a cocktail for her. At first I wondered if she was with someone but when we spoke it was very clear that she was on her own.

"This is Cindy," my father said as I sat down.

Cindy held out her hand and flicked back her long blonde hair. "Hey there, your father's telling me all about you and your trip."

She didn't say 'y'all' and her tone was very different to anyone local that we had spoken with over the last week.

"He's been having a busy week," I said.

"I'll say! And horse riding on a ranch – jeez, you guys really had a blast!"

"It was good. Where are you from?"

"I'm from California. I'm meeting other executives from our company in the morning. Oklahoma's in the middle of the country so we all fly here for conferences."

"Do you work for a big company?"

"It's a supermarket chain that's spread across from coast to coast," she said with a nod.

Her dress was businesslike, but she was in relaxed mode.

It amused me the way my father responded to what she said with intensity as if he could not only hear every word that she spoke but saw it too. After a few minutes I realised she had no idea that my father was visually impaired. She was the type of women who was used to men drooling over her good looks and yet my father's relaxed and easy manner seemed to make him more attractive to her.

They spoke to each other in an almost hypnotic trance and I realised that my presence wasn't needed the further they became engrossed in conversation. It was like they'd met before and this was a chance for a catch-up they hadn't had in a long time. Their chat was rhythmic, and I wasn't listening to the words they used as much as the harmony of their voices.

He still had it. He always carried a certain charisma that people are either born with or not.

Cindy reached out and playfully touched him on the thigh.

"Stop it, you know me too well," she said.

They continued to tease each other, and I excused myself to go outside and call my daughter. It was bizarre but I felt like I was the stranger in the midst of the little encounter at the bar.

I stood outside as the roars of the crowd in the stadium echoed across the road. I hung on, waiting for my daughter's response.

"Hello?"

"Thalia, it's Mum."

"Hi, Mum, can't wait to see you tomorrow!"

"How are things? Have you heard from your dad?"

"He called to check that I was okay but he's staying in London tonight so won't be back until tomorrow."

"I'll be home mid-afternoon. Do you want me to collect you in Emma's?"

"I might just get Emma's mum to drop me home in the morning – I'm looking forward to sleeping in my own bed."

Of course she was.

"How are the studies going?"

"Fine. I'm completely ready for exams next week. I can't wait for the summer holidays."

"Neither can I." I paused – not sure if this was the right time to bring up my suggestions for summer. "Would you like to go to Ireland for a couple of weeks?"

She let out a sigh that said more than words. "I'd love that."

I was shocked. I thought the sigh implied that she would hate to stay with her grandfather.

"Are you sure?"

"Absolutely. Mum, I need to get away from Oxford. I really want to go somewhere as far away from here as possible."

Now I was concerned. Why would she want to be away from Oxford?

"That's great, darling, I'll tell Granddad – he'll be delighted."

"We can talk when you get back," she said. "Have a good flight home."

As we hung up, I smiled. I was pleased that she wanted to go to Ireland. I desperately wanted to go back to my home-town and fix the part of me that I had left behind.

Cindy and my father were wrapped up in conversation and they hardly noticed my return.

I tapped him on the shoulder and offered to buy a round of drinks which was accepted by both. Feeling surplus to requirements, I turned to the bartender and propped myself up on a high stool.

"Your pa sure can tell a good story," the bartender said.

"He likes to talk," I agreed. "Can you give them the same again and I'll have a gin and tonic."

I'd taken it easy with alcohol on this trip but it was our last night and I wanted to kick back and relax. I would enjoy the freedom before returning home.

"He was telling us all about your stay at the ranch," the bartender said as he poured a long high shot of gin.

"I think that was the highlight of his trip." I took the glass from him, added tonic and drank.

"I've always wanted to go to Ireland. My grandfather came from there – lotsa folk did."

"I've been amazed by the similarities between Oklahoma and Ireland – yours is a rural state and we are largely an agricultural country, but more recently taken over by tech companies and Big Pharma."

"Agriculture is big here in the heartland. We love Irish music. We've got some music starting soon – could be a long night."

I shook my head. "I'm going to enjoy a couple of drinks but I don't think we'll be late."

"I wouldn't wanna bet on that," he said and nodded over to my father and Cindy, still engrossed in each other.

I drained my glass and shuffled across a few steps to be nearer to the couple.

My father acknowledged me. "Where were you?" he asked.

"I was talking to Tally and the barman. I think I'll just have one more then I'll hit the bed."

Cindy seemed disappointed. "Won't you stay?" she said.

"Which hotel are you staying at?" he asked her.

"I'm at the Hampton Suites – what about you guys?"

"That's where we are too," I said.

"My daughter is afraid to leave me because I can't see very well – I'm actually certified blind."

Cindy lifted her brows with surprise. "No way!"

"Yes, but he can see sometimes, can't you, Dad?"

My father laughed and explained about the complications of his condition.

"I'm going to bed – will you be okay?" I asked him.

He smiled and said he would see me in the morning.

Chapter 28

It felt like I had just closed my eyes when the phone beside my bed rang out. I stirred and realised that it was morning. I hadn't pulled the curtains over. My first thought was of seeing Michael at Chicago International later.

I lifted the phone.

My father was breathless and excited at the other end.

"Rosaleen, are you awake?"

"I am now," I said, resting up on my elbows. We'd stayed in so many different places during the week that I was disoriented each morning when I woke.

"I'm sorry to wake you."

"It's probably just as well," I said, looking at my watch. "Do you want to go down for breakfast?"

"I'd like that – I'm starving."

"I'll take a shower and call for you in fifteen minutes."

～

My father answered his door quickly. He stood taller than usual with a radiant beam from his cheeks.

"You must have had a good night," I said.

Was I jealous that a stranger had taken my father's attentions on our final night together?

"Rosaleen, I'm sorry that I got so carried away talking to Cindy –"

"It's okay," I interrupted. I didn't really want to hear.

But he held on to my arm gently yet firmly and pleaded with his eyes for me to listen.

"It was remarkable meeting Cindy like that. I swear it was like I knew her from before, a long time ago."

"Well, you did say that people are drawn to each other for a reason so maybe that was it."

We started to walk down the corridor towards the lift but he wanted to tell me more so I reluctantly let him continue.

"Even though she talked with a Californian twang there was something about the way she spoke that reminded me of a girl that I used to know. A girl I knew when I lived in Inniskeen – we were friends."

"Was she an old girlfriend?"

He shook his head. "It was all very innocent in those days. You'd be afraid to hold a girl's hand in case the parish priest caught you. But she was someone that I fell in love with. She was blonde and very pretty – it was unusual to have blonde hair in those days I mean there were few dyed blondes. Kathleen Joyce was her name and she had the voice of an angel. She used to sing at Mass and I always made sure I went whenever she was singing. She could have gone on to great things and been a famous star."

"What happened to her?"

"Shortly before I came up to Dublin she contracted TB

and spent a year in an institution. I wasn't able to go see her, but she used to write to me and I wrote to her. Although now I wonder if the nuns looking after her used to read the letters first, because sometimes pages were missing."

"I wouldn't be surprised at what the nuns got up to in those days, especially in institutions."

My father knew I had little trust of some characters in the religious orders and he didn't try to change my opinion – he was well aware of the gross injustices carried out by certain members of religious orders in twentieth-century Ireland.

"Well, she was only out a few days when didn't she get a relapse and the blasted plague took her – she was only twenty-two years of age."

My father stopped walking and felt for his breast. I thought that he was going to cry. Instead, he took a deep breath and smiled.

"Kathleen was an angel and we had a pact that if anything ever happened to either of us in this life, we would let each other know we lived on in some way." His eyes filled up and I reached out to steady him.

"What way? What do you mean, Daddy?"

"I think that Cindy could well have a lot of Kathleen roaming around her. She spoke of dreams she's had since she was a little girl, and I didn't prompt her on any of it. I never mentioned Kathleen to her. Instead she told me that she has been wondering about a girl from Ireland called Kathleen for most of her life."

"That's amazing, but it's just a coincidence," I said.

"Remember what I told you?"

I nodded. "There's no such thing as a coincidence."

"And the longer I'm alive the more clearly I see it."

I didn't want to rush him, but the lift had arrived. We stepped in and were joined by some other guests.

"We can chat about this over breakfast," I said.

Downstairs I searched for the cereal and made a pot of tea from the buffet. My father found a quiet table in the corner to sit at and when I joined him I was ready for the rest of the conversation because, whatever or whoever Cindy was, she certainly had a profound effect on my father.

"Cindy reminded me so much of Kathleen and that wasn't all. Cindy was born on the 27th September – ten years to the day after Kathleen died."

"That is a coincidence."

"But the song that she loved all her life was a tune her father used to sing to her at night and it was the very same song that Kathleen said she would sing for me on the other side of the grave."

"What was the song?"

"'She Moved Through the Fair'."

I knew it. It was a haunting traditional ballad.

"How did she know that song?" I asked.

"Because her father was from Monaghan – and wait, are you ready for this?"

I was.

"Cindy has a beautiful voice and last night she sang that song for me. I felt like Kathleen was there with us." He hung his head and closed his eyes before lifting his teacup to his lips. But he put it back down without drinking and continued to speak. His words were tinged with pain. "I don't want you to think I'm losing it or anything, but I do believe that there's a part of Kathleen in that girl. I've been feeling this way for a long time and now I'm convinced that we are all one and the same person. I needed a jolt or reminder to believe it but now

I know it to be true. We are all part of the same family of souls that leave our bodies and return again but with traces of the lives we lived before."

He stopped talking for a moment and rubbed his eyes to hide the drops that had formed at the rims of his lids.

"The night Kathleen died I was up in Dublin and I didn't need a mobile phone or telegraph or anything to tell me that she'd died. I knew inside and felt a pain in my heart that didn't go away for a very long time. To be honest, it never went away until now. To know that we live on and pass through other's lives and spirits is a great consolation when you come to my stage in life. I realise that I'm not long for this earth and that's fine too."

When he said things like that, I felt a pang in my chest, unnerved by the casual way he spoke of his own death.

"Daddy, don't speak like that."

"I'm not trying to be morbid or anything like that," he said. "I just want to say it like it is. I'm sure that I met that girl before in a past life and this isn't the first time I've met people that I think I've known before. The fact that we are thousands of miles from home and this girl shows up only proves to me what I already know."

"But don't you believe in heaven, like the Church says?"

"Heaven is peace of mind and peace in your soul and living a good life on this earth is enough to ensure you have a little bit of heaven while you're alive – nobody really knows what happens when we die. But I've seen enough evidence that we live on."

I shrugged. "I'm beginning to think that something happens to us after we die but I'm not sure what it is. Seeing the way Pam reacted to her father's picture moved me all right and I felt like he was there with us."

"I've felt your mother with me several times over the years but not so much this last two or three. I've felt Kathleen's presence several times over the course of my life but never as strongly as last night. I think it was the perfect ending to our wonderful week."

Then he put his hand out and rested it on top of mine. He knew instinctively where it was and I never felt so connected to him or anyone before. I was happy inside because I could feel his joy.

After breakfast, images of Michael crept into my head again and I started to dream about seeing him. He hadn't left my memory on many occasions since I'd met him two nights before. But I had to be realistic and we were from two different worlds.

Daddy and I returned to our rooms. We had an hour to rest and finish packing our luggage. I spent some time flicking through the photographs we'd taken and organising the literature that I'd picked up along the way. I would enjoy writing about Oklahoma and reminiscing with my father. I checked my diary and planned to take time in August to visit Ireland. A renewed sense of hope about the future had seeped its way into my spirit and at the same time I was fearful of the changes that were coming my way. These changes had started without my instigation, but I felt relieved that I was finally brave enough to make them.

The phone rang again. It was the last time my father would call on this journey.

"Are you ready, Rosaleen?"

"Yes, Dad. I'll get the porter to collect your bag."

"I'm well able to look after myself – just knock on the door for me as you pass by."

We brought our luggage down to the lobby and I went to get our car from the parking lot while my father stayed with the bags. We were quieter than usual with each other and I realised that we were sad. This journey was unique and time might not allow us the opportunity to do something like this again.

We were all set a few minutes later and on our way to the airport. I had left plenty of time to return the car to the rental garage and eat some lunch in the airport. My father found the crowds at the airport difficult to deal with – it was situations like this that caused him stress compounded by his condition.

I wanted to settle him in a nice restaurant that served a healthy lunch and found it at a grill bar.

"What's on the menu?" my father asked.

"Would you like a burrito or quesadilla?"

"I'm not sure what a burrito is – would I like it?"

"Yes – it's a tortilla with chicken or meat inside – whatever you like."

"That sounds grand. Chicken then, thank you, Rosaleen."

I ordered a large Caesar Salad for myself and brought our lunches down to where he sat. The crowds rushed around us but we were in our own bubble – a little oasis of calm.

"Have we plenty of time for our flight?"

"Yes," I said, looking up at the data screen. "And it seems that we'll be leaving on time which is great."

"When I was a lad in Monaghan I'd never have imagined that travel would become so easy. The world has changed so much in my lifetime. It will be interesting to know what it will be like when Thalia is my age."

"I do fear for the next generation with all of this technology . . ."

"Don't fear," my father interrupted. "You must never fear – fear only makes matters worse. It stifles progress and stops positive changes. What we all need is a little more faith and the right outlook. Which brings me back to what I wanted to explain to you at the hotel . . ."

I remembered. He'd wanted to tell me something. I said nothing and let him start.

"Don't let fear into your life, because if you focus on fear you will attract fearful situations. Remember I told you about a secret thought that I had which is now fulfilled."

I nodded.

"Well, I feel responsible for conjuring up this wonderful trip of ours. I've had a vision of you and me in a place like this for some time. One evening while I was watching *True Grit* on the TV and wishing I was in the Wild West, I thought of you. I wanted to go to a place where you could understand why I loved wide-open spaces and why nature has given me so much pleasure in life. I still listen to the audio books of Westerns as well as the other great authors that I love so well. Some time ago I put it into my meditation to focus on a place just like the Blacks' ranch. I started to really feel like I was going there – I found myself looking up exchange rates for dollars and going to the doctors to get checked out so that I would be fit and well for the trip. This was six months before you called and asked me to come with you to Oklahoma."

It sounded a bit farfetched but I didn't want to burst his bubble so I let him continue.

"I've always had the belief that if you truly set out to achieve or do something that you'll be successful, with the right attitude and frame of mind. When you think negatively then negative things are more likely to happen. When you focus on positivity and success, they will be your result. The difference between people who succeed and those who fail is that the successful ones don't stop trying after failure. With self-belief and focus you really can do anything in this life."

I began to understand why he didn't let his disability deter him from doing things. Enthusiasm and self-belief are probably the most important skills to take through life. I didn't interrupt him.

"So, remember. what you think about is what you bring into your life. It's called the 'Law of Attraction' by some people but I don't like using silly names for common sense. I focused on being with you in a place like Oklahoma and it happened. I changed the screensaver on my laptop to a long straight road several months ago and pictured you and me on it. I dreamed about such a lovely adventure and, Rosaleen, even in my dreams the time on the road wasn't as wonderful or special as the past week has been in reality. We spend so much time thinking about all the things that we don't want to happen and the things that we don't want in our life that we don't realise we are actually drawing them to us more with our thoughts."

I got it. I realised exactly what he meant. I'd heard of the Law of Attraction, like most people, but I hadn't understood it until now. If a blind man could rustle up a dream of going to the Wild West with his daughter without her knowledge, surely there was something to it?

"Did you really wish this?"

"I did and I tried not to influence you when we spoke on Skype or when you came to visit last time, but I really wanted this so badly and didn't know how it was going to happen. I even went to the travel agent's to see if they could come up with a package for us and then you rang me. So that is what I've been keeping from you until now, in case you thought that I was going insane."

I smiled. "You are insane, but that's why you're such a wonderful and inspiring part of my life and I'm glad you're my father."

It was a special moment. I felt my eyes well up, not with sadness but joy, and my father's smile was magical.

We finished our meal and joined the passengers plying back and forth with luggage on wheels and shopping in large carrier bags. But we walked at a slower pace than everyone else. I'd learnt to be more mindful of each experience and moment spent until our journey was complete. I would take this mindful way of being back with me to Oxford. It was all about perception and perspective and if my father could turn his disability into a positive, as he'd shown me on so many occasions during the last week, then I could do the same with my situation.

Our aircraft was a small commuter plane and it was packed with heavy luggage as many passengers were making connecting flights. We left behind sunshine and high winds as we buckled up into our narrow seats.

"Are we not meeting Michael?" my father asked.

"He's on the next flight out to Chicago."

"He'll be cutting it fairly fine then."

"He should be fine if he isn't delayed." I really hoped that he wouldn't be delayed because I couldn't wait to see him again.

My father fixed his seat belt and sat back with a quiet air of satisfaction.

"We didn't get caught up in a twister," he said with a gentle nod of his head.

"Aren't we lucky! The stormy weather seemed to go around us rather than follow our routes."

"I think we had angels at our side – did you feel them?" he said.

"It's funny you should say that because I did actually think of my guardian angel when we were in Sulphur. I hadn't for so many years but he just sprang to my mind when we came out of Mass."

"Never neglect your guardian angel. I don't know what I'd have done without mine. It's the one memory that I have of my father. Because I was the youngest, he'd sometimes put me to bed – a job usually only for the mother of the house in those days but we had a special bond. I sometimes think he knew that he didn't have long left on this earth and that he wouldn't have long with me being so small. He thought me the prayer *'Angel of God, my guardian dear'*. I've said it to my father every night of my life and sometimes the two blend into one and I think that my father is my guardian angel. He helped me through some tough times and gave me strength when your mother wasn't well."

I put my head back on the headrest and turned to him. I understood how difficult his life had been and how he'd made the best of everything. He had lived a good life and, regardless of my mother's condition, he did his best for everyone, even the people who worked for him or those that he came in contact with day by day.

"I never said thank you, Dad."

"For what?" He seemed surprised.

"For being such a kind father. And thank you for wishing up our little adventure. I think you did a good job getting us to the American Heartland, especially if you did it by positive thinking. Where are we going to next?"

"Ah, now, I'm not sure I've too many journeys left in me, to be honest, but I would like to see more of you and my granddaughter in Ireland."

I put my hand on his arm and squeezed. "I'd like that too and I'm going to make sure that it happens as soon as I get back to Oxford."

I meant it too.

Chapter 29

The transition lounge at Chicago International Airport brought back memories. I felt my heart pound at the prospect of seeing Michael again. I could picture his face clearly now. It had been a week of reflections, of thinking back to my past and memories of the things in my life that had moulded me and mattered.

We found a café and I listened to my father recount every detail of his time on the ranch as if I was hearing it for the first time and hadn't been a spectator.

We hadn't tired of each other as I'd feared but instead had settled in together like a comfortable pair of slippers on two sore feet. Our time together had nourished us both. I was feeling proud and content when Michael appeared in front of us.

"Patrick, Roz – well, we made it back to where we began."

My heart started to pound and I could feel his energy like an electric shock. I could sense the gentle wetness of his lips touching mine from our time in Bricktown.

"Hello, Michael," was all I said.

"Michael, good man," said my father. "Sit down here beside us and tell us what you got up to."

I wasn't imagining it; Michael was looking at me intently.

"I had a great time, thanks, Patrick. It was long overdue time spent with Claudia and I'm glad you got to meet her. Went to the movies with my niece and nephew one day. Kids really keep you young."

I couldn't help but think what a great father Michael would make and how cruel the rules of the Catholic Church were to deny him the chance to become one – although, as I knew, many priests did have children in the past and others were hidden and denied.

"God's greatest blessing," my father piped up.

"Amen to that," Michael said, staring directly at me.

I blushed. Michael smelt so good, a mixture of cedar wood and mint. His bright eyes and his infectious love of life shone through his charismatic smile. The Defence Forces were fortunate to have someone like him to look after their men. But if he was so good at his job and so absorbed in it, then he wouldn't have time to spend with children if he had them. I didn't necessarily agree with it, but I realised a character like Michael had so much love to give it would be impossible to maintain that energy and have some left over for his family.

"We're going to have to board soon, Rosaleen – can you see the boarding time?" my father asked.

"Yes, in ten minutes, Dad."

Then I walked with a man on either side of me and I felt swaddled and safe as we stepped onto the airplane.

∽

The aircraft wasn't full as we boarded and Michael was able to move seats so that he sat across the aisle from us. I listened intently to his tales of tours of duty and life in a parish. He made each story interesting and seemed to know everybody in Ireland. I didn't feel the time pass. We spoke easily, both knowing that we had kissed but it hadn't made us awkward. If anything, it had made us more comfortable in each other's company.

When the lights were dimmed, and passengers settled in under their blankets, Michael beckoned me over to sit on the empty seat next to his. My father had fallen asleep and was breathing noisily through his open mouth.

As the passengers around us dropped off to sleep one by one, our conversation took on a clandestine quality when we realised we were almost alone. These next few hours would be our secret time together and a journey that in itself was an adventure.

"I've been meaning to ask, what made you become a priest? It seems so unlikely in many ways."

"You don't know me all that long, or that well."

"I know but I feel like I do." I really did.

"It was natural for me. To be honest, I couldn't imagine myself doing anything else up to this point. Did you always want to be a journalist?"

"I always wanted to write. I thought I'd be a novelist one day, but that book never came to me."

"What's stopping you?"

It was an honest question but one that I couldn't answer. I could blame motherhood or my divorce or my own mother but really I only had myself to blame. I shrugged.

His head was pressed against the headrest and tilted towards me so that our faces were only inches apart. In the half-light his eyes twinkled and I felt as if he could see right into my soul.

"If you wrote that novel would you be happy?" he asked.

"Maybe, but I'm not sure that I've anything interesting enough to say."

"There must have been a time that you did if this is your ambition."

God, he was good. He really could see right into me.

"I carried around anger for years, anger towards my mother. I was so angry with her. It took seven years of therapy for me to figure that one out. Then I spent another three trying to discover why I was so angry when my husband asked for a divorce."

"Maybe you didn't have the right counsellors?"

"I mustn't have had. I see my father who is so at peace with his lot and his life and wish I could have some of that."

"You can, right now in fact."

"What do you mean?"

"You can be, have, do whatever you want – that's why God gave us free will."

"I'm not so sure about God, even after the week we've had and all the discussion with my father."

"But who do you think God really is?"

I didn't have an answer. I didn't think he would either, but he started to tell me.

"When you were a kid you were told that God is every-where – that's because he is. He is in everything and everyone and that means we are all a little bit of him."

"My dad said something like that, one night in Oklahoma."

"That's why Jesus said 'Whatever you do to the least of my brethren you do to me' – the answer is in all the scriptures.

Ironically it's the identical message in all religions – everyone says the same thing."

"My father said all that as well."

"It's simple really." He shrugged his shoulders gently. "People try to complicate it but it is all so simple. Life is simple too. We choose to be happy, choose to feel fear, choose to love and choose to hate."

Michael's philosopy was eerily like my father's but it resonated with me after hearing it a second time.

"So it's not your job to convert me?" I said.

"It's not and that's not why I joined the priesthood either. I just wanted to serve people. I love people, all people, and I wanted to spend my life enjoying and helping others."

"At the cost of marriage, of having children."

"It's a sacrifice in Europe and the States but there are plenty of priests in South America with families and wives. The closer you get to Rome the more orthodox the priest – it's like the closer you get to Mecca the more orthodox the Muslim."

"But what about you – what did you want?"

Michael paused and I swore I could hear him speak straight to my consciousness.

"It is a sacrifice to go through life without having children, but I helped kids when I was a school chaplain. I'm not going to lie and say it's all been easy and there are times when I've felt low about my life choice – but doesn't everyone?"

I nodded. "If I hadn't married I'd have had an easier life, but I have my beautiful daughter and if that's what I had to do to get her then it was worth it."

"A marriage is never a failure – it's a life experience – and not all experiences are meant to last forever. It was a great success if you have Thalia at the end of it."

"I like your way of looking at life," I said and smiled.

"If I'd wanted kids more than serving the Church, I would have taken that option. But with my way of life I can be of service to more people than if I had my own family."

Then he pushed up his sleeve on his left arm and revealed his tattoo. It was an intricately etched image of Jesus and covered his complete bicep.

"It's Jesus," I said. "Was it painful while it was being drawn?"

Michael shook his head. "It was nothing compared to what Jesus suffered for us. I try to live my life with him in mind. He's my inspiration. He was a man who gave his life to serving others. That's all I'm trying to do."

It was the freshest perspective I had ever heard. I couldn't believe that someone so warm and interesting could feel that way. I wanted there and then to be the one to change his mind and make him love me.

He saw the vulnerability in my gaze. Then he lifted his palm and put it on my left cheek as he had done in Bricktown. It rested there for a few moments as we just looked at each other.

"You seem to have it all figured out," I said with a sigh.

"Don't be fooled by what I say. I have all the normal desires and faults, like every other person that you meet. What if I said that I could easily fall in love with you?"

Then he stared into my soul and I melted.

"I'm only flesh and blood, Roz. It doesn't happen often but sometimes I meet someone who sways my perfectly ordered world. If I am to continue serving others in the way that I chose to live my life, there isn't space to love just one person. That upsets me."

My heart was pumping so loudly I was scared that he

could hear it. I didn't know what to say but I could feel a tear well up in the corner of my eye and trickle down my cheek.

"You're not the only lost soul on this plane, Roz. I saw it that day in the lounge when we first met. I wanted to run over and hug you so badly. We are all only trying to do our best in this life."

"Do you go around picking up lost souls out of the crowd and making us better?"

"I wish I could, Roz, but you are the only one that can make you better."

I knew that he was right. He let his hand slip away from my face but held my gaze.

"So what do I do?" I asked.

"You have the answer inside you. Trust your gut and yourself. I wouldn't make you happy. Nobody has the power to make someone else happy. Until you're happy with yourself, nothing else will fill that void."

I licked my lips and swallowed hard. It was the most connected I'd been with a man for a very long time – possibly since my teenage years.

"We must stay in touch. You can talk to me whenever you need."

"I'd like that," I said.

But really I wanted more. I wanted to physically feel his lips on mine again.

He leaned forward and placed the softest kiss on my lips. I wasn't sure if it was the kiss of a friend or lover. Then he put my head on his shoulder and he stroked my hair as I fell asleep.

∿

A few hours later our aircraft descended on to Runway 10 and the chief steward welcomed us to Dublin Airport. It had been a quick flight – too fast.

The salty morning air brought a sharp awakening to our return. I had two hours to wait before my flight to Birmingham and I was worried how my father would manage through baggage reclaim. But Michael offered to help him and promised he would stay until he found a taxi. I was grateful and yet worried about him arriving home to his small maisonette alone.

"Be careful, Dad," I said. Then I hugged him tightly, the same way that I used to when I was a little girl. After spending so much time together I realised how much I would miss him in the coming days.

He squeezed me so hard I felt his strength would help me to return home with confidence.

"You mind yourself, love, and give me a ring when you get back to Oxford," he whispered in my ear.

I turned to Michael who put his other arm warmly around my shoulder before leaning forward to kiss my cheek. "Don't worry about him – I'll make sure that he is alright."

I could feel myself well up inside as the two men walked away from me. I hid behind a pillar so I could see the two of them walk on for a little while longer. I wanted to stay in Dublin and not return to Oxford. But I had to.

As I took a left turn to Flight Transfers, I swallowed back my tears. It was a consolation that I would soon see Thalia.

Chapter 30

Oxford, England

When I stepped off the Boeing 737 at Birmingham Airport, I was returning a very different woman to the one who'd taken off from the same airport eight days before. Not only more reflective but a new person.

My father had shown me that life is not a dress rehearsal and it was no accident that we'd run into the characters that we met. I wondered what part Michael could have in it all because I knew that we were destined to meet again.

In less than an hour I was driving past the rolling green hills along the A40 motorway. The heavy traffic started to diminish and I was soon on the road through Kidlington and mere minutes from the village of Bladon.

My Cotswold cottage looked quaint as I parked in the empty drive.

I'd only just turned off the engine when Thalia flung open

the front door and ran out to greet me. I was so relieved to see her. I jumped out of the car and held her tightly.

She squeezed me and buried her head into my shoulder. Then I felt the guilt of leaving her.

When she pulled away I put my hands up to her cheeks and studied her beautiful face. Her skin was clear and pale, her eyes a bright translucent green. Then I noticed a gash on her rosy lip and caressed the scar with my fingertip.

"What is that?" I asked.

She hung her head and took two steps backwards.

"It's nothing." She shrugged. "I fell."

I knew my daughter well and I knew when she was lying.

"*Thalia, what is it?*"

She swallowed hard and shrugged again.

"Let's go inside to the kitchen and you can tell me all about it," I said.

I locked the car but left my bags in the boot because this couldn't wait.

We walked silently to the kitchen and sat at the table.

"Don't you want a cup of tea? You always like one when you come in." she said.

"I'm fine – I'd plenty on the plane. Thalia, what happened while I was away?"

She took a deep breath as if about to tell me then shook her head.

"Is this something to do with Dad?" I asked her.

"Okay then," she said. "The party we went to . . . just after you went away . . . was not what we expected . . ."

I slapped the table so hard my hand hurt, and I was glad. I deserved to be punished because this was my fault.

I looked deeply into my daughter's eyes – they were filled with anxiety and tension.

"What happened?"

Thalia looked down at the ground.

"Did someone hit you and gash your lip?" I asked.

"I can't say."

"Who did this to you? You must tell me."

"It's best if I don't."

"Thalia, you have to tell me. Was it a boy?"

Silence.

"Do you know this person well?"

She nodded.

I put my hand on her arm and tried to draw her to me.

She resisted.

"Was it a boy that you met at the party?

Reluctantly she said, "It was one of the guys who took us to the party."

"Which one? Was it the one who was driving? You told me his name before . . ." I couldn't remember it.

"I don't want to say."

I didn't press her for the moment.

"Where there any adults at that party?"

"The parents – but they were outside in the pool house and didn't come inside at all. I didn't want to go to them and make a scene."

"Did you say anything to Emma's parents?"

She shook her head.

I pulled her to me and held her so tightly she gasped for breath.

"This boy . . . did he do anything else to you?"

Thalia pulled away

"It's okay – he didn't rape me," she said.

I felt sick inside as she said the word *rape*.

"You have to tell me the truth – he didn't rape you?"

She shook her head harder this time. "No, but another ten seconds and he would have. He pulled my top off but Emma found me and disturbed him. I tried to scream but he held his hand over my mouth so I bit him and then he slapped me so hard he left me with this."

I brushed her fringe away from her forehead and looked more closely closer at her. I could see that her eye was healing from a bruise.

"Who did this?"

She shook her head.

"What about your body – did he hit you?"

She nodded. "My ribs are bruised."

My blood was boiling. I couldn't remember ever feeling so angry before.

"He can't get away with his," I said.

"Please, Mum, don't do anything. I'll be a laughing-stock."

I stood up and paced the floor. "This is my fault."

"No, it isn't anybody's fault. It just is what it is and I'm fine. Please, Mum, don't make it worse."

"But bullies can't get away with stuff this and he would have raped you. You said it yourself that if Emma hadn't found you –"

"She did find me and I'm fine. I'm glad you're back and everything can return to normal."

What was normal? Was it normal that a boy should be allowed to do this to a girl? I felt sick and so sorry that my daughter had to carry the burden of her attack alone while I was away.

"Did Emma's mother notice anything?"

Paula Stevens was a smart woman and I trusted her. She would surely have checked out this party?

"Yes, but we said that we were messing on the patio and I fell down some steps."

It wasn't Paula's responsibility – it was mine and I wasn't there for my daughter. I'd let her down.

"Have you seen your father yet?" I wondered what my ex-husband would make of the situation.

"Please don't tell him. I bet he won't notice the scar anyway."

I didn't want to make matters worse. Keith would definitely be furious and would twist the scenario around and make it out to be my fault. It was more than I felt I could stand. I agreed to say nothing but insisted that she took me upstairs to show me her other scars.

I wanted to cry when I saw her bruises. The thought of her in such pain and alone was too much to bear and I had to try hard to keep from crying. I should have been there for her. Why was it so difficult to be there for all of my loved ones? By giving time to my father, I'd neglected my daughter and there would be repercussions.

Then I wondered if I was being punished by God. My fixation with Michael was more than a schoolgirl crush. It wasn't how a middle-aged woman should behave. I would soon be forty-four but inside I was churning with teenage infatuation.

Thalia and I didn't speak but held each other close for a while longer.

Later that evening I rang my father to make sure that he was happy and settled in his home. He didn't need his spirits dampened with my news.

"How's Thalia?" he asked.

I fudged the answer. "She's fine – I'm glad to be home to her."

"That's good – a girl needs her mother."

She certainly did. I knew what it was like to have a mother that I couldn't depend on and from now on I would stay closer to my daughter.

"I suppose it's too early to ask when you're coming to Dublin."

"I'm just catching up on the news here, but I'll let you know as soon as I get organised," I assured him.

"What about Michael – have you heard from him?"

My father had posed an innocent question so why did I feel embarrassed?

"No. Did he put you into a taxi?"

"Of course he did. He even offered to swing by and help me get settled but I wouldn't hear of it. I'd left everything organised here and Mary-next-door left some bread on the table and milk in the fridge. She'd even turned the heating on for me last night."

"I promise we'll be over sooner rather than later," I said.

We chatted for a short while more.

When I put the phone down, I turned on the laptop to catch up on emails. As I flicked through my social media I saw that Michael had left me a message on Facebook. I remembered how it felt to be sixteen again and my stomach fluttered in the way that it hadn't since I was that age.

Hi Roz, I hope you got back to the UK safely. It can't tell you how great it was meeting you and your father in Okla-

homa. I'm blessed to meet such good people wherever I go. I'd like to stay in touch. Your father is a strong man and I'm in awe of his determination and strength of spirit despite his disability. He's a great role model and I think he could teach me a thing or two about life. I wanted to let you know that I'd like to be there if you need me. It's what I do.

Keep well
Michael

I read and reread the message. I had to pull myself together. It wasn't a holiday romance. It was one soul seeing another in trouble and reaching out to help. I couldn't read more into this situation than it was, one friend being there for another. It was a new perspective on relationships. Many of my relationships were based on giving help but with the promise of getting something back in return. What could I offer Michael in return? It seemed an unlikely friendship but at the back of my mind I was conjuring up other ridiculous scenarios that sent my imagination running wild. I wanted to answer his message immediately, but I couldn't. I had to think of my mental health and wellbeing. I couldn't reply because Michael was completely unattainable and I wanted more from him. If only life were as simple as he said it could be.

The days that followed were tense. I buried my head in work when I was at the office. The Oklahoma article wrote itself with ease as the memories of my trip flooded back. I enjoyed organising the photographs and the copy editor said it was one of the best travel features he'd read this year, which was positive.

However, my daughter was my main concern. Thalia became consumed by her exams, which I was relieved about. They took her mind away from her bad experience and gave her focus. She did, however, ask me to lie down with her every night for a short while before she went to sleep. She started to talk in her sleep and she clung on to her cloth rabbit that had shared her bed since she was two years of age.

I fought hard with the option of going to the police – the boy who had attacked Thalia could do it again to another girl – but she insisted on protecting him by not telling his name and I didn't want to cause her anymore distress than was necessary. I also had to deal with terrible guilt and the fact that Keith was right about the party. I'd given permission for her to go to a party that had disastrous consequences . . . when I wasn't even around to check things out or be on call if she needed me.

Keith and I barely spoke and I didn't tell him what had happened. At the back of my mind I was worried that I was avoiding confrontation and falling into my old patterns. One thing I'd learned from my journey with my father was that we are all connected, and I had a social responsibility to do something though it could ultimately end up hurting my daughter. It troubled me that a boy could be shielded by virtue of his class and the structure of society. I couldn't allow him to get away scot-free. My social conscience urged me to do something, but it pained me to do it without Thalia's permission.

Eventually I decided to meet Emma's mother during my lunch break and confront my demons. It had to be done and, even though it would be difficult for Thalia, I had to think of the 'We'.

At one o'clock Paula Stevens was sitting at a small coffee shop at the Covered Market as we had planned. She was an elegant woman with English tastes and sensibilities. I hoped that she would support what I had to do.

Paula stood up to greet me as I approached. Her blonde hair was rolled and tied at the back and she wore a smart Chanel suit. I couldn't have felt more unlike her if I'd tried. She leaned forward and barely brushed her lips against my cheek.

"Roz, we must do this more often, you know," she said as we sat down. "We never get a chance to chat."

"It's true but I suppose now that the girls don't need us to make their social arrangements for them as they did in primary school, we don't get the chance."

Paula had been kind during my marriage break-up with Keith, a lot more so than some of the other mothers at Thalia's school and I was grateful for it then and now.

"Paula, it's great to see you but I have to admit there is an ulterior motive for getting together. It's not easy to talk about this and I hope that you don't think I'm upset with you because you have been so supportive to Thalia and me."

Paula frowned. I could see she was taken aback by my tone, but I didn't know how to say what I needed to say.

"What is it, Roz?"

"Paula, first I just want to say thank-you again for minding Thalia while I was away but there was an incident and I know that the girls hid it from you . . ."

Paula's frown deepened."What incident?"

"Apparently one of the boys who took Tally and Emma to the party wasn't as nice as the girls thought. In fact," I paused because I didn't want to say the words, "one of them attacked Thalia and intended to rape her."

Paula's mouth dropped. She gave a polite laugh. "This can't be. I mean, Tom and I know their parents and those boys are attending the High School – they're young gentlemen."

"I know it's difficult to hear but I've seen the bruises on Thalia's body and injuries on her face and I've had to listen to her sobs at night. She was attacked, and if Emma hadn't disturbed them Thalia would've been raped."

"Emma knows about this?" Paula was consumed by shock– or at least appeared to be.

"Yes."

"Which boy was this?"

"Thalia won't say."

"Why not?"

"The girls decided that they wouldn't say anything in case they upset the boys and made the situation worse. But Thalia did tell me when I got home – but wouldn't tell his name."

Paula shook her head. "I'm sorry, Roz, but that party was supervised by parents. I was assured."

"Apparently the parents were outside in the poolhouse and didn't come into the house at any stage. It was a well-to-do event but all kids are capable of doing things like this."

Paula still shook her head and I realised that she wasn't going to be as supportive as I'd hoped.

"I really don't know what we can do. It's up to Thalia to tell who did it."

"Well, I was hoping that you could talk to Emma about it and find out the boy's name. I could then go to the police –"

"Go to the police?" Paula seemed startled.

Suddenly the penny dropped for me. She didn't want anything to do with this. These were people that she admired and respected and she didn't want her daughter or anyone else's saying anything against them.

Then I remembered what my father had said in Oklahoma. The reason why bad things happen is that good people sit by and allow them to. It made me more determined than ever to find out the name of the boy who had done this to my daughter and see that he didn't do it to anyone else.

"Paula, I can't rest at night knowing that this kid thinks he's got away with it. Thalia is the innocent victim in this and it's obviously painful for her to discuss it. I'm sure that Emma hasn't come away unscathed –she must be traumatised in some way too."

"Well, she has said nothing to me."

"That's why I'm telling you now, Paula."

"I really don't think that I can do anything."

I got it. What she was really saying was that she didn't think she *would* do anything about it. It had happened to my daughter and hadn't affected her personally. I was disappointed. What hope was there for our daughters if our sons were allowed to behave like this? Where was the moral compass for parents?

I realised as I sat and looked at Paula's perfectly manicured countenance that there was a time when I would have felt like she did now. There was a time when Keith controlled who I was friends with and who we should and should not associate with. I had turned a blind eye to things all my life in different circumstances, but this was a test and I had to do what I felt was right.

"I think I see, Paula. I'd hoped that we could tackle this together, but I understand your position."

Paula let out a huge sigh of relief. "Oh good, I'm glad that you see it sensibly now." Then she lifted up the menu and scanned it. Without looking up she asked me, "What are you having?"

Chapter 31

On the last day of her exams Thalia asked to go to Emma's house for dinner to celebrate. I was reluctant at first. Now that she had finished her studies, I intended to pursue the boy who had hurt her and that might destroy her friendship with Emma Stevens and her relationship with her parents.

"I'll be ringing Granddad to tell him we are coming over soon," I said. "Do you mind when we go?"

"I'm fine with whenever. I can't wait to see him. It's been ages."

I hesitated. "I was hoping we might deal with the boy from the party before we go?"

Thalia frowned. She shook her head. "No, Mum. I don't want to speak to anyone else about it."

That left me with a dilemma. I couldn't do it without her cooperation. I was also aware that if she did cooperate and we went to the police, I'd be throwing her to the wolves for interrogation and her word would only be as good as the boy's – and perhaps his friend's. I wouldn't have the support of Emma as witness or her parents either. I had to decide what the best way to deal with it was.

But for now better let her enjoy the night with her friend in peace.

"Alright, love, enjoy your night and I won't do anything without your permission."

When Thalia had left, I took the time to catch up on my backlog of messages. I sat and turned on my computer as dozens of emails started to file up in orderly piles on my screen but one in particular caught my eye. It was from Pam Allen and I scanned back quickly to open it.

It read as if Pam was speaking to me.

Dear Roz

It was so great to meet you at our center. You and your father have been in my thoughts since that special day we spent together. I returned home to my family that night and told them what happened. I said that I'd met a deeply spiritual woman and her father, and you'd helped my father to connect with us. We all prayed for you that night and gave thanks to the Great Spirit for you coming into our lives. I really believe that my father was waiting until your arrival to explain to me that he is still at the centre every day and walking with me.

Thank you, Roz, for your gift and thanks to your father too for making the day so special.

Best wishes from Oklahoma

Pam

. . .

I felt a lump in my throat as I reread the email. I was afraid that I was going to burst into tears as emotions were building up inside me all day. I needed to do something and decided to go for a walk to one of my favourite spots. Blenheim Palace was a short walk away.

I grabbed a jumper and set off, walking briskly. I thought of Casey and her father as I passed the creamy-stone Cotswold cottages covered with clematis and other creepers. They were picture-postcard-pretty and only a stone's throw from Winston Churchill's grave that the Blacks had visited years before. It was comforting to be in this place and a reminder of my time in Oklahoma when I was happy and not in the turmoil that I felt now.

I wandered through the gateway hidden for use by local residents and started to trek through the long grass to the river's edge. In the distance a couple walked across the hump-back bridge. I loved Blenheim this time of year, as the sheep and their long-limbed lambs frolicked over the acres of lush green grass. Perched high on the hill in the distance, the beautiful grand house observed all below.

I started to walk the winding pathway through the trees. This was where I came to think. I had done so since we'd moved to Oxford. When Thalia was small, she loved to come and chase the baby sheeps, as she called them. So much of my life had been here and, although it offered me a good home and means of making money, I couldn't continue this existence. Oxford was tainted now for Thalia and me. It was time to tread new water and find out who I was.

Walking past the giant oaks and sycamores was a spiritual experience – my father had reminded me of this in Sulphur country. As I did, Michael came to my mind. This was a lovely time of year to be in England, but it would be more beautiful beside the salty coast in Dublin. I knew that I would be tempting fate by moving back to Dublin with Michael Williams so close by. But I needed to address my future and I had to do it right away.

Keith's car was in the car park of his apartment block when I pulled up and I braced myself before getting out. I was pained by the truth that Keith had been right about the party – nothing was black and white – he wasn't a bad man, but he was a sad man. He valued and respected things that didn't matter but was doing his best on his journey. When I stepped outside of my situation and observed my life I wasn't sure who I was but I would never find myself staying here. I knew there would be a struggle with what I was about to do but I needed to take my daughter to Ireland.

I tried to remember all that Martina had said to me in Oklahoma about power struggles and relationships. I couldn't decide what my condition was. If Keith was an intimidator then I was probably aloof for most of our married life, covering up and ignoring all the incidents that had been warning signs.

I pressed the buzzer attached to Keith's apartment and waited. My heart pounded and I took a deep breath to steady my nerves.

"Hello, oh, it's you," he said through the intercom.

He pressed the release on the front door of his apartment. I walked in and could hear him clattering around the kitchen as cupboard doors were opened and slammed. When I got to the kitchen I stood at the door and watched him as a stranger.

He no longer had a hold on me.

"I've decided to spend some time in Ireland and I'm taking Thalia with me."

"You could have phoned to tell me that," he replied, while taking food out of the fridge to start cooking.

"I thought it best to clarify with you that it will be several weeks and more likely months."

"Roz, I don't give a damn how long you go for and if you are taking Thalia then it's your responsibility – you're always telling me that you are responsible for her, so do whatever. I've more pressing things on my mind."

I realised he was was right. What was I doing there? How much of my attachment to this man had been my doing? I completely released.

As I sat back into my car and drove home, I was in a clear state of mind and ready to cut the strings.

I dialled my father's number and waited.

When he answered his voice was gravelly as if he was coming down with the flu.

"Are you feeling okay?" I asked.

"It's funny that you should ask," he replied. "I've a bite on my leg that swelled up last night."

"When did you get bitten?"

"I'm not sure – but when I was coming home from the market yesterday I noticed my calf muscle was itchy. I scratched it and it went hot. I think I was bitten by a tick. I hope I haven't contracted Lyme's disease."

"I'm sure you haven't but you'd better go to the doctor tomorrow to check anyway."

"Tell me some good news – when am I going to see my

granddaughter?"

"Sooner than you think."

I could hear his joy sweep down the phone.

"Well, that's great news. I'm so glad – and Thalia is alright with it?"

"She's really looking forward to coming to Dublin."

"And what about Keith? How did he take it?"

"I was surprised at how easy it was. I expected a barrage of abuse and accusations from him when I called around to his apartment but, instead, I was met with *ennui*. Perhaps he's lost interest in his daughter, or maybe there was another reason. Either way he didn't seem to care that we'd be leaving."

"So have you got a date?"

"Next Wednesday."

"I'll put that in my diary," he said.

After we hung up, I pictured him going over to the large print calendar that hung in his kitchen with massive numbers in each box that represented a day. He'd ordered it from the National Council for the Blind, like so many artefacts in his house.

I tried to hand in my notice at work but Gerry wouldn't let me. He gave me three months leave-of-absence and a chance to change my mind if I needed. It was more than generous of him and it gave me something to fall back on if things didn't work out in Ireland.

The easterly flight path into Dublin Airport made a spectacular descent. When the tiny chocolate-box houses in Howth became visible, warmth enveloped me that I hadn't felt for a very long time on returning home. I'd made my father promise that he would stay in Skerries and not come to the airport to meet us. It was a twenty-minute journey to his house and I'd organised a hire car for our three-month stay.

Thalia was quiet when we eventually set off on the M1 towards our destination. Taking her away from Oxford was a positive move, but I was concerned that she'd miss her friends. We needed to take stock of our situation and we both needed to be away from the trauma that was the attack. Thalia eventually gave me the boy's name: Alan Grant-Smith. Perhaps a warning was all the boy would need. I did hope so. But turning a blind eye would not have been doing anybody any favours.

So before leaving I paid a visit to the boys' parents. They seemed reasonable people but of course defended their son totally and said that they would deal with the matter in their own way. I wasn't satisfied that I had done the right thing but unfortunately dragging my daughter through a court would have been more traumatic for her in the long run.

The taxi took us on a road to Skerries that had changed dramatically over the years and I started to reminisce when we came onto the older, more familiar terrain. The car swung around the roundabout and in the distance the wheels of the windmills stuck out on the horizon. I was home in a new and uncertain sense.

My father must have timed the flight to perfection. The door of his maisonette swung open as we pulled up and he appeared wearing a striped black-and-white apron. The pinny protected his clothes as he said he often made a mess when he cooked.

His greeting for Thalia was a marvel to observe and, as they embraced tightly at the front door, I knew that I was doing the right thing for everybody.

"You'll never guess who I met in the doctor's!" My father beamed as he dished out a chunk of gorgeous homemade vegetarian lasagne.

"Who?" I asked.

"Carole Kenny."

I hadn't heard my old-school friend mentioned in years.

"Carole! How was she?"

"Well, I couldn't make her out properly but she recognised me of course. She sounded exactly the same and had her daughter with her. She's about your age, Thalia. Anyway, she asked for you and I said that you were coming over."

"That's a coincidence . . ." I hesitated, reminded of our little chats about coincidences in Oklahoma.

"She was a grand girl. You used to be such good friends."

"What's her daughter like?" Thalia asked.

"I haven't seen her for years, so I don't know," I said. "I'm sure we will meet up and you will get to know lots of young people around the town."

Carole was like a secret friend. I was different when I was with her. She talked about all sorts of strange things when we were growing up. I remembered that she was obsessed with the apparitions at Medjugorje in the 1980s and the prophecies of the wrath that was coming if children didn't help their parents and stop watching TV. As it turned out the message of the apparitions were correct and the genocide that followed in the old Yugoslavia was the worst seen in Europe since the holocaust.

I hadn't thought of those days for a long time, days that we had spent in the school chapel, on our knees praying. We prayed that all the children in the world would be good. It was naive and foolish of us to believe that our prayers could help. We were secretly afraid that the world was going to end and that the Russians and Americans would press the buttons and start World War III. The past three decades hadn't panned out as dramatically for those in our little corner of the world but it had changed beyond recognition for so many in other countries.

"Anyway, Carole said that she'd love to see you so I gave her my number and she said that she would call in the next day or two," my father said.

I came back to the moment. "I wonder if she'll contact me. I'm not sure I'd know what to say to her."

"Well, it will be nice for you to have a friend your own age and maybe her daughter will get on with Tally."

My father the Fixer. How I loved him. "What did the doctor say about your bite? I take it it's not Lyme's disease?"

My father laughed. "No, not at all – just a hive, but it was driving me mad at night. Tally, will you have another bit of lasagne?"

"Yes, please. It's delicious, Granddad. When did you become a vegetarian?"

"Well, I'm not but your mother went off meat when we were in Oklahoma and she said that you had become one, so I made it veggie."

Warmly and happily the three of us sat around the table, until suddenly the landline phone rang during a silent moment.

"I'll get that," I said and stood up. "Hello, Patrick's phone."

"Roz, is that you?"

"Who is it?" I asked although my heart was pumping fast and I knew who it was.

"It's Michael."

I tried to pull myself together but it wasn't working. "Lovely to hear from you."

"Your father said that you were coming back. I was ringing to see when but you're obviously here."

My father had been speaking to Michael and he'd never said a word about it to me.

"Yes, I'm here and my daughter is with me."

"I look forward to meeting her. I'm going on tour in ten days and I hope that we'll get a chance to meet up before then. I could come out to Skerries?"

"I thought you were going to Thailand?"

"I had to cancel that trip because they brought our tour forward."

I was shaking inside. I didn't want my father or Tally to see my reaction.

"We aren't going anywhere quickly – when were you thinking of popping out?"

"I have a funeral tomorrow and a night out but what about the day after?"

"Yes, great."

My father knew who I was talking to. "Is that Michael? Tell him to come out soon to see me."

"Is that Patrick in the background?" Michael asked

"Yes, it is. I'm sure the day after tomorrow would be great. Do you have my father's address?"

"Yes, he gave it to me. I'll pop out around twelve, providing there are no emergencies here."

"Great," I said but I couldn't make myself sound calm no matter how I tried.

When I sat back at the table Thalia and my father looked at me and I hoped that they couldn't read my mind.

Chapter 32

Two days later

The doorbell rang and I jumped up to get it. I'd been counting the hours. It was foolish but there was a void inside me that Michael filled. My father sat without moving while I answered the door.

Michael stood wearing a pair of faded denims, a green Aertex shirt and black bomber jacket. His tan had held since his return from Oklahoma. We stood silent for a moment while his eyes connected with mine in that warm loving way that only he had.

"Michael, it's great to see you," I said, as he leaned forward to peck my cheek.

I sensed that he was as nervous as I was.

"Roz, you look amazing – you always do. So, how's the man himself?"

"He's just inside there, go on through. Thalia is out at the moment with the girl who lives two doors down, but she'll be back later."

I followed him into the kitchen where my father was now standing at the kettle.

"I've made us a bit of lunch, Michael. I hope that you've got an appetite."

"I'm hungry alright, just come straight from a funeral – that'd be great."

My father pulled on his pinny as he went over to the oven. "I've asked Mary-next-door to join us. She gets very lonely – you know how it is for old people living alone."

This was exactly my father in his element. He didn't see himself as an old person at all. He had amazed me by heading off to peel potatoes for the 'meals on wheels' only the day before.

"Isn't she lucky to live next door to you, Patrick?" Michael said while giving me a knowing look.

"I don't know how she'd manage at all really without me!" my father replied.

I wanted to have Michael all to myself but our time would come. We both knew it and the glances we gave each other confirmed it.

Mary-next-door's hair was dyed a blue-rinse shade and looked almost trendy in a strange and 'hunger games' sort of way. She wore the black-rimmed glasses that had come full circle and become almost fashionable.

When she was introduced to Michael she started to flap about uncontrollably.

"It's wonderful to see such a fine young man like yourself in the priesthood. I wish you were in our parish – we only seem to be getting priests on loan these days."

I could see that Michael was put on the spot, but my father deflected the conversation perfectly.

"Mary, are you going to try my vegetarian hotpot or would you rather I put some ham in with it?"

"I never feel that I've eaten properly unless I've meat with my dinner," she said.

"Fair enough."

I went over to help my father take the ceramic pot from the oven. We placed it in the middle of the table and Michael picked up the ladle that rested beside it.

"I'll serve if that's any help?" he said.

"That would be good, thanks," I said and went over to the fridge to get the bowl of salad.

Michael ladled a portion onto Mary's plate and my father brought her some ham to add to it.

Michael served the rest of us and we all began to eat.

"Patrick, this is lovely – a little bit of pepper would make it perfect," Mary said.

"Is there no pepper on the table? I sometimes think I've put something out and then see a shape and think that's it." He started to get up.

"Stay where you are, Dad, I'll get it," I said and went over to get the pepper.

"How long have you been in the priesthood, Father?" Mary said, taking control of the conversation again.

"I'll be ordained twenty-two years this October. The time has flown really but it has been enjoyable."

"My brother Seamus was a priest – he served in Dún Laoghaire for years – did you know him?" Mary asked. "Seamus Gaffney?"

"I did actually, met him a couple of times. We concelebrated at a funeral once."

Mary seemed pleased about that and turned her attention back to her hotpot.

"So tell us about your 'tour of duty' coming up, Michael," my father asked. "Are you nervous?"

"I actually had good news on my way out here. I thought we would be based inside the Syrian border but it looks like we will be staying at the Golan Heights which is much safer."

I was relieved but didn't say anything.

After the hotpot, my father produced a pot of stewed plums which he served with custard for dessert. He had spent hours making the meal just right for everybody.

Then Mary-next-door announced that she had to go because the electrician was coming around to fix her light.

My father started to tidy up after Mary left and then he made a suggestion. "Why don't you show Michael around the town? It's a lovely bright afternoon and I'll be here when Tally gets back."

"I'm sorry that I didn't get to meet her," Michael said.

"She'll be back in a while and you'll see her then. Do you want to go for a walk?" I hoped he would.

"Yes, I've never been out here would you believe? It's a pretty town."

"Take him down to the harbour," my father said.

So that's what I did.

We strolled past the boats and Stoop Your Head, my father's favourite pub. As we came to the pier we stopped, and Michael leaned against a railing.

"You must be disappointed about cancelling your Thailand trip," I said. I had never been and would love to bask under the Asian sun with Michael by my side.

"It was a pity. I had hoped to do a different yoga course. I've a special interest in Eastern Philosophy."

"So there would be no clubbing or seedy bars involved?" I couldn't believe I'd just said that. It sounded terrible.

"What do you take me for, Roz?" Michael said coyly with a naughty wink.

I laughed and gave him a look that covered a multitude of emotions.

"How does it feel to be back?" he asked.

"It feels good . . . well, apart from what happened to Thalia while I was away and that was the last straw really." I took a deep breath before telling Michael because it still caused me so much pain to talk about it. "When I arrived home from Oklahoma Thalia told me that she had been attacked . . . and almost raped by a boy at a party. I felt so upset and guilty because her father hadn't wanted her to go to the party."

"Don't feel guilty," Michael said, shaking his head. "I know it seems terrible but sometimes things happen for a reason. Was she badly hurt?"

"A few bruises and a cut lip. Thank God she wasn't raped but if her friend hadn't come upon them right then it could have been much worse." I sighed. "The odd thing was her father didn't go mad when I said I wanted to take her to Ireland. I was surprised by his reaction."

"What did he say?"

"He said that he had more pressing things on his mind and she was my responsibility. I couldn't believe it because he had always put me through hell in the past when I wanted to take her to Ireland. Then I had a text the other day where he admitted that his new girlfriend wanted to move in. She's only thirty."

"So it suits to have Thalia out of the equation?"

"Exactly," I nodded. "Everyone has their own agenda at the end of the day."

"That's how most people see the world. Everyone has a different perspective on any given situation. It suits him now and it may not in a few years' time. But I like to think that there is a rhyme and reason to it all. It's like we are one big massive organism pulsating on the earth and moving in different directions that help us to keep the whole world together."

"I'm not sure what you mean?" I said, though I realised he was voicing a more convoluted variation of my father's ideology.

"Everything happens for a reason and this new move by the girlfriend has come along at the right time for your husband to allow you to move on with Thalia. I'm sure the new surroundings in Dublin will help her after the attack."

He moved against the railing and propped himself up on his left arm. Then he stared at me with his head slightly tilting. I thought he could see right through me.

"You've changed from that first time that I met you in Oklahoma," he said.

I couldn't refute that. Though I still saw the man in front of me with rose-tinted glasses and as we had walked by the shimmering water my heart had pounded in my chest.

"I was restless after meeting you, Michael."

He smiled that cheeky grin that lit up his face.

"I sometimes think that if a man wants to meet a woman he should slip a wedding ring on to his finger and he'll become much more attractive to the opposite sex."

"Are you saying that women only want what they can't have?"

He shrugged. "Aren't we all a bit like that? When something is there for the taking it seems much less desirable. Don't you think?"

"I won't argue with you because you have more experience of that than me – but don't you wish you could have relationships with women?"

Michael stared again. "I do have relationships with lots of people. Men and women." He was teasing me now.

"But you don't have sex with them."

He laughed again. "I'm not saying there aren't celibate priests in the priesthood but the majority do have sex lives, albeit clandestine."

I wondered if he would consider a physical relationship with me. His kiss was still a clear memory on my lips. I wanted to hope that. My brain was conjuring up forbidden scenarios.

"But, Roz, I told you before that I became a priest because it suited the life that I want to live. What I didn't tell you was that I was almost engaged to a beautiful girl that I dated for four years."

"And what happened?" My heart went out to her. I couldn't imagine having Michael and then losing him. He must have been so handsome in his twenties.

"I couldn't commit. I didn't want to spend my entire life with just one person. I knew who I was and I love people and this is the way that I wanted to spend my life."

To someone who didn't know him this sounded selfish. He had tried to explain it to me in Oklahoma, but I understood now.

Even a little bit of Michael for a while would be nice. I edged over closer to his side of the railing and allowed our elbows to touch.

"I think I'm probably more like you than I realise. I used

to think that to be accepted and live a happy life I had to have a husband. I tried to be like normal people."

"I've yet to meet a normal person." Michael gave a little laugh.

"When my marriage broke up, I was worried about how I would feel and how people would see me. It was easier living in England because so many people are divorced but it made me anxious about returning to Ireland."

"Ireland is catching up with divorce rates – but divorce shouldn't be seen as a failure. To stay in an unhappy marriage is a failure. There's always ways to make your life better."

"I'm beginning to realise this. I feel like a weight was lifted from me when I was in Oklahoma with Dad. He has a great way of looking at life. I'm not going to try to be like him but I see merit in the way he lives that I didn't before. He did his best for me always and I'm becoming more mindful of how I live my life now."

"I like that. Mindfulness is something that is missing in the world today and if we were all a little more mindful there would be more solutions and fewer problems."

"It's a buzz word, isn't it?"

"It is and I think we've lost the use of the word *spiritual*. It's spirituality that is missing from so many people's lives." He shuffled on his feet a little, altering his position. "I'm not preaching but mindfulness is a way to find spirit. We don't have to use the word *God*. I quite like to use it but that's my personal choice. The reality is that spirit is needed to live a full life. The Father, Son and Holy Spirit are all the same thing. The scriptures all say the same thing. Every religion says the same thing. We just need to learn to love."

"*All you need is love?*"

He nodded slowly and, as he moved his head up and

down, I was entranced by him. I tried to hold back but I couldn't. I wanted to taste his lips. I needed to feel a closer connection and I slid forward until I could feel his breath on my cheek. He didn't move an inch. Instead his breath became slower, steadier. I brushed my nose against his cheek and still he didn't move. Was I being too forward, did he want me to kiss him? I couldn't tell but I couldn't stop and I didn't care if passersby saw us.

I stopped moving when I was about to touch his lips with mine. The tension was electric between us and I closed my eyes as our mouths pressed together. Suddenly I was lifted. I was brought to a place that energised every particle in my body. It felt different to that gentle teenage-crush kiss in Oklahoma – we had reached a new plateau. Intense, moving and slow.

As I pulled back the emotion fell away like a veil and I had to look at what I had done.

Michael looked at me calmly.

Inside I had turned numb.

"I'm sorry," I said.

He reached out and touched my face. "Don't be but please just accept me faults and all."

When we stepped away from the railings at last, he put his arm loosely around my shoulder. It was solace and comfort more than just a romantic gesture.

We strolled along the harbour's edge, past fishermen with pots of crustaceans and nets unravelled. There was no need to talk because there was nothing to say. We were moving as one with the energy of love and bliss surrounding us.

∾

When we arrived at my father's house Thalia was home and eating a sandwich at the kitchen table.

I took my jacket off and shook it down, along with my conscience. Had I taken Michael into the dark side – taken him away from his vows once more?

"Hello," Thalia said on looking up.

"Thalia, this is Michael who we met in Oklahoma."

She looked him up and down in a friendly manner and said, "You don't look like a priest, Michael."

It was enough to make me feel uncomfortable but not Michael who just laughed.

I rubbed my palms along my thighs and brushed my hands together but could not wipe away the awkwardness.

"Right so, cup of tea, anyone?"

Michael pulled back a chair and sat down solidly on it. "Sure, thanks."

"Not for me," Thalia said.

"So, Thalia. What does a priest look like, tell me?" He glanced up at me with a wicked grin and I pretended to throw the tea towel at him.

"Well, I haven't seen that many. I'm not baptised or anything like that. Mum's not religious either," she said defiantly.

I could understand her need to protect me, but I didn't need protecting. I was already lost in love.

Chapter 33

My father ensured that I made contact with Carole and arranged for her to call around to see us. I suspected that he'd picked up on the chemistry between Michael and me, and he was trying to keep me distracted. But my head was in a spin with thoughts of Michael and the realisation that we had so little time to see each other before he went on tour.

It was good grounding for me to meet Carole again and miraculously her daughter Aoife and Thalia hit it off.

"It can be such a gamble introducing teenagers, can't it, Rosaleen?" Carole said. "I'm sorry – Roz – I keep calling you by your old name."

"It's grand. I'm used to it again – my father never calls me Roz."

Our daughters had decided to go to the Main Street for a coffee and it was good because we got a chance to chat properly.

"It's difficult bringing the kids up alone though, don't you agree?" Carole said as she picked up a biscuit and dipped it in her tea.

Carole's husband had died when she was only thirty-eight, leaving her with Aoife and a young son, Philip.

"I'm sure it was horrendous for you at the time. I'm sorry that we didn't keep in touch." I did feel guilty.

"Don't be. I was no use to myself or anyone else for the first three years after George died but now it's just the way it is, and the kids are doing fine. If I was left destitute I'm sure it would have been different but George provided for us before he died. It takes a lot of pressure off – not having to work."

I noticed how relaxed and well she seemed. Five years was a long time and she was obviously coping better with widowhood than I had done with my divorce.

"Have you decided how long you are staying – do you need to sort out school for Thalia?" Carole asked.

I hadn't thought that far ahead. I needed more time to decide if this was to be a permanent move – this was only meant to be a three-month holiday but already my father was making suggestions that we should stay until Christmas. But it would be the end of summer soon and Carole was trying to be helpful.

"Where is Aoife going to school?"

"She's at the local convent and she's happy. I can give you the headmistress's number if you like?"

"I'm not really sure yet if we are staying," I replied. Being put on the spot like this made me realise that I didn't really know what I wanted.

"It's no harm to be prepared."

"I realise that. Maybe I will call her."

"Roz, you remind me of me. I know how hard it can feel when you are firmly in your forties and wonder what is ahead. Our daughters are at an age where they'll consume our lives for the next couple of years and then they'll be gone. Try and get something for yourself."

"What do you have for yourself?" I was curious because she was so together and seemed so content.

"I do Tai Chi and meditate. I'm also training to be a Reiki master and I surround myself with like-minded people who don't drain my energy."

"That sounds interesting," I said.

When we were in school Carole would have been afraid of alternative things like this. I always thought that she was religious. Someone had given her a pack of tarot cards for her birthday and she'd burned them – afraid that they carried some type of Black Magic. But that was a long time ago and I had changed too.

"Reiki changed my life. It's made me content with myself and healed parts of me that were damaged before George died. I think George helped me from the other side too."

Even Carole was on her spiritual journey while living in a little seaside town. She had to deal with a huge trauma but had found herself possibly because of it.

"I must try it," I said. I was curious.

"My Reiki healer is marvellous. I can give you her number if you like?"

I would take the help and hopefully be able to figure out what I wanted to do with the rest of my life.

"I think you are incredibly brave and so together," I said.

"It has taken time to get to where I am now, but I don't think I've ever felt happier."

"Do you ever feel resentful or cheated that George was taken from you? I mean, are you happy? I found it incredibly difficult being a divorcee and I'm only coming to terms with it now."

Carole took a deep breath and a sip of her tea. "Roz, I know you're going to think this a bit strange because what I am about to say is not what you would expect from a grieving widow . . ."

I was all ears.

"Well, that's the odd thing. I am happy. Don't get me wrong – I was happy with George but I've got used to coping with life without him and looking after the children on my own without interference. I see so many of my married friends and their frustrations with their husbands and I think I'm probably happier than they are."

"So you're happier being a widow?" I was incredulous.

"I'm just saying I was happy then but I'm happy now too. I'm not sure that I would be as happy if George was alive. I would never have had to heal myself. I was caught up in a whirl of pleasing him and other people who all seemed to be doing the same thing in the world of couples. It's nice to just be alone and find yourself. It's something that's difficult to do in a relationship."

I admired Carole so much and wished that I had evolved in the way that she obviously had. I was still yearning to be loved and part of someone else. Maybe because I'd never been truly connected in a healthy relationship, I wanted to know what it felt like. Carole was someone who had and yet didn't resent when it was taken away from her. It was no wonder that my father wanted me to talk to her.

That evening at dinner my father had a hundred questions for me.

"Will you be seeing Carole again?" he asked.

"We didn't set a date but she'll arrange for me to go to her Reiki teacher."

"That's a great idea. Anything like that will help give you a lift."

Thalia let herself in through the front door and entered the kitchen with a clatter. She kicked off her shoes and sat down at the table without saying a word.

"I hope you're hungry, Thalia," my father said. "I have your favourite vegetable curry for dinner."

Thalia grunted without looking up.

"Where were you?" I asked.

"Walking."

"Where?"

"Down the pier."

I had seen her in moods before but this was something serious. I wanted to know what was bothering her but didn't know how to ask without upsetting her more.

"I can't find the salt," my father said.

"I'm sorry, Dad," I said. "I was using it earlier."

"You have to remember to put things back into their place or I won't know where to get them," he berated me.

It was easy for me to take my sight for granted and every day I needed my father to remind me.

I filled some glasses with water for us all and dished out the rice onto our plates. Then I placed the curry in the middle of the table.

"Dad rang me this afternoon," Thalia said. She looked straight ahead, not making eye contact with me.

"Is everything okay?" I asked.

She huffed a little and then slapped her fork down on to the table. "His girlfriend's going to have a *baby*."

The last word landed with a thud and I was speechless. I didn't think this news would affect menthe way it did but suddenly I felt really dispensable, old and barren. I didn't know what I expected to happen. His girlfriend was young and it was natural she would want her own child. My thoughts were for Thalia and I wondered how she felt inside: obviously shock and sadness. It made sense to me now why Keith was happy for Thalia to leave Oxford.

"Good, that will keep him busy and I hope he makes more effort with this one than he did for you," my father said.

This wasn't the reaction Thalia needed. My father couldn't see the tearstains around my daughter's eyes.

Thalia jumped up from her seat and ran upstairs to the room that we shared.

"I'll go up to her," I said and left my father eating his dinner.

Thalia was lying on the bed with her eyes closed. I sat down beside her and stroked her head gently.

"I'm glad we came to Dublin," she said. "I'm never going back to Oxford and I want to start in a new school too."

"Whatever you want, Tally. We can start looking around on Monday."

A tear trickled down her cheek and I brushed it away.

"Dad told me that Stacey is having a boy," she said, her eyes doleful.

There was no reply to that.

Michael called me two days after our kiss and we arranged to meet at his barracks. The cold brick-buildings didn't seem like a place where he would belong but, as he sauntered over to me at the barrier, I realised that Michael was at home everywhere.

"This is my friend, Paul," he said, pointing to the private in charge of the gate.

"Yes, sir," the young man said and raised the pole so that I could drive through.

Michael slid onto the passenger seat of my car and told me to park over by a dark grey building. His presence instantly energised me and filled me with love.

We got out and walked over to the barracks, each as anxious as the other.

"Thanks for coming out all this way to see me."

I blushed. "I wanted to see where you hide out."

"That's my pad over the other side of the square. Come and I'll get you lunch."

There it was again. That smile. I was melting inside.

"Or something stronger!"

I had lost myself completely and yet I was finally beginning to find myself.

"It's this way," Michael said, gently taking me by the crook of my arm.

Every soldier that we passed nodded at Michael and smiled at me.

I wondered what his apartment would look like. I didn't have long to wait to find out.

The door was heavy and not like an entrance to a private residence. Inside it had been freshly refurnished and painted in muted creamy tones.

"I've made us some lunch," he said, steering me towards his clean new IKEA-style kitchen.

Laid out on the island were two green salads and a basket of crusty bread. Michael went over to the fridge and took out a bottle of cold white Chardonnay.

"Will you have a glass? I know you're driving but maybe just one?"

I nodded. This was the first time a man, who wasn't my father, had made me a meal. I sat up on the high stool while he screwed the opener into the cork.

He poured without saying a word and any awkwardness between us disappeared.

"How is Thalia doing?"

"Ah, my poor girl has had to deal with more this summer than any teenager should. Her father rang yesterday to say that his girlfriend is having a baby."

Michael seemed unfazed. "And how do you feel about that?"

I shrugged. "I haven't had emotional feelings for Keith in a very long time. I was shocked initially but now I think I feel a sense of relief. The pressure is off me or something. He won't be so controlling with Thalia, I hope, and I am free."

"That's good but I can understand how Thalia must be feeling."

I knew that Michael did understand because he was a grown-up. He was a man who had seen and experienced so much of the world and had compassion for everyone in it.

We ate and joked and laughed about life until he brought up the subject that stood between us.

"I've been thinking about our last kiss a lot," he said.

My heart pounded. I'd found it difficult to think about anything else since.

"I have to apologise –"

I put my hand up to his lips to stop him from saying anymore.

"It was my fault. I made the first move," I said.

He pulled my hand away and let it fall onto his chest.

"I didn't stop you. This has happened to me before. I wonder if it has anything to do with temptation from God. Whenever I'm about to go on a tour of duty I seem to have doubts about what I'm doing with my life."

"And do you have doubts now?"

"They come in waves – but doesn't everybody have doubts about the choices they make in life?"

I nodded. "What do you want to do?"

He didn't answer with words but instead move forward and kissed me gently on the lips.

I was frozen and aching and couldn't move.

This time he didn't move away, and our kiss developed into an embrace. I was whisked into a whirlwind and hardly felt my feet move along the floor as we walked into his bedroom. Time slowed as we stopped and stared into each other's eyes. The bed seemed huge beside us – the elephant in the room, along with the crucifix on the wall.

But all was forgotten as he peeled back my shirt and unhooked my bra. I shivered with each brush of his fingertips against my skin. The smell of him brought me to a safe place – somewhere I had only dreamed of going before. Naked and breathless, our bodies rolled into one on the bed. The union of our souls was a new experience and with each joyful turn and twist of our lovemaking I learned for the first time what it really means to make love.

～

Thalia sat into the passenger seat and put on her seat belt.

Our little rented Nissan Micra was a far cry from the Volvo that I drove in England. Everything had changed dramatically but with it came a realisation that worldly goods meant nothing. My daughter and I had been through so much together and we just wanted a car to get us from A to B for now.

"So which school did you like the best?" I asked.

"The last one."

Michael had put me in touch with the principals of all the schools in the locality and they all seemed willing to offer Thalia a place.

"It's not as close. There is a bus but you will have a short walk at the end of it."

"I don't mind. I liked the feel of it."

"And Aoife is there."

"Yeah."

I just wanted Thalia to be happy and I realised that I would have to do something about our living arrangements sooner or later because the tiny house that we shared with my father was not going to work out long-term.

"That's decided then. You won't have too long to wait either. Schools start back here the end of August."

"Will I be able to go to Oxford and get the rest of my stuff?"

I nodded. "And we need to go back and sort out things about the attack."

Thalia winced. "I want to forget about that, Mum."

"I know you do, pet. But we have to see it through or that Alan boy will be allowed to get away with it and do it again to some other girl who might not be so lucky next time."

"I don't care, I'm staying here."

"We can't run away from our responsibilities –"

"But isn't that what you did? You told me that you went to London as soon as you finished college because your mother was an alcoholic!"

Thalia was right. My father had stuck with his responsibilities and I had run. I was probably running away from Keith now. I was happier everyday at the prospect of his new family and the hope that he would leave Thalia and me alone.

I was back in my father's house and a burden on him when he needed help.

"It was different, Tally. Look, I don't want this boy to get away with what he did. That's all!"

Thalia nodded and suddenly I felt that everything was going to be okay. Until I thought of Michael and what had happened at the barracks.

Chapter 34

Michael was due to leave for the Middle East in a few days. We had spoken every day since we'd made love. My mind was in a haze. It was like I'd been given a strong drug that sent me into a state of delirium. It lasted days and even my father noticed the change in me. Suddenly my phone rang.

"Roz, it's me."

The sound of his voice made me feel like I was home. I wanted to see him. I hated that we had agreed not to see each other again before his flight. I felt cheated because this was the most love I had experienced for years.

"Hi, you." I couldn't think of anything else to say.

"It's such a nice day and I thought we might walk down that pier again if you're free?"

This wasn't what we had agreed but I didn't care. I wanted to see him so badly.

"Oh darn, I'm meant to meet Carole." I thought for a moment. "She won't mind if I change the day. I'll tell her that I can meet her tomorrow."

"Are you sure?"

"Yes. See you for lunch?"

"I'll be out at one if that's okay."

"I look forward to it," I said and held the phone to my chest after he hung up.

My father appeared out of the kitchen but his acute sense of hearing he had probably heard Michael's voice as well as our plans.

"Be careful," he whispered as he passed me by but continued on walking.

How could I be careful when I was playing with fire? He was expecting too much of me.

"Be careful," Carole said when I rang and told her that I couldn't meet her.

"That's exactly what my father said."

"You're a big girl and he's got his own conscience to live with, but I don't want to see either of you hurt."

"I know what you mean, Carole – it's just that he's going on tour soon and I might not see him again for a long time."

"Don't worry about me. I can meet you any morning. Just take care!"

I appreciated Carole's concern but I had to do what felt right. I trusted my gut more each day and I had felt safer and happier back home in Dublin than at any other time in my life. I wondered how much of it was being with my father and how much of it was my infatuation with Michael. I would know soon enough as Michael would be gone in a few days.

Thalia had arranged to meet Aoife and my father discreetly told me that he would go for a walk with Mary-next-door.

I fixed my hair and rolled some gloss on my lips before the doorbell rang.

As I opened the door I was met with a burst of glorious energy. The type my father had described in Oklahoma. I was enveloped in light and love and the simple act of walking into the kitchen with Michael filled my soul.

"Is Patrick here?"

I shook my head. "I'm home alone. My father and daughter have tactfully left."

"Oh dear. I feel bad about this."

I suddenly felt deflation. What was he going to tell me now?

"Would you like a cup of tea?" I asked lightly.

"Thanks, I will." He took a seat at the kitchen table while I put on the kettle.

I wanted to talk about something bright and easy. I didn't want a heavy conversation but I could intuitively feel a heart-to-heart coming on.

I filled our cups and put them down beside the milk and sugar. I'd prepared some wraps and left them in the middle of the table but could tell that neither of us had much of an appetite.

Michael moved about in a fidgety manner and wasn't his usual composed laid-back self.

"Roz, I've been in an awful wonderful mixed-up place since we last met and I have to be honest with you . . . I think I'm addicted to you."

Addicted! Was he for real? Addiction is a bad thing, a bad word. I was mad at him for using a word like that.

"That makes me sound like a drug," I said frivolously.

He took my hands in his to try and calm me down.

"That sounds wrong but addiction is the best word to explain the whirlwind of falling in love."

I knew then exactly what he meant.

"Please, Roz, I've been thinking about you non-stop and imagining our afternoon together. It was amazing to feel that kind of love again. It never happened like that before. That feeling of love is heaven on earth and we all yearn for it. I fear that we both would be drained of energy too quickly if we stayed together."

I had never felt such love before – why did he have to call it energy?

"So what are you trying to say?" I asked.

"I'm about to go away and I have a job to do. I won't do it properly if my head is full of you but there is nothing I can do about it."

"I'm sorry for messing up your plans," I huffed. This isn't what I wanted from this afternoon. I wanted love. I wanted more of what we'd shared in his barracks.

"It's not anyone's fault. It's unfortunate that I'm a priest but I forget how to be me when I'm with you. And I have to put my work first – it's what I've got to do."

I just stared at him coldly because I was hurt. He was taking away from me the one piece of happiness that I'd enjoyed for a very long time.

"Don't be angry with me, Roz. I'm telling you the truth. I'm hurting."

"And what about me? I have feelings too!" I said defensively. "You make it sound like it is all my fault and I have messed up your plans. I've messed up my own head too."

Michael nodded and closed his eyes. "I'm so sorry. I just wasn't ready for this. I was smugly in control of my emotions until you came along. I feel like I've been hit by a bus."

"That's exactly the way that I feel."

"Would it be easier if I just went?" he said.

I shook my head and he put his hand up to my face again, the way our other kisses had started before. This time when our lips locked it was so natural and right that I knew that he didn't believe a word that he had just told me. He was as consumed by me as I was by him and my intuition told me how love was meant to feel. I wanted him and missed him but still I felt him with me in everything that I did.

After he left we didn't speak again and the day for his departure came and went and I continued with my life and tried not to think about him all the time. It was futile. My father noticed the change in me and instinctively knew who was responsible for my maudlin mood.

"Michael is a lovely fella but you mustn't go from the frying pan into the fire," he warned.

He'd caught me unawares.

"Of course not, Dad – he's a Catholic priest."

"Ah, and so was Father Michael Cleary and Eamonn Casey was a bishop but it didn't stop them from messing with women's hearts."

"This is my problem with your stupid religion, Dad." I could feel my eyes well up and I regretted lashing out at him. It wasn't his fault.

"There's no perfect religion, my love. Maybe Michael should've been a Protestant vicar if he wanted to share his life with someone but I'm not so sure that he does. He's too big a character to spend his life with only one person."

And then I doubted my father's wisdom. I adored him but

he wasn't the Oracle and he didn't know what Michael and I had shared. Maybe we were caught up in the physicality and emotion of our relationship. To my father, Michael was in his perfect profession. Things Michael had said to me confirmed that, but I knew that he felt a deeper love when we shared our bodies and I couldn't forget it. Even if I was seeking something completely unobtainable, Michael hadn't said it but I could feel his love for me. How could I stifle a character that had so much to give the people whose lives he touched?

I gave my father a kiss on the cheek and we said no more on the subject.

Thalia and I were due to fly to Birmingham a couple of days later to pick up the rest of our stuff, the plan being to drive it back in my car. I had to deal with telling my boss our news and deciding what to do with our house. I put the wheels in motion to rent it on a yearly basis. I feared that Keith would want it back even though he had signed it over to me after the divorce. It was the most decent thing he had done in our years together. With house prices the way they were in the UK it was a solid investment and I wanted to keep it for Thalia in case she decided to continue her studies in Oxford one day. The current blip would pass with time and I knew that.

Without Michael in my life I was drawn back to the mundane world that I had inhabited for so long. The estate agent who would look after the rental of our house was waiting at the front door as the taxi dropped us home.

Mrs Higgins had left the house in good shape and I felt bad about letting her go. She had been a part of all our lives in Oxford but it was time to move on.

Keith was too busy to meet me but said that he would take Thalia to lunch before we left.

In some ways it was like I had never lived in this city at all.

~

I had left Thalia at Emma's house and didn't relish the thought of meeting Paula Stevens again.

If I ever got my hands on Alan Grant-Smith I wouldn't be responsible for what I'd do to him. But then I would be sent to prison in a heartbeat because I was not connected with the right people.

As my father came into my head, my phone began to ring.

"Rosaleen, how are you getting on?" I loved to hear my father's comforting voice, reassuring me from across the Irish Sea and over the Cotswold Hills.

"I'm okay but it's been a frustrating day."

"Pack up your car and *'Get the heck out of Dodge'!"* my father said.

He made me laugh for the first time since Michael left.

"I'll be back soon. I've found an incredible packing company that will take care of everything and leave the house in perfect order for the estate agents. I've been told that I'll get £2,500 per month in rent."

"Will that cover the mortgage for you?"

"Yes – and the costs – and it will leave me with some to put towards renting our own place in Dublin."

Suddenly silence at the end of the line and I knew that I should have warned him first.

"Dad? Are you okay?"

"Grand, love. I just thought you might stay with me but of course you will want your own space."

"Thanks, Dad, I knew you would understand." I felt bad but I couldn't stay with him any longer.

"Do you think you might stay in Skerries?"

"Of course we'll stay in Skerries. What's the point of being in Dublin and not being close to you?"

"Ah, that's great news altogether. It will make a big difference to me."

"I'm actually looking forward to the drive back. It will be a fresh start for Thalia too. We'll be like Thelma and Louise!"

"That's the spirit. Have you seen that eejit that you were married to yet?"

"No, and I don't think he wants to see me either."

"The poor girl who's lumbered with him now has no idea what she's let herself in for."

I didn't envy her. I was at peace with him and the marriage that was now finished.

Instead I was in a new drama with my gorgeous unobtainable man hundreds of miles away. He had sent me one message on Facebook and that was all that I needed. I knew that I was in his thoughts and he was firmly in mine. There was such a bond between us I was certain that I could feel it every time that he was thinking of me.

Whatever the reason we had for being in each other's lives, it would unfold with time. I was proud of myself for my logical thought on the affair. Maybe I had grown up over the course of my travels to Oklahoma. I'd definitely changed my thought processes.

There was one other thing that I had to do before I left Oxford.

My boss, Gerry, had been very good to me but I couldn't ask him to keep my job open any longer. However, there was one favour that I needed from him before handing in my notice.

I took the walk through the windy lanes that led to the office of the *Oxford Times*.

Gerry was a kind man and stood up warmly to greet me when he saw me. Once we'd embraced I was ready to present my request.

"I have written a piece about teenagers and sexual attacks," I said. "And I'd really appreciate it if you would publish it as an opinion feature."

I had used Thalia's scenario as a basis for the piece. It was highly sensitive to use her case and I'd used false names but maybe this would help other mothers to be aware of the risks involved and prevent an attack happening to someone else.

Gerry glanced over the sheet that I had handed to him.

"Send it to me by email and we will run it this week," he said, taking off his glasses and putting them down on his desk. "I'm sad that you're leaving, Roz. I looked over that travel piece again and it's really interesting. You should do more travel, you know. In fact, you can still send some my way and I'll publish it."

"Thanks, Gerry, maybe I will. I never thought of being a full-time travel writer but it would be nice to do more. I might write to you about travel to Ireland? For the moment though I need to be with my father and daughter."

"I understand. I will miss you around the place. Do you think you'll ever come back?"

I shook my head. "It's taken me so long to even consider moving back to Ireland but now I think it's somewhere that I need to be."

He gave me a warm hug and I realised that he was probably the only person in Oxford that I would miss.

"Take care, Roz."

"Thanks for everything, Gerry, especially for sending me to Oklahoma!"

As I walked down the narrow stairs and out on to the High Street, I realised that I wouldn't be going up those stairs again or at least for a very long time. It was the first sense of reality that hit me since I'd decided to leave. For an instant I could recall the days I had walked up and down those stairs carrying my sadness while I was in my unhappy marriage. I thought of all the time that I'd wasted trying to hold myself together. I was very much a changed woman since that day that I saw the dead bird on my doorstep and Gerry invited me to travel to Oklahoma.

Chapter 35

When we arrived back in Skerries my father was all business. He had been to see Séan Doherty the estate agent and found a place for Thalia and me to live, down by the harbour with a sea view. It was tiny, and expensive for what it was, but it was also spotless and newly decorated with all modern conveniences. Even without his eyesight my father had great vision and I applauded him. He'd made an appointment for us to see it the day after we returned to Dublin.

When we did go and see it, he stood proudly in the kitchen, pointing out the window at the pretty harbour view.

"I love it, Dad – thanks so much for putting down the deposit. I'm sure lots of people would snap this up."

"I had a feeling that it was just right and with a lovely view too. Not that I can see it, mind you. I did have a look at the website on the computer and saw boats and it has a parking space that should fit the Volvo."

"I think I'll trade my car in for something smaller anyway, Dad. What do I need a big car for? It's silly."

I meant what I said. My values had changed, I was on

retreat in my old country and would seek out new ways to be happy and satisfy my soul. Carole had set me up with a Reiki session and I'd agreed to go with her to a meditation class on Tuesday mornings.

Séan, the estate agent, came into the kitchen and seemed pleased with my reaction.

"So, are you happy to sign the lease today, Roz?" he asked.

"Yes, thanks, it really is lovely – and did you say the heating is gas?"

"Yes, gas, and the boiler has just been serviced so you shouldn't have any problems."

"When can we have the keys?"

"Tomorrow if you like?"

My father had found our new home so easily – it felt completely right to be living here.

"When something is meant to be the Good Lord will always provide," Dad said.

I didn't reply but there was a synergy about my move which did imply that I was meant to be living in Skerries. But if the stars were really in alignment then Michael wouldn't be so far away and he would not be in the priesthood.

Thalia pulled on her wine-coloured jumper and then her uniform was complete. There was a definite nip in the air, as if autumn had decided to come early to Dublin.

I watched her put her lunch into the back of her bag and handed her a bottle of water.

"Do you have everything that you need?" I asked.

"Yes, I'm fine now," she said with a nod.

But I could sense her anxiety.

"First days can be difficult, but at least you know Aoife."

Thalia nodded. She liked Carole's daughter.

"Ready to get in the car?"

"I'm all set, Mum!"

We drove to Thalia's new school – she would be getting the bus in future. Everything would be fine, I could tell. She smiled and gave me a peck on the cheek as she jumped out of the car and walked into the school.

I sat back and turned on the radio. Neil Young's 'Heart of Gold' blared from the speakers – a song that I hadn't heard since I was in Oklahoma. I'd found one but it was unfortunate that he was posted to a war zone near Syria and not near me.

I pulled my car into my small parking space. My father had said that he would call by for lunch and I had that to look forward to. At some stage I needed to find a job and get my act together if I hoped to support myself and my daughter on a permanent basis in Dublin.

The house smelled of lavender from the pots in the driveway and the small boxed garden out the back. The scent wafted in as I opened the door and made my way over to put the kettle on. My laptop was open on the kitchen table and I turned it on. I could start reaching out to some newspapers and try to find work, although from what Carole said all businesses seemed to be going online and a glut of journalists around the country were without work.

I poured myself a cup of tea as I browsed through the mail and went over to look at Facebook. The little red square was lit up. I opened the message. It was from Michael. He had been up for several hours and he'd sent me a message while I was taking Thalia to school.

I shook in anticipation as I read the words. He was thinking of me. I was thinking of him and had been for some time. His message was simple and he described where he was staying. He was safe considering how dangerous the area was and he had a prefab to himself – same as the other senior officers.

I read on . . .

We never know what's going to happen from one day to next. The group before us had to pull out as the rebels were fighting too close to the border. During the day the sound of gunfire becomes like background noise and we don't even notice it. Then at night sometimes I'm woken up by a loud mortar and I remember that I'm here. It's difficult being so close to the action and not able to do much to help. In the Lebanon we could help schools and communities – we built wells and did positive things. Here on the edge of Syria we're simply dressing the wounds of the refugees before they are sent to a camp. The camps are dismal places and full of women and children. Their men have either been killed or are fighting in Syria but a disturbing number leave their responsibilities behind and are desperate to start a new life in Europe without their dependants. It's a crazy war. Lately I've been thinking about what your father told me in Oklahoma. You were a clever kid when you said that there should be no more soldiers and then there would be no wars. If everyone laid down their arms, then there would be no more fighting.

The day after we arrived in Tel Aviv we had the afternoon off and I went to the beach with one of the other officers. There were two young girls lying near us in their bikinis, enjoying the sun. They went down to the water for a swim and when they came back they dried off and

changed into their clothes – army uniforms – and as they shook down their towels they revealed two heavy-duty rifles. They shook the sand off their weapons as if they were parasols and strolled off without a second glance.

It really is a twisted world when you go to a place like this. It makes Oklahoma seem like Leitrim! We've been told to expect the snows early this year which is terrible for those in the tents and camps. I feel blessed with my life – there are so many with lives torn apart.

I'll try call some evening.

I miss you, Roz – give my regards to Patrick.

Michael

I reread his message a few times and pondered my safe little world in Skerries.

Michael filled my head while I went to the supermarket. When I was finished I called on my father. He was in good form but said that he had nuisance calls from someone selling stuff from India who wanted his bank-account details.

He was well versed in what to do in such situations but I think boredom had led him to making a game out of nuisance calls. I think he enjoyed tormenting those on the other end of the line.

I mentioned Michael's message and then my father started to preach.

"I'm glad you get on so well with Michael. You need to have a man friend – but someone who will be your friend because they want to be with you and not for any other reason."

I felt terrible guilt because we both knew that there was

another reason why Michael was such a fixture in my mind and my life.

"He will be a good person to officiate at my funeral when my time comes."

I winced. "Don't say that, Dad. We both know you aren't going anywhere."

"I have to be realistic too, Rosaleen, and I'm not getting any younger."

"But don't talk about that."

"I'd like you to know my wishes," he continued, ignoring my pleas. "I heard a thing on the radio about wicker coffins – nice and biodegradable and much better for the planet."

"Sounds awful."

"What are you talking about, Rosaleen? It's the best idea I've heard in an age. I'm looking into getting one."

I couldn't listen to this – it was too upsetting. I stood up and made an excuse. It was nearly time to collect Thalia from school.

"I mean this, Rosaleen, and don't be upset. I also want Michael to be the celebrant – I seem to have outlived any other decent priests that I knew over the years."

"Okay, Dad, I'll remember that."

Then I stooped down to kiss him on the forehead and made my way out to my car. I knew that he was only being helpful in his matter-of-fact sort of way but I had only just reconnected with him since Oklahoma. I couldn't stand the thought of losing him.

I was early to pick up Thalia and waited in my car outside the wall of her school with the other mothers of fourth-year students. It was a nice place to go to school with rows of sycamore trees lining the driveway up to the main building. The treetops were starting to turn yellow on a couple of the trees and I felt so happy and relaxed inside. I couldn't remember the last time that I had felt so content in this way. Michael's email had moved me. His inspiring words would linger and help me through the impending winter months until I could see him again.

Chapter 36

Thalia was finished her first month in her new school before I realised how long we had been living in Dublin. The nights were drawing in and I was getting used to my new life.

I walked the pier most mornings and I'd even made friends with some other walkers. One man always walked with a plastic bag and pick-up tool, taking away the litter left by tourists. He said he did it because it made him feel good to give something back to his community. It was nice to talk to someone about ideas and philosophical notions. After a couple of weeks I found out his name was Jack. He was a writer too but of schoolbooks. I really looked forward to meeting him and it was pleasant to have some male company with no agenda other than enjoying a walk.

I wasn't having much luck finding a job. Everyone seemed to like my pitches but didn't want to pay me much for them. I realised that I would have to find some sort of work soon or I would run out of money fast. I'd made great savings by coming to Dublin. Thalia's school looked for a nominal voluntary contribution, whereas in Oxford the fees were £20,000 a year. Keith was happy about that as he said that he needed to set up a fund for his new baby when he arrived. Thalia hadn't expressed a desire to visit Oxford and I certainly didn't want to either.

We were happy with our simple life. We spent weekends with my father and Thalia had a good social life at the local youth club. Carole encouraged me to try some night courses. I tagged along with her to Pilates, under duress initially and then found myself really enjoying it.

I hadn't heard from Michael for some time and he hadn't phoned me. Then one evening out of the blue I heard a strange tinny tone from my phone. It was a Viber call.

I shook when I saw that it was him and ran my fingers through my hair which was ridiculous as he wasn't going to see me.

"Roz, hello . . ." His voice faded away and then returned again. "Roz?"

"Michael, hello, yes, I can hear you fine."

"Hey, that's great, I'm so pleased to get through to you. I lost my phone and had to get a replacement SIM and phone sent from Dublin. I had to wait until one of the lads was travelling back home to get it. How have you been?"

"I'm good, thanks."

"And Patrick? And Thalia?"

"He's well – they both are. Tell me what you've been up to."

"Everyday is hectic over here, Roz. It's a bit nerve-racking. We've been in a Code Red in camp since we've arrived. But I've been doing a good bit of travelling with the lads, taking them to the religious sites and they love it. We've been all over the Sea of Galilee and Nazareth and Jerusalem."

"Sounds lovely, it's got really cold here."

"It's cooled down a lot here too. It's October now but they told us to expect snow at the end of December this year."

"When will you be home?"

"I'm getting leave in about six weeks but I've no plans to go home. It's busy and all hands on deck. I might go to Thailand."

I felt my heart sink. Why didn't he want to come home and see me? Then I realised that I was craving energy from him. All the words that Martina and my father had said in the Paseo District came flooding back and I shook my indulgent thoughts from my head.

"Thailand must be beautiful this time of year," I said.

"It will be good to rest. I've seen some terrible things. And what about you, Roz? How's the job-hunting and how is Thalia settling into school?"

"Thalia couldn't be happier. She's made lots of friends."

"That's a relief."

"This has been a really good move for her. I haven't got a job yet but I'm hanging in there."

"So the media hype about things turning around in Ireland isn't exactly true?"

"Nah. There's an election looming. Dad has it all sussed. He said he's seen it dozens of times before and they are talking shite! He nearly threw the remote at the TV when they announced a €3 increase in his old age pension in the Budget last week."

"I'd like to have been a fly on the wall to see that. You know, Roz, when you see how the people live over here things at home seem comical. This war is a complete farce. Everyone is fighting each other. It's a proxy war and nobody can win this. I'd be worried that the destabilisation of Europe is the real endgame behind this mess."

"It does look like that."

"Think about it, Russia and America are at loggerheads again and flexing their muscles at each other. If Europe is busy looking after the refugees, they won't be one of the big world players."

"Oh, Michael, it's difficult to think about things like that."

"But do think about it, Roz. You have the time to write about this. You can't quote me but I can give you information. It might be the sort of juicy topic that will help you get a job."

He was talking sense. I did want to write real journalism.

"Okay. Tell me all that you can say," I said and took out my notepad.

I wrote notes as he spoke and told me what it was really like in the war zone. I felt inspiration bubble up inside me as I jotted down each word. This was something that really mattered to everyone and again my father's wise words resonated with me: *We are all part of the great We.*

"My father told me '*We are all connected*', "I said to Michael. "Sometimes I think I can feel you are thinking about me. Is that connected too?"

"You know it is. I miss you, Roz."

I clung to his words.

"I miss you too, Michael. It's good to have someone special."

"Our bond won't be broken, however far we are apart."

"Call me again."

"As soon as I can, I will."

When Michael hung up I was sad that we hadn't indulged in our feelings for each other a little more but that wasn't the message that Michael had for me this time. I went straight to my laptop and started to write down words.

I thought of *The Grapes of Wrath* and all that my father had said while we were in Oklahoma. I thought about all the greed and wealth division in the world today. I thought about my father's favourite quote from Hegel and the fact that the only thing we learn from history is that we don't learn from history. When the truth was unravelled in the schoolbooks in my grandchildren's generation what would I have done as I watched?

Michael was correct. I had an opportunity to print the truth. Most people didn't want to hear it but that didn't matter. I had to do something that mattered. I wrote until Thalia came home from school and was so motivated that I didn't want to stop to make the dinner.

My father called around and together the two of them made dinner while I stayed writing. I edited the article and edited some more and found that the words had a life of their own. I was so absorbed in my work I hardly noticed my father leave and my daughter get ready for bed. When I had finally finished, I read it a couple of times and saved it. I couldn't remember the last time that I'd felt such a sense of accomplishment.

The next day I met my father after Thalia left for school. We'd organised a walk down the pier and had wrapped up well to protect ourselves from the cold northerly wind.

When I told my father about my call from Michael and then the article, I thought his eyes filled up.

"That's the best news you could have told me," he said. "Now send that around and get it published and if it gets people talking then you will have something good for your CV. But what matters the most is the fact that you've written something that will make a difference." He paused and looked proudly at me and it was as if he could see clearly. "It's important to make a difference. This is how you will feel better about yourself, Rosaleen."

I finally understood all the wisdom that he had imparted to me while we were in Oklahoma. I was part of the great *We* – we all were.

We hugged the shoreline and I described the smouldering grey and blue hues of the north Dublin coast to him. My father pointed out the sounds that I was missing along the way and the sound of the gulls squawking overhead.

I felt completely at one with him and reminisced about the time we had spent in Oklahoma.

"That really was the most wonderful experience of my life," he said.

I agreed that it was the most special trip.

We arrived back at his maisonette all too soon. I wanted the walk to last forever. He hugged me and then he released me.

"You have lots to do with your day, I'm sure?"

"I suppose I could send the article off?"

"You do that," he said and nodded.

"Will you come over for dinner tonight?"

He shook his head. "Not tonight. Stay safe and happy." Then he kissed me on the forehead and went into the house.

I felt a shiver when he walked away. I dropped into the local grocer's and bought some vegetables for a curry. I had an uneasy feeling until I got to the door of my little house and there it was: a tiny bluebird dead in the doorway.

I smiled because it was like my story had come full circle. I didn't feel the usual dread because I was home and with my father now, in the place that I was meant to be. I went into my kitchen and poured myself a cup of green tea. Then I went back to my laptop and wrote a couple of emails to the *Sunday Times* and the *Business Post*. I hadn't contacted those newspapers before. But the words I had written the previous day were powerful and filled with Michael's truth and my father's truth and also mine.

I attached the article and pressed send and then went to my room to lie down.

I woke to the sound of the front door slamming. I looked over at the clock beside my bed and realised that I had been asleep for three hours. It was the most glorious sleep and I felt refreshed in every cell of my body.

"*Thalia, is that you?*"

"*Yes, Mum. What are you doing?*" she called up to me.

"*I lay down for an hour and fell asleep. Did you call in to see Granddad?*"

"I knocked on the door but he wasn't there so I came home."

That wasn't like him. I went downstairs to my daughter and took her coat and made her a sandwich.

"Give Granddad a call and see if he's okay," I said as I made some tea.

She did as I asked and I heard her voice in the next room.

"Grandad, hi. I did call around – didn't you hear me knock?"

A pause.

"Okay, then I'll come and see you tomorrow."

Thalia came into the kitchen and plonked down on a chair. "He said that he fell asleep and didn't hear me call."

"That's grand then. How was your day, sweetie?"

"Really good. We're having a dance-off next week during lunchtime . . . and I didn't get much homework."

I put some tea down on the table as Thalia started to devour the sandwich I had made her.

"Are you settling in well?"

She looked at me wisely. "You don't have to keep asking me and checking up on me, Mum. I'll tell you if I'm not happy. So far it's going really well."

"I'm relieved. I just want to do the right thing."

"Have you heard back from any of the newspapers?"

I shook my head. I'd been asleep for most of the afternoon. "Actually, I'll check my email."

I picked up my phone. There was a message from the *Sunday Times*. I braced myself for a polite rejection. Many of the editors hadn't the manners to even reply to my pitches so I felt some sort of gratification. But it wasn't a rejection. It was applause for my clear and concise writing style and powerful message. Included were details of payment and invoice submission. I'd sold my first piece in Ireland and I had Michael to thank for it. I wanted to punch the air.

I looked over at my daughter and smiled. "The *Sunday Times* is going to publish my article."

"Great! How much are they going to pay you, Mum?"

"Two hundred and fifty euros. It's about the going rate at

the moment, so I've been told, but maybe if I get one a week it would be a good start."

Thalia got up and went over to hug me.

"Well done, Mum."

As she wrapped her arms around me I felt so loved. It was sweeter knowing that Michael had inspired me. He was helping those at the coalface of the Syrian War and maybe I was doing my little bit in the only way that I could.

Chapter 37

My weekly piece in the *Sunday Times* couldn't be called a salary by any means but it was a start. I sent Michael a message on Facebook about the article and he was thrilled and wrote more snippets to me as the weeks flew by. He would be going to Thailand soon and I was getting some work from Gerry in Oxford which meant that I had to organise my writing time for straight after my walks each morning. My father wasn't always up early so I usually met him for a bite of lunch or he came around for dinner.

One evening, when Thalia was staying at a friend's, he asked if I could come to have dinner in his house. It was nice to take a break from cooking and I wanted to chat about other things with him. I'd noticed that the winter was a difficult time for him and older people. The weather had an impact on his bones and his mood was affected by the bareness of the trees and smell of decay in the air.

"You know, Rosaleen, I've not been feeling great this last couple of weeks."

This was news to me because he had never complained. "In what way? Have you been to see the doctor about it?"

"No, I haven't because it's difficult to put into words what's wrong. I feel uneasy in my gut."

"Maybe you have an ulcer?"

"It's not really a physical pain. It's more a gnawing inside of me. I noticed it first that lovely day when we went for the long walk a few weeks back. I had a long sleep that afternoon and I felt strange when I woke up."

"How did you feel strange?"

"I had a kind of dream that my mother was in the room. I could sense her, smell her. It was as if time stood still and I wasn't on this earth. I felt myself hover over my body for about thirty seconds and then I heard voices whispering in my ears."

"It must have been a dream."

He shook his head vehemently. "I might have been in a half-sleep but I was definitely in awaking trance."

"What did the voices say?"

"They were loud, like speaking on a tannoy at a train station, and there were several of them."

A year ago I'd have dismissed him as crazy but now I was more willing to listen to alternate suggestions of this universe that we occupied and how little we truly understood it. I was certain that our dream world and spiritual state had real substance. Michael and my father had helped me to see that.

"What happened then?"

"I heard the doorbell and that must have been Thalia calling around. Then a powerful vacuum sucked a pile of energy from my stomach and I was wide awake."

"Maybe you should go to the doctor?"

"I think it's a priest I need. I might go to Confession. It will be the first Friday soon."

I laughed. "What on earth would you need to tell in Confession, Dad? You are goodness itself!"

"I just think it will help. It's a pity I won't be seeing Michael again."

Now he was starting to freak me out. "He'll be home in three months – of course you'll see him again."

My father just nodded. We ate the fish pie that he had made and he spoke fondly about the people we'd met in Oklahoma. I had a strange feeling that he was giving me a crash course in his philosophy before I left. He kissed me on the forehead as I got up to leave, the way that he used to always kiss me as a child.

"Sleep well, Rosaleen, my love."

All this talk of death was so unnecessary. He was in fine health and I hadn't moved back to Dublin so that he could go and leave me.

My father rang me the next morning in buoyant mood.

"How did you sleep?" I asked.

"Very well," he said."But I got a lovely surprise this morning. Michael called me on Skype."

I was instantly jealous and cross with myself for being this way. He was entitled to call my father but I would have loved to hear his voice.

"What did he say?"

"He told me about his work and all the places he'd been. I'm so pleased that he rang me."

"How did he have your Skype name?"

"I sent him an email and asked him to call."

This was very bizarre but my father was an adult and entitled to his own conversations with Michael. I had a short message from Michael only the day before on Facebook.

"Why did you do that?"

"I wanted to chat to him about a job that I need him to do."

I hated it when my father was cryptic like this. It usually meant that he was trying to protect me from something. I was a grown woman who'd been through enough life experience to handle whatever troubled or irked him.

"He's going to Thailand at the end of the week."

"Yes, he said that. Michael also said that his chats with you are helping him a lot."

"What else did he say?"

"Eh . . . he said that you did great with your article and stuff like that."

I couldn't figure out what he was keeping from me but he certainly had a hidden agenda for the call.

"Do you want to do something today? I've got to go to the Pavilion Shopping Centre – do you want to come?" I thought the jaunt would occupy him.

"No thanks, Rosaleen. You know how I don't like those shopping places – too many trolleys and buggies."

"Alright then – will you come around for dinner this evening?"

"That would be grand. I think I'll make a bit of brown bread first."

"Oh lovely," I said.

When he put down the phone I dressed in my comfortable clothes for my walk down the pier.

The sky was a creamy grey twinged with pink and the sea a snotty green. I recognised Jack's figure in the distance, with his little white Scottie dog by his side, and his black plastic bag in his hand, ready to gather the rubbish. The air was crisp and calm but bitterly cold, in contrast to the time I'd walked the pier with Michael. Sometimes I'd picture him there when I saw Jack. A friendly companion, but Michael was much more than that.

"Hello, Roz, I haven't seen you the last couple of days."

"Hi, Jack. I've been writing opinion pieces for the *Sunday Times* actually and I have to start when the mood takes me."

Jack nodded sympathetically. "I know that feeling. Sometimes after walking I go home and my mind is blank after being down here and I can't write a thing."

Jack's little dog Snowy jumped up against my shin and wagged his tail frantically. I leaned forward and petted the little animal who loved this morning ritual with his master.

"Aren't we so lucky to live in such a beautiful place, Jack?"

"I never tire of it. Think of all the people in office blocks in the city now with fluorescent lights blinding them and noisy traffic outside the window. I wouldn't swap my life with anybody."

Jack was right. There was a good quality of life to be enjoyed in this corner of the world. Jack and I shared a privilege while walking the pier most days, one that the majority of people in fulltime employment couldn't appreciate.

"I'm thinking of writing a book," I said. "Now that I've got my mojo back and I'm writing with a newspaper I feel I might tackle that novel that's been niggling at me since I was in college."

"What do you want to write about?"

"Something about mothers and daughters maybe – I didn't have a great relationship with my own mother for several reasons but family is a good place to start."

"Exactly, you could be the next Anne Enright."

I heaved a sigh. "Irish families are complex and do lend themselves to twisted characters and plots."

"From what I can see all families are complex, Roz. Every generation has its issues and every gender in it. I think you should write it. It will be cathartic at the very least."

I nodded in agreement. "Did you ever want to write a novel?"

"I would like to write about history or something factual. It's difficult to find the time when I've so many commissions for the language books and they pay the bills. I'll see how it goes."

I strolled with Jack for a while longer but he was taking the long route. After I left him I walked back to my house via the pier and stopped at the spot where I'd kissed Michael in the summer. I closed my eyes and tried to imagine him standing beside me. It was strange because, as I took a deep breath in, I could almost imagine the scent of his skin close to mine.

It was a foolish pipe dream to imagine having a relationship with him. Would I be willing to play second fiddle to his Church? It would be a thwarted relationship and a disrespect of his vows.

Michael had changed me. He'd helped me to find my voice and my father had given me the guidance to have something worth writing about. I felt a strong shift in my thoughts about myself and the world was now a positive place full of possibilities.

When I returned to my house I sat down and started to write a few words with relish. They were meant to be about my mother but funnily enough they were about my father. He was my guide and I let the words flow. They came so easily I didn't notice the time race by and only realised at two o'clock that I hadn't stopped for lunch. I wasn't hungry. I was being filled with sentences from somewhere out at sea and they were rushing through me and into the laptop.

My description of my father's young life, the time that my editor Gerry asked me to go to Oklahoma, scenes were playing in front of my eyes and I was dictating them all down. This wasn't a piece of fiction that I was trying to write, this was autobiographical, and I didn't want it to stop. As I came to the part about taking the horses out to the range with my father I heard the front door open. I glanced at the clock and was surprised to see that it was four o'clock already and Thalia was home.

With lightness in my step I rushed downstairs and hugged my daughter tightly.

"Hey, Mum, I'm pleased to see you too – what was that for?"

"Do I need an excuse to hug my daughter? I'm just so happy, Thalia. I've had the most wonderful day and I've started to write a book."

She smiled at me. For a moment it was like I was the child and she was the proud parent.

"Good for you, Mum. I'm so pleased that you're happy. I haven't seen you smile like this since Michael was around this summer."

She grinned at me cheekily and I blushed.

"I'll start the dinner. Granddad is coming over."

"Good, I'll do my homework now then."

I peeled the potatoes with a renewed sense of accomplishment. I was mindful of taking the vegetables out of the fridge. Feelings of a new life woke inside me and I couldn't explain it but emotionally I was on a high."

I put the hotpot of root vegetables into the oven and poured myself a cup of tea. It had been a wonderful day and one that I would never forget. I didn't realise then that that was not the reason why I would never forget that day.

Chapter 38

"What time is it?" I asked Thalia.

"It's twenty past six."

"Granddad should be here. Give him a call, will you? He's never late."

I set the table and, when Thalia said that my father hadn't answered either his mobile phone or the landline, I thought it strange.

"Will you finish off here? He might have fallen asleep. I'll go get him."

I jumped into my car and drove to his house. It was strange that the lights weren't on inside as night was creeping in.

I put the key in the front door and pushed it open.

"*Dad, are you there?*" I called to him.

The faint smell of freshly baked bread lingered in the air so I went into the kitchen. Resting on a grill were two loaves of brown bread. I touched them; they were now cold. I turned on the lights upstairs and climbed the stairs to my father's bedroom. He lay asleep on the bed. I smiled as I looked at him, so peaceful and relaxed. He wore a grin on his face and I wondered if he was dreaming about Oklahoma.

I sat down on the edge of the bed and turned on the lamp so that the light shone directly on his face. His skin appeared clear and almost translucent like an angel, without a wrinkle around his eyes or on his forehead. He was particularly still and I put my hand on his chest but that too was still.

Suddenly I realised the dread reality. I put my hand on his face and it was stone-cold. I couldn't bear to think the impossible – not right now, not like this. I put my hand over his mouth and my worst nightmare was confirmed: he wasn't breathing.

I started to shake and sob and threw myself onto his chest but still he didn't move. I didn't know what to think, or to do or who to call. All I could do was sob while I clung to his chest. I'm not sure how long I lay there because my sobbing was interrupted by a knock on the front door. My mind was in a haze and eyes flooded with tears as I went downstairs and opened the door.

Mary-next-door stood there and I fell into her arms.

"What's after happening? Is everything alright with your father, love?"

Sobbing into her shoulder, I said, "He's dead."

"Oh, dear sweet divine Jesus!" she said and clung to me tightly. "What happened?"

"I don't know. There's bread made downstairs and it looks like he went to take a nap and didn't wake up."

"Oh dear God! Should we ring an ambulance?"

I nodded. I didn't know what to do. We went upstairs and Mary confirmed that he was gone.

We went downstairs and Mary sat me down at the

kitchen table while she rang the emergency services. When that was done she came over, sat and put her arm around me.

"We've been looking after each other for years now and it was our job every evening at half past six to check that we were both still alive. I never thought that he would go first."

I couldn't answer her – my mouth was dry and my voice had disappeared.

"What about your little girl?" Mary-next-door asked.

"Oh dear God, Thalia, I'll have to go home to her. I don't know what to do."

"Let's ring your friend Carole."

It was a huge relief to have Mary there. She took my phone, called Carole and asked her to go to my house to get Thalia.

Mary took my hand and guided me up the stairs. In the bedroom she took Rosary beads from her pocket and handed them to me.

"Will I start?" she said, as she knelt down at the side of the bed with her clasped hands resting on my father's arm.

I nodded.

She began with the Glorious Mysteries and I recited the answer to the Hail Marys after her. It was automatic and seemed like the right thing to do. At this moment in time all my thoughts about the Catholic Church didn't matter. This is what my father would have wanted. I was in a daze and repeating the words of the prayers steadied me – until Carole came to the house with Thalia.

Poor Thalia was devastated when she saw her grandfather, still and cold on the bed.

I put my arms around her and hushed her calm.

"Thanks for coming, Carole," I said.

"Of course, sure I'm only down the road. Is there anything I can do?"

I shrugged. "I don't know what you're supposed to do at times like this."

"The paramedic will come soon and declare him dead and then we can keep him here or he can go to the hospital," Mary informed us. "Would you like me to call Father Hurley?"

"I hadn't thought of that – yes, of course." My mind was very clear about what Daddy would have wanted. He had a firm belief in his Church and I had to do things his way. "I'll stay with him."

"I'll go and call Father Hurley – it's such a pity that lovely young priest isn't around," Mary-next-door said. "What was his name?"

"Michael," I said.

There was so much to do that I just didn't know where to start and I was still in a horrible state of shock. For now I had to ring Evan and in the morning I would call Michael.

I lay awake for most of that night. Thalia slept in the bed beside me in my father's house and I was happy to hear her breathe evenly in her sleep.

Life had a cruel way of throwing a curve ball when it was least expected. My father had such good health that the paramedic couldn't give a cause of death; all he said was that he had died of natural causes. To die in your sleep was a blessing in my father's eyes and I couldn't fault the way it had happened for him. He didn't have to endure some lengthy disease like many of his peers. He had been well enough to bake bread only a few hours before.

I realised that I hadn't had any dinner so I went downstairs and cut myself a slice. I put a thin layer of butter on top
and ate it carefully. It was delicious. I felt emotions well up
inside me as I realised that I would never get to eat his brown
bread ever again. I hadn't asked him for the recipe so I
couldn't even make it. He always said that his mother handed
it down to him and now nobody would be able to keep up the
tradition.

I longed for Evan to be present to shoulder some of this
burden. Mary-next-door rang the undertakers before she left
and they would be here in the morning to dress him. There
was nothing else that I could do.

I decided to go up and lie with him a while and talk to
him. If there was an afterlife then he would hear me. I climbed
the stairs carefully so as not to wake Thalia.

The lamp was on in my father's room and for some
unknown reason I thought it best to light a candle. My father
always had a torch and a lighter and nightlight beside his bed
in case of a power cut. It was one of those things that he
always did. Since his sight had left him he found it easier to
see in candlelight. I remembered him telling me about the
butt of a candle that he used to see his way to bed as a child
and how he would try make it last a little bit longer so that he
could read a few words before going to sleep.

He'd seen so much change over the decades and lived
through so many different milestones. All that wisdom and
knowledge would pass now with him to the other side, wherever that was. I wanted to believe that there was another side.
Death didn't impact me this way when my mother died but
Daddy was different, I wanted him here with me so badly I
needed to believe that he hadn't vanished into thin air.

I looked at the mark that Father Hurley had left on my

father's forehead with the ashes and the smell of incense still filled the room. I had felt a whoosh sweep by me as Father Hurley said his final blessing and I wondered if that was when my father's soul had left the room.

"I will write down everything that you taught me, Daddy," I said. "I started today. I probably started as you were taking your final breath. I'm so sorry that you were alone and that it happened now. We didn't even get to spend Christmas together for the last time."

I stopped speaking out loud because I was welling up again and the tears were my only source of comfort.

Evan called me at ten o'clock the next morning and was full of apologies.

"I tried to get an earlier flight but honestly, Roz, it's going to be Saturday before I get there."

"Don't tell me that with so many airlines and options it's going to take you four days to get here!"

I could hear his sharp intake of breath at the other end of the line.

"It's an interview and I have to take it on Thursday, I don't have a choice."

"But you do have a choice," I replied adamantly. "Our whole life is a series of choices." I was speaking with my father's voice now.

"Please, can you put it off until Saturday morning? I'll probably make it for Friday night."

I was the one being left with no choice. I didn't want Daddy going to a funeral home so I would stay and hold vigil with him. I realised how difficult it would be when my time came and my hope was that Thalia would be fortunate enough to have a good man at her side by then.

"Okay, Evan. See you when you get here."

"Thanks, Roz."

When he hung up I knew who I really wanted to talk to and I wondered if he would have WiFi. I went first to my Facebook and sent him a brief message.

Michael, can you give me a call if you get a chance. I know it's difficult for you but I would like to ask your advice about Daddy.

   Best Roz x

I went in to see my father. I wanted to wash him but Mary advised me against it. She told me to leave it to the undertakers. I sat for a while beside him, stroking his cold lifeless hand. It was like he wasn't my father anymore, just a body that had once had life in it. But I could feel him all around me. Something niggled at me to open the drawer beside his bed. It was like a voice telling me that I had to see what was there. I slowly pulled it open and sticking out was a white envelope with my name on it. Across the bottom was written *'To be opened in the event of my death'*. It wasn't a new envelope; it looked like it was written some time ago. I peeled it open, careful not to rip it. Inside were three pages of parchment paper, filled with instructions written carefully in my father's hand. It must have been written before his eyesight deteriorated too badly. My eyes welled up as I went through each paragraph. He sang the praises of all of his family and the people that he had shared his life with. He was clear that he wanted to be buried in the home plot in Inniskeen and he had even written down the songs that he wanted played and the readings at the Funeral Mass.

I felt a kind of solace with the instructions. I read on to the end and spotted an addendum written in black marker in his now familiar large font that he used since his eyesight faded.

I WOULD LIKE TO BE BURIED IN MY OKLAHOMA CLOTHES AND WEARING MY HAT AND MY COWBOY BOOTS. AND IF POSSIBLE IN A WICKER COFFIN. THANK YOU.
PATRICK CULLEN

The last part read like a note to Santa Clause that Thalia would have written when she was small. It was so sweet and yet so like him. I smiled to myself and pictured him looking down on me.

This process would help me to say goodbye to him properly in the way that he wanted. Suddenly my phone rang. It was a foreign number and I was overwhelmed by the possibility that it was Michael.

"Hello, Roz?"

"Michael, oh thanks for getting back to me!" I started to cry with relief on hearing his voice.

"Roz, are you okay?"

"It's Daddy, he's dead."

"But I was only talking to him the other morning . . . how did it happen?"

"I asked him around for dinner yesterday and when he didn't arrive I called over to his house and he was lying there on the bed. He must have gone for a nap and didn't wake up."

"That's incredible, Roz. Was he ill and hadn't told you?"

"Not that I know of – he'd mentioned a sensation in his stomach but said he didn't need to see a doctor, that it wasn't actually a pain."

"He asked me to give him the Last Rites over Skype. I'll admit that I found it a bit odd but he must have felt that he was going to die."

I knew that my father liked to take control of things but to time his death sounded a bit exceptional. "I don't know . . . the paramedics said he died of natural causes."

"It's exactly the way Patrick would have liked to go. I know that's not much consolation at this time but it might be in the future."

I knew that Michael was right but now I felt hopeless and sad. "I wish you were here."

"I'll come over – when is the funeral?"

"It's not until Saturday because my brother has an interview that's more important than my father's funeral."

"Don't be cross with your brother – it might be helpful for me because I'm not officially on leave until Friday."

"Aren't you going to Thailand?"

"Roz, Thailand isn't going anywhere. You're my priority."

I didn't say anything else. My father only had one sister still living and she was in Inniskeen. He had outlived all his other siblings. There were a couple of cousins that I would like to see at the funeral but I didn't think that it would be a big affair. At least if Michael conducted the ceremony I could make sure that all my father's wishes were carried out properly.

Chapter 39

Thursday arrived and the previous two days had been the longest of my life. Keith didn't ask if he could come to the funeral and I told Thalia that it was better anyway that he didn't. She had come to terms with the fact that her father had his own life and she wasn't going to be a big part of it anymore. It saddened me to hear her say that the only reason he ever wanted to see her was to make life awkward for me. I was delighted that I didn't need or want his shadow hanging over the proceedings. I had moved on and had my father to thank for it.

I'd put the news of Daddy's death in RIP.ie and the *Irish Times* and sorted out the administration. Thalia made a beautiful card with a picture of him on his horse in Oklahoma on the front. She printed a bunch of copies and said that she would leave them around the church. I didn't think that she needed to print too many because I had no idea how many would turn up to the funeral.

But, over the course of preparations, I began getting calls

from people that I never knew and had never heard my father mention.

He was obviously more of a celebrity in the town of Skerries than I had realised. People were coming out of the woodwork with cakes and cards and flowers and I felt a little strange about the whole proceedings. I had put in the paper that he would be reposing at home on the Thursday evening and that was when I started to meet the people who had encountered Patrick Cullen. Some hadn't seen him for years but were visibly upset to hear of his passing. Each of them had a story of some way that he'd helped them, either with a piece of good advice or putting his neck on the line to help with a contact to bring them to where they needed to go in their life. The neighbours hailed him, thanking him for taking in their bins when they were at work. My father was a veritable hero according to those who called and they said that he always wore a smile.

My father lay in the front room downstairs dressed in his cowboy gear like a waxwork Clint Eastwood.

I was overwhelmed and the feeling of love from each of the callers helped to confirm to me that my father had lived a rich and full life. He had constantly striven to do his best. He must have been so burdened with me the past few months and I hadn't realised it. I probably drew the last bit of energy that he had left in him. As the final callers got their coats and left, I went into the kitchen to help Thalia tidy up the mess.

Then the doorbell rang and I wondered who would be calling this late.

I dried my hands in a towel and went out to the door. There he stood in full uniform and looking more the picture of manhood than I remembered. I flung my arms around his neck and snuggled my head into his shoulder. In turn he held me tightly around the waist and our souls merged into one.

"Thank you so much for coming," I sobbed. "I'm so relieved that you are here."

Michael kissed my forehead the way my father used to always do and the same way that he had the last time we'd been together.

"This is what I'm here for, this is my job, and it's what I do."

And I let out a sigh and buried my head in his shoulder again as the tears rolled down my cheeks. I didn't want to speak and he seemed to know exactly what I needed. We slid upstairs to the empty spare room and lay down on the bed. He put his arm around me and indulged my sorrow. I wasn't alone. I had a man that really cared about me. It wasn't about sex – that isn't what love is about. Michael would show me how true love copes with loss and grief and how my worst fear would be made bearable while he held me.

Next morning, after I'd given Michael something to eat and while Thalia went home to get some fresh clothes, we were ready to speak.

"Patrick timed it all so perfectly. I mightn't have been able to get here if I was already in Thailand," Michael said.

"I know, it's like he had planned the whole thing. He'd written a letter and left it in the drawer beside the bed and he'd even had a conversation with me a week ago about wicker coffins. He had it all worked out."

"I got quite a shock when he asked me for the Last Rites, I wouldn't normally do it via Skype but he seemed to want me to bless him so I went ahead and did it. It isn't unheard of though – some people just know when they are going to die."

Michael turned to me and put his hand up to my face the same way as he had in the past.

"I'm so sorry, I really liked Patrick."

I nodded. "Thank you for being here."

"This is what I do, Roz. This is me at work. My life is about helping people on their journey and this is the toughest journey that anyone has to take. The death of a family member is traumatic and I'm so sad that you were just beginning to enjoy spending time with him before this happened."

"I didn't think the Church mattered to me but the last couple of days have been all about the Church. I've been getting music ready and proceedings for his funeral. I realise that if he didn't have a funeral I'd be lost."

Michael understood. But he'd always understood the importance of his role in the people's lives that he touched. He just happened to touch mine in a deeper way.

"And that's what the Church is really about, not the hierarchy or dogma," he said, brushing his palm gently along my cheek."It's a place to mark the important milestones in our lives. There is none more sacred than coming into the world as a new life or leaving it with a life lived."

"I think I get it. Funny but when Mary called by the other night, the first thing we did was say a decade of the Rosary."

"And that was exactly what Patrick would have wanted. You're doing it all the way that it is planned to have a happy death and that is what Patrick had."

"Sure, he even left some brown bread for us."

It was true. He'd lived his life well and made a spectacular death, if there was such a thing.

"Last night I came here straight from the airport so do you think I could take a shower?"

"Sure," I said and stood up to lead him upstairs.

Slowly we took each step together in perfect time.

We were alone again. Daddy's body was reposing in the living room but the tension was evident between us. I needed a release and it had been months since I'd shared my body with his. We stood at the bathroom door and paused. Our faces close enough to feel each other's breath and enjoy the warmth of desire between us. We couldn't deny each other, this was meant to be.

"This is completely wrong, you know?" he said.

I shook my head. I didn't agree. He leaned forward and kissed me. I was back where I wanted to be and is this instant the pain of my loss was lifted. We made love for an hour and when we were finished I no longer felt lonely or sad. I'd lost my rock, my father, but found my rock in Michael. I didn't want to share him with God anymore and he looked at me with eyes that said he would love me forever.

Evan arrived at six o'clock on Friday night and Michael had gone back to the barracks for the evening. It was our last night with Daddy and I was relieved that Evan was finally home. I didn't feel so alone and Michael had worked out all the details for the ceremony the following morning.

Daddy was lying in his coffin now and we had left it open so that Evan could see him one last time. My brother was taller than my father and as he aged he was starting to look like Clint Eastwood too, but with a thinning fringe and receding forehead.

"It's hard to believe that he's gone." He leaned over Dad and whispered something that I couldn't hear. Then he straightened up and examined the coffin. "What is this thing?"

"It's a wicker coffin – Daddy's instructions."

Evan shook his head. "He really was quite an exceptional man. I could never understand the way his mind worked. I think I became a more conservative person as I grew up because of his eccentricities."

"I think Daddy would say that you became the person that you needed to be in the big scheme of the great 'We'."

"The great what?"

"Daddy spoke to me about a lot of things while we were in Oklahoma. He gave me a crash course in his philosophies on life. He said that we each had to realise that we are part of the great 'We' and whatever we do it has a knock-on impact on others."

Evan looked down at my father and then back at me.

"I don't think I ever will get his philosophy now," he sighed. "I'm not looking forward to tomorrow either. I haven't been in a church since I was last in Ireland and that has to be when Mammy was buried."

"Funny but I would have felt the same about the Church before I went away with him. I realise now the importance it has in society. I was even more secular than you when I lived in Oxford but I honestly can say I didn't understand what it was about."

Evan turned to me, shocked. "What? You! You were always giving out yards about the oppressive and tyrannical Catholic Church."

"Well, maybe Daddy has helped me to see it differently. Let's face it, Evan – isn't it nice to be able to bring Daddy somewhere peaceful to celebrate his life and to say goodbye?"

"They're doing it for the money. I bet it's going to cost a fortune."

I shook my head. "That's not what it's all about. I've spoken with priests too and I think I know what they do a little bit better –"

"Don't tell me you've become some Holy Joe!"

I was astonished by what I was saying but for Daddy's sake and my own I had to continue. "Maybe I've learnt a little bit of tolerance. There's no perfect religion and practising one of the religions doesn't mean that you have to be against the others. I'm not a practising Catholic and I don't agree with much of the rules and doctrines of this Church but it was Daddy's choice and I'm glad that we have it for tomorrow."

Evan seemed to understand. Or maybe he just didn't want to discuss it with me anymore.

"So what time are we going to the church?"

"The hearse is coming to collect Daddy at ten fifty. We will follow in a car – you, me and Thalia."

"Okey-dokey, I'm going to get some sleep. See you in the morning."

Evan went into the front room to sleep on the couch where Michael had slept the night before. My brother had no trace of my father in his manner or his personality. But I was happy he was here.

Chapter 40

Michael walked up the aisle carrying a smoking censer that oozed incense. With each serious step that he took he became more removed from the man that I'd met in Chicago Airport or in Oklahoma and he wasn't like the man I'd made love to the day before either. His vestments clothed and protected his body from my secret perceptions and I watched him as an envoy of Christ taking my father home.

One of the ladies from the local choir sang 'Pie Jesu' and I heard sobbing around the church. Even my wonderfully composed daughter broke down as she watched her grandfather's coffin shrouded in incense.

A Catholic funeral is an event to meet and rejoice over a person's life. I was overcome with pride at such crowds filling the church. People continued to pop up out of nowhere and tell me things about my father and it came as a great comfort to me. Thalia had been right to print more cards and if she had printed twice as many it still wouldn't have been enough. There were people standing in the aisles who couldn't get a seat. It was good that the funeral was held on a Saturday because people who worked nine-to-five could make it. Everything was slotting into place and I was watching like an observer from the outside.

I was so relieved when Michael said that he would like to speak about Daddy though I couldn't focus properly on his words. It meant that there was a little bit less for me to say. I was feeling emotional about standing at the pulpit and talking to strangers but Daddy would want me to send him off with a eulogy, rather than his son who he had drifted from so long ago.

I almost missed my cue from Michael to come up to the altar. Thalia went first and read a beautiful prayer to her grandfather, Evan had read the second reading and I was shaking as my turn came. I had never wanted to do this but it would be closure for Daddy and in the days and months to come it would be for me.

When I reached the pulpit Michael came over and adjusted the microphone so that it was at the correct level to my mouth. He held my arm firmly in a gesture of support and I suddenly felt stronger.

I started and, although I felt my voice quiver, I was ready for this.

"I'd like to thank you all for coming today to help us to say goodbye to our dear father and grandfather. I've been overwhelmed for the last couple of days by the good wishes that we have received from those of you whose lives he touched. I always knew that he was a character but I didn't realise all that he was getting up to in Dublin while I was living in Oxford. I'm blessed to have had the last few months in his company and I've learned so much from him in this time. It is only when something is taken from us that we can understand what we had. My father was a sage, full of wisdom about the best way to do something and get what was needed. He marvelled in new inventions and took great delight in success of any sort. He was a positive person and from the stories that some of you have told me over the last few days he was a general Mr Fixit. I'm proud that he was my father and lucky to have spent time with him in America recently, where we visited the Heartland. He was a country man and he never let anyone forget that. He was happiest in nature and around animals and little people. He knew the true enjoyment of the simple things in life. It's only now that I'm beginning to understand what a heartland is and although you are gone, Daddy, I know that you'll always remain in my heart and the heart of everyone's who you touched. Thank you."

I didn't hear the clapping – it was only afterwards when Michael told me that the congregation applauded that I realised I must have said the right words.

The final journey, out to the car, I spent in a daze. Michael sat with me and Evan and Thalia as we went to the local hotel to meet people and eat soup and sandwiches. We would be going on our journey to Inniskeen in a couple of hours because the nights were now drawing in and we had to bury him before it was dark.

I can hardly recall the people I spoke to or the things they said. I was in a daze and all the time Michael came over to check and see that I was alright. He was such a support and really there for me and I understood that this is what it would have felt like to be married to someone who cared about me.

We set off at two o'clock and made the churchyard in Inniskeen by four-twenty.

Evan thought it strange that I was so friendly with this priest but he didn't suspect our true feelings for a moment. In his eyes, Michael was a robot who had been brainwashed into a cult.

I didn't try to explain my situation because there was nothing to explain. I wasn't sure what Michael and I shared but it was a happy place where we knew we were special to each other and that was all that I needed now.

The churchyard was small and it had been several months since someone had been buried in it. We had secured a spot in the corner beside my granny's plot. The gravediggers were shocked when they saw the coffin and asked were we sure we wanted to bury my father in that?

I could feel my father looking down and laughing at the spectacle. He must have especially enjoyed the embarrassment on Evan's face. My brother couldn't wait to get back to Dublin and he'd organised a flight back through Dubai for that very night. I would have minded in the past but not anymore.

Evan's taxi arrived to take him to the airport and Thalia, Michael and I waved him goodbye. I was exhausted and I could tell that the others were too.

"Go sit inside and I'll make you both some tea," Thalia said.

"Thanks so much, honey," I said.

My daughter was a rock. She had blossomed into a woman during her short time in Skerries and with it a sense of maturity had come that filled me with pride.

Michael sat opposite me on an armchair while I put my feet up on the settee.

"Don't you think that it was all perfectly planned by your clever father?" he asked.

"Well, it is strange to think that a few months ago we didn't know each other and if we hadn't met in Oklahoma you wouldn't be here today."

It was true. There seemed to be some sort of divine presence in all of the events of the summer.

"Think about it. The trip to Oklahoma, the decision to leave Oxford, even the terrible attack on Thalia, it all needed to happen in order for this day to go the way it has," Michael said.

"That sounds like something my father would have said."

"What would he say about us?"

I shook my head. "I don't know. Do you think he knew how things had developed between us?"

"Your father was no fool. I do believe he understood and accepted us."

"What about us, Michael? Is there an 'us'?"

"I love you, Roz. I think you know that. And it is a conversation that we need to have. I tried to keep you out of my head while I was in Syria but I thought about you everyday. It was like you were there present with me – even though we only spoke with time and distance between us, you were always there with me."

His words brought so much comfort. When someone speaks sincerely there is a difference that I had not realised before. But he was wonderful at his job and the support and love that he gave to so many people was a great service to the big 'We' as my father called us all.

"I felt it too – all the time that you were away I felt that you were here with me."

"So what do I do? I have to consider leaving my job if we

are to be together properly, the way that we deserve to be."

I needed to touch him and walked over and wrapped my arms around his neck. Our eyes were close now; close enough for our lips to kiss. We fell into our happy place and I was whisked into the greatest part of the universe where only love resides.

I eased myself away. "I couldn't ask you to do that. I love you, Michael, but it would be selfish for me to take you away from the great work that you do for others. I'm always here for you."

"And I am for you but –"

I put my fingers to his lips and stopped him.

"Tell me the truth. Do you love who you are? Can you deny that you are doing the best job for you?"

Michael paused. He was overcome and so was I, but I needed him to be truthful with me.

"I love my job and my life. Things are still the way they are in the Catholic Church and unless I leave my job I can only give you a part of me when I see you."

I soothed his cheek with a gentle brush of my palm.

"That's all I need to know. I hadn't expected anything more from you. When you love someone deeply and truly you don't need to be married or have a piece of paper to prove your love. We may have to remain clandestine, but others have had to suffer worse. I can share you with the world because there are other people who need you to do the job that you do."

I'd made up my mind. He would have to accept it or lose me. I couldn't take him away from the great 'We' as his job was more important than I'd ever realised.

"Bereavement is your speciality, isn't it, Michael?"

I'd sensed it earlier. He was so at ease with the situation.

He was so good at his job and had made every part of the cere-mony special and personal and it wasn't anything to do with how he felt about me. I could tell that this was how he made every family feel when they lost a loved one.

"It is what I do. I prefer the happier jobs like weddings and christenings but funerals are the really important ones. It's a dirty job but someone has to journey with the bereaved and it's what I'm good at."

"You know, you helped me realise something important today. I realised that I've been alone for a very long time. I felt your love on the altar today so strongly that I don't think I could have got through the ordeal without you."

"You are stronger than you think, Roz. I must finish my tour of duty and when I return I will have to do some soul-searching but, even if I can't give you what you deserve, I'll always be there for you. You have found your voice now and you need to do something with it."

He spoke the truth. I had started to write my novel while my father had taken his final breaths. I needed to continue with that book, writing his wisdom and sharing his message of love with the world.

"I think I know what you mean. I've actually started writing a novel. It's called *Journey to the Heartland*."

"That's a beautiful title. What's it about?"

"It's about finding love and finding yourself." I felt my eyes well up because I was speaking my truth.

Michael put his arms around me again and we held each other tightly. I hadn't cried all day and now the tears just rolled and wouldn't stop.

"It's perfect, Roz. It's what you're meant to do. I can feel it and you know that I'll be with you always."

I knew that I would never be alone again.

EPILOGUE

I looked over at the picture of Sitting Bull pinned to my wall and felt overcome by the wisdom and knowledge of the tribes who had gone before. They stood for a time when old age was revered and respected and something that was cherished. Beside it I stuck the photograph of my father at Stockyards City with his check shirt, cowboy boots and Stetson. He was the picture of happiness that day and that is how I like to remember him. Sometimes I think these wise old men's spirits are in this book. While I wrote it, I felt them look over my shoulder, urging me on to put down the words.

But the beginning of this story isn't that long ago and yet it was a lifetime ago – a full circle created like the circles in nature and the circle of life. As my daughter starts her summer exams in a couple of weeks' time I know that I have brought her to a safe place which she will one day leave and find her voice.

I thank my father every morning as I sit down to write this book. He gave me life and he helped me to find my voice. I didn't know then that in the process I would end up finding myself. I feel sad as I come to the end of this book but hope that some of my father's words will have been written for you too.

Michael didn't ever go on another tour of duty. Much as we tried to do the right thing by the Catholic Church, our love was too powerful, and Michael requested to be relieved of his duties by the bishop three months after Daddy died. Not everybody is given the opportunity to meet or spend their life with their soulmate and putting each other first was the right thing to do. He is still in the force as a counsellor and helping the troops and their families, just with a different role and title.

I've been lucky to be given a soulmate to share my life with and Thalia has a father figure who is proud and privileged to be there for her.

Life is a circle, an experience of beginnings and endings to be enjoyed whole-heartedly. There is always a way to change your life and follow a new path. I hope that you have a happy life because it goes too quickly, and it is up to each of us to make the most of this gift every single day.

The End